baa baa

~~black~~ Sheep
rainbow

baa baa ~~black~~ rainbow Sheep

PC Tales from the Unhinged Kingdom

David and Gavin Mortimer

**ROBSON
BOOKS**

First published in the United Kingdom in 2007 by
Robson Books
10 Southcombe Street
London
W14 0RA

An imprint of Anova Books Company Ltd

ISBN 10: 1 90579 802 4
ISBN 13: 9781905798025

A CIP catalogue record for this book is available from the British Library.

10 9 8 7 6 5 4 3 2 1

Typeset by SX Composing DTP, Rayleigh, Essex
Printed and bound by MPG Books Ltd, Bodmin, Cornwall

This book can be ordered direct from the publisher.
Contact the marketing department, but try your bookshop first.

www.anovabooks.com

Contents

'Mankind are greater gainers by suffering each other to live as seems good to themselves, than by compelling each to live as seems good to the rest.'

John Stuart Mill: *On Liberty*

WHAT'S IN A NAME?

Language is a dangerous substance in modern Britain. Indeed, language abolitionists seem to be at work in certain places, though they are unlikely to proscribe 'inappropriate', one of their terms of deepest censure. But be warned – only open your mouth after a careful risk assessment of the company in which you find yourself, and on no account within hailing distance of the local council chambers.

All We Like Sheep Have Gone Astray

Birmingham City Council got their comeuppance in 2000, and from a most appropriate quarter. 'Baa,' it said, jointly and severally, and, when the bleating had died away, announced that 'Baa, Baa, Black Sheep' was racist, and 'portrayed negative stereotypes', and must therefore be removed from the age-old canon of rhymes children could be allowed to sing. Rubbish, said the black parents of the city, displaying a commodity in short supply until that point, namely common sense. They probably pointed out that a black sheep is black, a white one white, a grey one grey and a brown one brown, so why try to pretend otherwise? Shocked by this riposte, Birmingham City Council suddenly realised it had been dragged through the sheep-dip backwards and climbed down, suitably fleeced.

Oxfordshire is close enough to Birmingham to have absorbed the lesson, but you can't keep determined pc persons down. Biding his time until 2006, Stuart Chamberlain, manager of the Family Centre in Abingdon and nursery school Sure Start Centre in Sutton Courtenay, ordered that henceforth 'Baa, Baa, Black Sheep' was to be converted to 'Baa, Baa, Rainbow Sheep'. He declined to explain what a rainbow sheep was, or how to explain to your little ones why, however many walks you took through fields heaving with black, white, grey or brown sheep, you never seemed to see a rainbow one. His main concern, as he explained to his local paper, the *Courier Journal*, was that 'no one should feel pointed out because of their race, gender or anything else'. One can foresee the time, not far distant, when something impossible will no longer be likened to hen's teeth, but to rainbow sheep. Happily, parental indignation was so great, and council support so conspicuous by its absence, that Mr Chamberlain leaped the fence and fled the field.

Not even an Aberdeen nursery school risked going to quite the same extremes as their Oxfordshire personhood. It merely decreed 'Baa, Baa, Happy Sheep'. Undoubtedly a sheep is capable of being happy, irrespective of whether it's black, white, grey or brown. How you can tell is difficult to answer, though let's not get too technical. But, as Margaret Morrissey of the National Confederation of Parent Teacher Associations said, 'It's really sad.' Indeed it is, in both meanings of the term.

Enough said

'We haven't often sung rainbow sheep as that is not their actual colour of course.' – Felicity Dick, *Project Co-ordinator, Sure Start Centre, Sutton Courtenay*

'To approach all these tiny little politically correct things wastes time and is irrelevant.' – Paul Phoenix, *Black Parents in Education*

'This is a madness that is creeping into our society, but this is not wanted in Oxfordshire.' – Keith Mitchell, *Leader, Oxfordshire County Council*

Vindictive Farmers' Wives

When Birmingham, Oxfordshire and Aberdeen launched their assaults on sheep they may have been doing no more than follow the lead given by Maidstone Borough Council in 1999. To be sure, 'Baa, Baa, Black Sheep' escaped being shorn at Kiddies Zone in Maidstone, but only by a barely heard bleat, since a new verse had to be composed to provide 'racial balance'. Otherwise the list of casualties was impressive.

'Three Blind Mice' got the chop in rather a different fashion from the way the words of the rhyme suggested. In it, the three blind mice 'all ran after the farmer's wife, who cut off their tails with a carving knife'. Although Group Manager Donna Carr admitted singing it to her own children, she had since recanted, because 'the words are vindictive and some children were upset by them', though who was more vindictive – the mice for chasing the farmer's wife, or the farmer's wife for winning the day – is somewhat open to question. Ms Carr went on to explain: 'Lots of children have pet mice and hamsters, and it is not very nice to think of their tails being cut off.' (As a matter of zoological fact, hamsters have tails so tiny you would be hard pressed to see them, let alone cut them off.) Perhaps the words of the rhyme could have been adjusted along the lines of 'they all ran after the farmer's wife, and scared her nearly out of her life'? That would at least have had the virtue of being fashionable metropolitan thinking about the value of farmers and their wives to society.

'Goosey, Goosey Gander' also got itself blacklisted in Maidstone on the grounds that, in an excess of violent cruelty, the unspeakable gander took an old man by his left leg and threw him down the stairs. 'I think it is taking things too far. Where do you draw the line?' asked Teresa Hay, mother of three-year-old Kirsty. 'Humpty Dumpty falls off his wall and hurts himself – do you stop singing that?' Well, yes, Mrs Hay, you do. Not in Maidstone on this occasion, but elsewhere Humpty was roundly condemned as illustrative of the violence involved in falling off a wall. In 2003, the Mothercare chain decided that 'Humpty Dumpty' was altogether too upsetting and added an extra verse in their tapes containing the rhyme. Now Humpty gets a big surprise, counts to ten and gets up again, none the worse.

Seeing things in a new light

In yet another blow to the freedom of expression of dogs it seems that lampposts have become things of the past, in Bury St Edmunds at least. In a TV interview, Councillor Julian Swainson said they were not banning hanging baskets to stop them falling on people's heads, but for the safety of the 'lighting columns' from which they were suspended (see p. 223).

Hot Cross Bakers

It was pancakes that started the rot – at least in the schools of London's Labour-run Tower Hamlets where, in 2003, the local council welshed (if the inhabitants west of Offa's Dyke will allow us this intemperate term) on Shrove Tuesday pancakes and, as Easter inexorably followed, hot cross buns as well. That shadowy figure, 'a spokesman', claimed that 'a lot' of people had complained about the pancakes, but when asked exactly how many came over all vague and forgetful. He (or she?) became noticeably more eloquent on the subject of the provocation posed by hot cross buns. Although they have been a feature of British life for nearly 650 years, the spokescreature stated: 'We are moving away from a religious theme for Easter and will not be doing hot cross buns. We can't risk a similar outcry over Easter like the kind we had on Pancake Day. We will probably be serving naan breads instead.' And that's the giveaway – fear that the symbol of the cross 'will spark complaints from Jewish, Hindu and Muslim pupils and their families'. That seems insulting to the many members of those faiths who have lived in Britain for many generations – certainly in the case of Jews and Hindus – without raising an eyebrow at the sight of a hot cross bun. In any case, if the poor bun is liable to offend, why replace it with naan bread, which simply transfers the supposed offence on to other groups?

Could it be that fear of upsetting Muslims was the dread Tower Hamlets dare not speak? Not that it was alone in its actions. The councils of Liverpool, York, Wakefield and Wolverhampton have never been slow to spot a bandwagon on the move, and a cartload of hot cross buns was irresistible.

Wakefield, indeed, showed a truly innovative turn of mind in announcing that it was replacing hot cross buns with IT buns. 'This Easter term we chose information technology,' said another of those ubiquitous spokespersons proudly, 'and didn't even consider putting hot cross buns on the menu.'

The Muslim Council of Britain called the decision 'very, very bizarre'. 'British Muslims are hardly going to be taken aback by a hot cross bun. (They) have been quite happily eating and digesting hot cross buns for many years and I don't think they are suddenly going to be offended. Unfortunately actions like this can only create a backlash and it is not very thoughtful. I wish they would leave us alone. We are quite capable of articulating our own concerns and if we find something offensive, we will say so. We do not need to rely on other people to do it for us.' So yet again, interfering councils had managed to offend everyone. Manchester, on the other hand, seemed to hear the voice of reason, or maybe simply took the trouble to consult. They kept hot cross buns on the menu while catering for other faiths as well, and pulled off the three-card trick into the bargain by keeping the local bakers happy.

Heavens above!
Manchester may have scored in the hot cross bun saga, but it gave away an own goal in 2005 when Howard Monks and Julie Sagar-Doyle turned up at Dukinfield Registry Office in Greater Manchester to tie the knot. 'Their tune' is the Robbie Williams number, 'Angels', and that's what they wanted to be played as they signed the register. Fifteen minutes before they were due to be married their choice was banned because it contained the word 'heaven', giving it 'religious connotations'. Might it scare the wits out of other faiths?

Bonfire Night Without a Fire

In 2005, Laura Heaps was enthusiastically outlining the history of Guy Fawkes Night on the MyVillage.com page of the MyTowerHamlets – yes, it's them again – website. She concluded with a rousing call to the citizens of the North London borough to 'get that bonfire burning . . . and look out for the best bonfire near you'. Her enthusiasm might have been dampened had she known that one year later Guy Fawkes would not be perched atop his bonfire in Victoria Park. He and it had been usurped in the affections of the council by the tale of a Mogul emperor and his tax collectors, and it was they – together with a spectacular tiger – who would be occupying Victoria Park, without a bonfire to be seen.

Councillor Lutfur Rahman enthused that 'the vibrant, brightly lit tiger will arrive in a stream of light and colour, fire will illuminate dancers and drummers and an impressive fifteen-metre-tall emperor, whilst firework effects will light up the skies as the compelling tale unfolds. It promises to be a memorable occasion.' At a cost of around £75,000 it should, indeed, have been both memorable and spectacular. Its creators, Manchester arts charity Walk the Plank, had already presented it at several London events, notably the Trafalgar Square Festival, and planned to include it in the Lord Mayor's Show a week after the Victoria Park performance, so its pulling power was not in doubt.

The only question was why the denizens of Tower Hamlets had been denied their traditional opportunity to scorch Guy Fawkes' trousers? A spokesman for the council was indignant when asked: 'It's utter nonsense to suggest the council has banned Guy Fawkes or is acting politically correctly in relation to bonfire night.' It was Liz Pugh, a producer with Walk the Plank, who may have given the game away. Bonfire Night was, she said with the conviction of those certain of their own infallibility, an anti-Catholic celebration and 'we no longer want to be involved in that'. Well, maybe in Lewes, East Sussex, it is, but there they had a history of violent persecution at Catholic hands to assuage. Elsewhere in the country it's an excuse for a good night out and, if anyone is concerned with the history, which is doubtful, surely it's more likely to be either a celebration of parliament surviving an attempt to send it skywards or, as MyVillage.com put it, 'in sympathy with [Guy Fawkes'] plans to overthrow the government!'

Rude pudding

Women out on hen nights are famed for the bawdy humour they exchange among themselves. Hardly surprising in a society that has thrived on sex and innuendo – very openly these days – since the days of Victorian music hall. So how to explain Tesco's extraordinary conclusion in 2001 that a traditional British pudding, on the menu for at least the last 150 years, is causing fainting fits at the checkout? Naughty, naughty Spotted Dick has been banished from the shelves, and readmitted only under the nice polite title of Spotted Richard. Spokesman David Sawday was the unfortunate chosen by the supermarket chain to step forward and explain that 'female customers were too embarrassed to ask our staff if they had any spotted dicks'.

Safeway Treads Gingerly

It's surprising how the most innocuous things can be relied on to upset somebody, somewhere. In 1999 Safeway fell foul of the rent-a-complaint mob for threatening to withdraw gingerbread men from sale. These familiar biscuits are, if in the traditional mould, undeniably in the general shape of men, with two eyes, two arms and two legs all present and correct. They could, at a pinch, be taken for women in trousers, although Professor Deborah Cameron of the University of Strathclyde (rather chillingly described in one newspaper as 'an expert in politically correct language') thought the problem of sexism in Safeway's biscuits might be solved by adding gingerbread women in skirts to the gingerbread men already in the range. Presumably she had in mind the kind of skirt seen in the doll-like silhouettes on the doors of motorway loos rather than a clinging, pencil-line skirt because, as she said, 'they probably won't do that because putting on a skirt would mean extra ingredients'.

Professor Cameron turned out to be a staunch defender of leaving gingerbread men well alone, and she was in good company as linguists, fellow academics and the local MSP (Member of the Scottish Parliament) Ben Wallace all sang a lusty chorus of disapproval featuring the familiar refrains of 'sad', 'barking' and 'political correctness gone mad'. They also pointed out that Safeway risked angering their customers by turning their backs on centuries of familiarity. 'Gingerbread men are traditional,' said Professor Cameron. 'People remember them from when they were kids and become nostalgic.'

Safeway remained tightly buttoned up, but were finally prevailed upon to rescind the ASBO on gingerbread men. 'A spokesperson' was pushed out through the curtains to face the derision for the volte-face. 'This was not a politically correct decision,' said the s-person, before contradicting itself in the very next sentence. 'We had had some complaints from customers and changed the name on our own brand accordingly.' It makes you wonder which to shake hardest – the spokesperson or your own head in disbelief!

Unmentionable covers

You wouldn't think a modest manhole cover could lie there in the road causing offence to half those who drive over it, would you? You would be wrong, at least if you live in Hackney, North London, where the council has decreed that the modest manhole cover is henceforth to be called a Personal Access Chamber. This will come as a nasty shock to several generations of female cricketers who will have to change their affectionate nickname for a vital piece of sporting equipment . . . but best not go into that.

How to Speak Proper

In November 2006, the National Centre for Languages told us that more than three-quarters of pupils in almost a third of UK state schools have opted out of learning foreign languages by the time they are fifteen. Perhaps the gap in the timetable left by this fall could be filled with teaching an understanding of another kind of language, one that sometimes seems as difficult to comprehend as, say, Dutch, but that is spoken in a lot of our town halls and council chambers. An acquaintance recently attended what was intended to be a quick, one-hour briefing from the Adult Education department of West Sussex County Council, only to find the first thirty minutes taken up with a recitation, with examples, of the four pages he was handed covering the acceptable language of equality and diversity. There were fourteen separate points concerning general language, a further six on stereotyping and, just to be sure nothing had been missed, another seven summarising all that had gone before. Thus the supposedly quick briefing was extended by a raft of instructions having nothing to do with his purpose for being there in the first place – for example, that stereotypes should be broken down by referring to 'Brian, a nurse, as well as Ann, a nurse', and 'Serena, the architect, as well as Bill, the architect'.

We've long since become accustomed to the idea that meetings can only be run in the presence of a chair (but have yet to hear a satisfactory explanation of whether an inanimate object can have a casting vote and, if so, how). But here, as presented by the Plain English Campaign over the years, is a handful of the expressions you should commit to memory in the event that you are intending to have, or might at some future point find yourself unable to avoid, intercourse, primarily of an oral nature, while admitting that it may at certain times or in certain contexts be written, and which may or may not prove to be meaningful, with a personage whose command of language, while possibly limited, is deemed to be unobjectionable in its inclusion of politically acceptable phrases. To be fair, one or two come from the USA, but most are home-grown. You may enjoy covering the right-hand column and trying to guess the 'proper' term:

Christmas tree *	Horticultural festive element
Christmas tree lights *	Festive embellishments of an illuminary nature
Dinner ladies	Midday supervisors
Lollipop ladies	Crossing patrol attendants
Old age pensioners	POPS = post-occupational persons (UK); or chronologically gifted (US)
Good schools	High-quality learning environments
Good education	Facilitation and enhancement of the learning process
Students who have failed exams	Emerging students
Students who have passed exams	Extending students

Only applies to those councils that have not yet abolished Christmas (see p. 132)

Down with gender-specific words!
If, like it or not, a chairman or a chairwoman is obliged to be a Chair, why do we still have salesmen, fishermen and midwives, never mind the spokesmen and women that lurk around every corner? Why should they not be called Sale, Fish, Mid and Spoke? What's wrong with a Spoke appearing for Gritshire County Council? Or a Fish for the Trawlermen's Union? And while we're about it, it's high time films and comics were re-titled – *Superperson*, *Spidercreature* and *Bat and Robin*, for example.

Who's a Pretty Yob, Then?

To be sure, we don't really know how to describe a yob. We know the word's a Victorian invention, being 'boy' spelled backwards, for denoting something unpleasant you wouldn't want in the house, but what exactly is it? Is it a teenage thug, or just a teenage fella hanging about with other teenage fellas looking vaguely antisocial? Prime Minister Tony Blair must have known once upon a time, because it's only a year or two since he woke up one morning with a wizard plan for ridding the nation of 'yob culture', and suggested the police drag an offending yob to the nearest cashpoint in order to relieve him of a hundred quid or so. Just for a moment the superintendent of police funds felt quite jolly. When the prime minister's Big Idea for Today failed to ignite popular enthusiasm, he forgot about it and left the police to worry about yobs in their own good time.

They did their best, wrote various reports and hatched plans up and down the country, without seeming to produce much by way of visible difference. But by now pc PC Sir Ian Blair had appeared on the scene as head of London's Metropolitan Police, and the inhabitants of that large city became aware that the problem was far simpler than anyone had ever guessed. Briefly put, the solution lay in the name. First to be shown the light was Chief Superintendent Stephen Bloomfield who, in September 2006, delivered to the Metropolitan Police Authority his report on making neighbourhoods safer. This recommended 'proactively tackling gangs and yobs across London'.

At this there was much pursing of lips in the MPA. Deputy chairman (or so the papers reported, though surely they intended deputy chair?) Cindy Butts said the term was 'alienating', though her explanation was hardly calculated to bring clarity to what she meant. 'I have a problem with the language of "yobs". It sort of sets up and defines too much of "self" and "other".' Assistant Commissioner Tim Godwin was quick to agree with whatever she was trying to say: 'I agree. I'm sorry. We won't use that again.' He later confirmed the Met's ban on the word. 'It can reflect on groups of youths who congregate, rather than those who carry out criminal activity.' By the simple device of eliminating the word rather than the problem the Met had delivered every politician's dream – the actual achievement of a manifesto pledge. Before the 2005 election, the Labour Party had promised to 'exclude yobs from town centres'. Et voila! Done and dusted. Since Sir Ian Blair was already a knight, a life peerage surely beckoned? One small cloud appeared on the horizon just one month later when the Institute for Public Policy Research published the outcome of a survey showing Britain's fifteen-year-olds to be way ahead of their Continental counterparts in underage sex, drunkenness and violence. But, hey, we mustn't alienate them by calling them yobs.

Heated heathens

With Halloween and Guy Fawkes Night plodding inexorably towards them, police in Ashford, Kent, launched Operation Pagan in a bid to contain crime and disorderly behaviour. 'Grossly irresponsible', wailed the Pagan Federation on behalf of the 5,000 members it claims. The police were obliged to remove their helmets, scratch their heads and think of another name. It can't be long before a spokeshumanoid claims on behalf of villains everywhere that it is offensive to use the word criminal.

Farnborough Banishes Birthdays

We all have them, like it or not. Whether you are a crumbly wanting to slow time down, or a youngster wanting the party to come quicker, birthdays potter round on an unalterable 365-day cycle. Whether we celebrate the fact or not should be up to us – unless you're down Farnborough way in Hampshire, in which case tread carefully with those candles (see p. 211).

In October 2004, the Hart Male Voice Choir was engaged to join forces with singers from a local primary school and perform in a show for charity. The choir selected Paul McCartney's 'When I'm Sixty-Four' because it's got a catchy, familiar tune and, as its secretary Dick Knight said, 'it was easy for kids to learn'. Easy to learn, maybe, but hard to perform when supersensitive teaching staff are looking for things to squirm over. Sing the song if you must, was the gist of their complaint, but only if you change the line 'Birthday greetings, bottle of wine', otherwise it's a no show. The Hart Male Voice Choir studied the offending five words for hints of a problem. They probably looked at them upside down and back to front, but the more they looked the more they couldn't see one.

'Why?' they asked eventually. Because there was a boy at the school from a family of Jehovah's Witnesses, and JWs don't celebrate birthdays because they consider them a pagan custom. Leaving aside the frisson of outrage that must have troubled the 5,000 spines of the Pagan Federation, this seems tantamount to saying that the rest of the birthday-celebrating members of the school must be pagan. It shows, as Sir Walter Scott wrote, 'what a tangled web we weave, when first we practise to deceive'. But the supersensitive staff at the primary school, evidently blissfully unaware of the pagans swarming all over the premises, were determined that their JW must not be caused 'embarrassment or upset'.

The UK Jehovah's Witness movement said: 'We would not expect the school to accommodate individual students.' But that was later. In the here and now the Hart Male Voice Choir had a problem. They had permission to use the McCartney song, but under the terms of the performing rights clearance the lyrics must not be altered. The only way out seemed to be to skip the line altogether and so, on the night, they stayed mum when the words 'Birthday greetings, bottle of wine' came round, and left the pianist to play on alone while the audience (90 per cent of whom must have known the words) probably sang it to themselves. Naturally, all the usual exclamations flowed as news of yet another gaffe was broadcast – 'this country is going mad, all a bit crazy, political correctness gone mad,' etc. (though curiously the popular favourite, 'barking mad', was missing on this occasion).

Police witness Mrs Grove's big sin

On Christmas Day 1974, Jehovah's Witnesses had the temerity to bang on Mr and Mrs Grove's front door in Burlesdon, Hampshire, just as they were sitting down to the annual turkey. Not themselves believing in Christ's birthday, or anyone else's, the JWs probably reckoned this was a good day to find more people at home than usual. The Groves were not amused at having their digestion disrupted on such a day and, every year since, Jean Grove, now a widow, has put up a sign reading 'Our dogs are fed on Jehovah's Witnesses'. In 2006, the police ordered her to remove it because it was 'distressing, offensive and inappropriate'.

The chairman of the local parish council was surprised by the police's demand as 'we don't have the same responses to what, to many people, are more pressing matters in the village, such as vandalism and trouble with yobs.' Once the officers had gone, Mrs Grove put the notice up again.

Half-baked Home Cooking

Over the years Liverpool has served a variety of concoctions to tickle our palates, sometimes scrambled, sometimes spicy, but one of the quirkiest to be cooked up was Liverpool City Council's politically correct assault on home baking in 1994. It appeared to come out of the blue, or perhaps red, when it was decided to put a park café out to tender. This particular café had hitherto been noted for its traditional afternoon teas and MP David Alton, a Liberal Democrat, wrote in to propose that whoever won the tender should be required to continue the tradition of outstanding home baking. To hear the squawks and hoots you would have thought a kitchenful of birds were being plucked alive.

Mr Alton received a reply from the council's Development and Environmental Services Department. Home baking, it considered, was a dangerous concept in 'a multiracial society wherein people of different ethnic groups may wish to tender for the contract'. When Mr Alton had recovered breath he enquired, 'How on earth can anyone take offence over the words "home baking" on the grounds that we live in a multiracial society?' He hardly needed to add that 'some of the best home-made food I have ever eaten is that which Asian families prepare'. He might just as well have asked if the department did not consider it at best patronising, and at worst insulting, to imply that home baking was alien to ethnic minorities. Across the city in Calderstones Park, meanwhile, Peter Wright, who had run the café there for 29 years, was coming to the boil nicely. 'Home-baked must be the most self-explanatory phrase in the entire English language,' he simmered. 'My customers have come from all over the world and none have taken offence, nor misunderstood, when I have told them my scones are home-baked.'

Before the whole affair could become overdone, the inevitable council spokesman stepped forward and performed a series of linguistic gymnastics to add to the chaos in the kitchen. Some people, he claimed, could confuse home baking with 'fast food, hot dogs and hamburgers'. This novel thought might indeed have wrong-footed the opposition had not Eileen Devaney, the chair (that word again) of the Environment and Consumer Protection Committee summarised matters briskly and succinctly: 'I believe a mistake has been made. It would seem that home-baked humble pie is the order of the day.'

Pub grub

In 1994 a pub in Eynsford, Kent, was said to be advertising its 'ploughpersons platters'. By the year 2000, similar sightings were being reported from outside pubs in Devon. All of which suggests a sense of humour is, despite it all, alive, well and as strong as the ale in Britain's country pubs.

Censorship Rules, OK?

The distinguished novelist Lynne Reid Banks wrote eight books for children, winning an award for *Indian in the Cupboard*. On the basis of the title, a man in Canada complained that it was racist, and the story was threatened in that country with a cover sticker reading 'contains material which may be offensive'. In this particular case all turned out well because librarians actually read the book instead of relying on assumptions about it but, as the author said, 'This kind of thing is so insidious. The freedom of expression is about the freedom to be offensive, whether accidentally or not.'

In 1993, the English arm of the writer's association, PEN, disclosed the result of a survey showing that 60 per cent of children's authors had been censored by 'politically correct publishers'. Among the examples was Gillian Cross, author of *The Great Elephant Chase*, winner of the Smarties Award for children's literature in 1992. 'I was once asked to change an illustration so that a West Indian child was eating an apple and not a banana,' she said. 'This kind of censorship is a very scary thing, and anyway children are not easy to fool.' Alison Prince, author of *How's Business*, told the survey she once began a story: 'Things were looking black . . .' and was told to change it to: 'Things were looking bad . . .'

Anne Pilling, one-time winner of the Guardian Prize, wrote the popular *Vote for Baz*, but another story of hers, *On the Lion's Side*, was declined by a leading children's publisher because it didn't take books about 'a mother, a father, children and three meals a day'. Luckily, a braver company risked this subversive concept, and was rewarded by seeing the book nominated for the Carnegie Medal. The one that rejected it may have felt a twinge of guilt when, thirteen years later, British fifteen-year-olds turned out to be more violent, more promiscuous and more alcohol-fuelled than any of their Continental counterparts. The cause, according to the Europe-wide survey run by the Institute for Public Policy Research in 2006, is that they spend significantly less time with their families than do their counterparts in France, Germany and Italy. Maybe three meals a day have their virtues after all.

Another children's author, Andrew Matthews, with *Wolf Pie* to his credit, regaled the PEN researchers with his attempts to satisfy the censors. 'In the first draft, Mrs Monster tried to make a cake and couldn't do it. I was told to redo that bit because it was sexist. Then I had Mr Monster trying and failing to make the cake but apparently that was also sexist . . . I think this sort of thing does happen frequently.' It makes one wonder if 'they' ever stop to ask themselves how the average meal gets cooked in a normal household.

Snow White and the Seven Vertically Challenged Persons
In her 2003 book *The Language Police*, Diane Ravitch, a senior education official under George Bush Snr and Bill Clinton, points out some of the ways in which American schoolbooks have been sanitised. The word 'dwarf' is out, of course. 'Dialect' is objectionable (ethnocentric) and should be called 'language', despite the two words meaning different things; 'brotherhood' is sexist and 'community' must be substituted; while 'Adam and Eve' is simply beyond the pale and must be replaced by – wait for it – 'Eve and Adam'. 'The result of this relentless purging is dishonesty,' writes Ravitch, 'a purposeful shielding of children from anything challenging, controversial or just plain interesting.'

Censorship Still Rules, OK?

Midnight Circus is the work of prize-winning author and illustrator, Peter Collington. He jumped the first hurdle, his publisher, but fell at the next when London's Lambeth Council ordered its libraries not to stock the book, claiming it reinforced racist messages and offended animal rights. The Young People's Services Librarian, Steph Smith, explained to the wondering author: 'We were surprised you chose to use a circus with performing animals. In our experience this is now widely disliked by most carers, who recognise that it raises issues about animal rights.' She then rolled up her sleeves and got stuck into the big one. 'The storyline of the child being threatened by this creature [a gorilla, normally pictured – as in this book – in fetching black fur] and saved by a little white horse seems to be very insensitive. The presentation of a black, apelike creature as evil and a small white creature as good have obvious overtones which many carers may find offensive, and which they would not wish to use with children and young people because they may reinforce racist messages.' Phew!

'They are seeing things that are just not there,' said a perplexed Peter Collington. But, my dear sir (if we may use this sexist terminology), surely the main reason inner-city councils exist is to see things that aren't there?

If it's any comfort to Mr Collington, Lambeth was not alone in its righteous crusade to sterilise the minds of children. The Inner London Education Authority was hot on the case in 1981. Its triumphs included the blacklisting (wicked term) of:

- *Beauty and the Beast* – the beast should have been coloured green.
- *Little Doll* – sexist. Well, you can tell from the title, can't you?
- *Here comes Dolly* – sexist. See above.

By 1982 and 1983 another inner London borough, Brent, was feeling aggrieved at being left out of the fun, and weighed in with some banishments of its own:

- *Dip the Puppy* (by Spike Milligan, no less) – banned, sexist.
- *Asterix* – sexist, *and* enjoyed by kids. Away with it.
- *Tintin* – sexist. See above.

The banning plague crept towards the Midlands as *Thomas the Tank Engine* was ousted by Dudley Council for its rampant sexism. All those nasty male engines forcing the carriages to be mere compliant females? Absolutely! Thomas the Tank Engine is 'a sexist male stereotype'. Now we know what Thomas reminds us of. All those tank engines in drinking clubs, thrusting their macho wheels across the counter and demanding another pint of engine oil in their tankards. Where Dudley Council led, Derbyshire followed, sending *Dr Dolittle* into exile for being – in a welcome change from sexist – racist.

Everybody had a go at Enid Blyton, of course. However many times she topped the list of the world's bestselling English-language authors, her shade was surrounded by librarians metaphorically kicking the corpse. Her executors surrendered and, once she had been 'cleansed' of racism, sexism, 'gayness' (sic) and almost anything else you can think of, she was readmitted to the library shelves. She is no longer among the world's most read children's authors.

I give up

In 1993, Gillian Avery, author of *A Likely Lad*, said she had stopped writing for children because of the rise of political correctness, and what she had seen happening to other authors. 'It started when a book of mine was published in America. It was a story set in Victorian times. The little girl's father says to her: "Don't bother about school because you're a pretty little thing and will make someone a good wife." The American editor took it out. It was quite ludicrous.'

A Very Fuzzy Problem

In 2002 John Denham, whose ministerial responsibilities then included the police, poor man, was addressing the annual conference of the Police Federation. Like any good politician, he was anxious to promise to do anything until he was safely out of the room and, in the course of his speech, announced that it was 'time to get down to the nitty-gritty of training'. 'Allo, 'allo, 'allo, what's all this? thought PC Chris Jefford, and rose to his feet. 'If I used the term "nitty-gritty", which you used a moment ago, in our modern politically correct society I would be facing a disciplinary charge,' he said. The minister turned – we were about to say white – a paler pink than usual, and his lower lip may have quavered as a hubbub of constables broke out around him. PC Jefford kindly explained the problem. 'Nitty-gritty is a prohibited term in the modern police service as being a racist term.' A susurrus of 'slavery' whispered around the room. It seems the police, ever alert for ways of reducing language to its most basic and colourless components, have decided that 'nitty-gritty' is a term coined by American sailors to describe the detritus left at the bottom of the ship once its cargo of slaves had been discharged.

Now what – or who – on earth put such an idea into the heads of our law enforcers? Slave trading is as old as history, but as an activity involving British and American traders was finished by the middle of the nineteenth century. According to Dr Jonathan Lighter, editor of the *Historical Dictionary of American Slang*, the first example of the term 'nitty-gritty' in use is in 1956 and, as another American lexicographer, Michael Quinion, says, 'It is inconceivable that it should have been around since slave-ship days without somebody writing it down until the mid-twentieth century.' It's not just 'nitty-gritty' that gets the police so excited either. 'Egg and spoon' is out (so, for that matter, is calling someone 'a good egg', and not because it's such a toe-curlingly old-fashioned expression). In their infinite wisdom, the police have decided that 'spoon' rhymes with 'coon' and therefore, despite a complete lack of evidence, 'egg and spoon' must be cockney rhyming slang for that naughty word.

So it goes on. There's a raft of things you mustn't say if you're in the police, nor may we say them to the police. What are they? Ah, thought you'd never ask. Nobody knows! That's the beauty of it. As David Nixon, with plenty of experience of hearing disciplinary cases, said on behalf of the Police Federation, there is no formal list of banned words. It is, he confessed, 'hugely problematic. You can find officers in trouble through no awareness that they were doing something wrong. Nobody knows what the standard is and so you just don't know the rules.' In a nutshell, therefore, you can make them up as you go along! Little wonder that, as John Harrison, national chairman (sorry about this insensitive, sexist term, but we're only reporting what he called himself) of the Sergeant's Section of the Police Federation, said: 'Officers have been withdrawing from policing and avoiding encounters that could lead to complaints.' So don't dial 999 unless you want to check out a correct Scrabble term (see p. 174).

(see p. 174)

Blackboards blacklisted
Haringey Council in North London does not like the racist implications of blackboards in schools (and they are pretty mad about black bin liners as well). In some schools, blackboards have therefore been replaced with chalkboards. What colour chalks may be used to write on them, one wonders?

Take Care of the Pounds and Forget the Penny

Two centuries ago, Liverpool was one of the two or three richest cities in Britain. Its huge wealth came from the shipping business. Cargo ships sailed in to load and unload rather as planes fly in and out of busy airports today, and among its successful entrepreneurs was James Penny. As a one-time benefactor of the city, he was rewarded by having a lane named after him, and in the 1960s the Beatles made 'Penny Lane', and Liverpool in general, world famous. Ever since, tourists have flocked to Liverpool, spending their money to visit the places made famous by the group, Penny Lane included.

In 2006 the city faced a dilemma. James Penny was a slave trader. There's nothing new in the knowledge, but maybe it would be best to forget he ever existed? Liverpool cannot escape the fact that a considerable part of the city's former wealth came from slave trading and it took an almost masochistic delight in apologising for the fact in 1999. Go through it all again for Mr Penny? But then they'd have to take the famous street sign down, ban all the postcards and generally run the risk of forgoing the lovely loot the tourists bring in. So, after a lively debate, the City Council decided to rest on the laurels of its apology. After all, it's the height of fashion to apologise for long-gone generations, and these days we can hardly get enough of it. In 1997 Tony Blair apologised for the Irish famine 150 years earlier; and the Queen is terribly good at apologies – in 1995 she rattled off two, one to India, and another to the Maoris. How big is that? Moreover, to celebrate the millennium and make sure the Brits didn't get too far ahead in the apology stakes, the Pope apologised for the Crusades – though at least he remembered to mention the number of Christians massacred by Turkish Muslims in the century preceding the First Crusade. So come on, Liverpool. As we're in the mood for stonkingly good apologies for things none of us had a hand in, why not rerun your 1999 effort? Or perhaps it would be better to heed Simon Jenkins, writing on apologies in the *Guardian*: 'We look ridiculous when we start awarding marks out of ten for the moral behaviour of those who lived and formed a view of a very different world from our own. Why cannot we generate the same moral fervour over the consequences of today's iniquities?'

Bristol has a more matter-of-fact approach to name-calling. Eighty-odd councillors and staff from Kidderminster and elsewhere in Worcestershire were packed off on an equalities and diversity course in 2005. The training company running it decided that 'all shipshape and Bristol fashion' was a most incorrect saying and should never, ever be used in politically correct society because it referred to black people ready to be sold as slaves. This came as news to Bristol. The city's lord mayor dismissed the idea out of hand, and he did so on good authority. Local historian Gerry Brooke explained that the term came from Bristol's excellent reputation for shipbuilding, and Brewer's *Dictionary of Phrase and Fable* states that 'the expression derives from the port of Bristol's reputation for efficiency in the days of sail'. As for the Kidderminster trainees who were the victims of the training company's vivid imagination, Worcestershire County Councillor Stephen Clee spoke for them when he said, 'A lot of the councillors thought this was political correctness gone mad. I am inclined to agree with them. No working practices will change.'

The language of flowers

In April 2005, a week or two before the General Election, a woman took some spring flowers to the Medway Council offices in Kent. She had received helpful advice from one of their departments and wanted to show her appreciation. 'We can't accept those,' she was told at reception. 'They're the wrong colour. It shows political bias.' Yellow, the colour of springtime flowers, is also the colour of the Liberal Democrat Party. Whatever induced the Labour Party to call an election when the countryside was awash with daffodils advertising the Liberals? What with red Labour, blue Conservatives, yellow Liberals and the Green Party, the poor woman really should have known that dead brown leaves were her only option.

The Biters Bitten

Don't you just love it when the boot is suddenly rammed onto the other foot? Thanks to the diligence of the *Romford Recorder* we have an inside account of what happened one day in September 2005, when Havering Council in Essex met in solemn conclave. Among other things on the agenda was an application to put a mobile home on a farm rearing rare breeds of horses and sheep. As the discussion made its ponderous way towards decision or deferment, the well-warmed air flowing upwards to the ceiling was suddenly intermingled with the unmistakeable sound of bleating. Disappointingly, it was not the bleating of genuine sheep but rather a male councillor, evidently becoming upset by the tenor of the discussion, performing a passable imitation of a woolly quadruped.

Now there are many things that get the goat of the average modern-day British town council but sheep, unless they are failing in their duty to be rainbow-coloured, are not generally high on the list of banned substances. This was different, however. It was clearly a human sheep, and it was 'making unhelpful baa-ing noises'. Worst of all, it implied disrespect to a body so powerful it could, on a whim, ban undesirable books from its libraries and declare Christmas not to exist within a sizeable area around Romford. Councillor Jeff Tucker, in particular, was so enraged that he reported the incident to the Standards Board for England. Until the perpetrator was found and punished, normal business had little chance of being resumed. The Standards Board knew a waste of time when one was dropped on its desk and, before you could say 'Grow up, lad', had batted the problem straight back to Havering Council – and like a zealous sheepdog, they weren't letting go.

One year, 300 pages and £10,000 later, the results of their dogged investigation were ready for inspection and the perpetrator of the Great Baa was about to be unveiled. Except he wasn't. The net result of this exercise in wasting time and local taxpayers' money was to narrow the possible list of suspects to four. Prime among the four was Denis O'Flynn, who clearly has a praiseworthy talent for stating the obvious: 'This has been an extremely expensive example of the worst kind of council bureaucracy. The fact that this investigation has cost so much time and money is the height of stupidity.'

The biggest laugh for the audience at this pantomime performance was that if indeed Mr O'Flynn was ultimately adjudged to be the scapesheep, there was nothing the council could do about it, since he was no longer a councillor. A persistent investigative reporter prised a critical admission from the council, who denied the report had been 300 pages long, but conceded it had been 'substantial'. Let us settle for 295 pages then. One can only hope that the residents of Havering have at least had a good laugh, although they may well ask what all the fuss was about. After all, the freedom to say what you think is supposed to be the essence of our democracy, and if it's good enough for humans, I'm sure Havering Council wouldn't want to upset the animal-rights lobby by denying our woolly friends a good baa.

Nostalgia time

Oh, for the dear dead days of the 1980s when North London's Brent Council kept us in stitches. In December 1983 a Brent disciplinary committee wanted a disillusioned lecturer sacked for recommending a dog be promoted on the grounds that it was 'mostly black'. This followed the council's 1982 decision to train four black teachers whose combined total of O and A level passes came to exactly zero. In December 1984 posters for a tea dance created shrieks of protest in Brent because they showed a man and woman dancing together. ('Gays and lesbians do not get a look in.') Only three months later another poster caused uproar for the racist sin of displaying a clown in a Union Jack bow tie. Those were the days, my friend, we thought they'd never end . . .

Pork Chopped

This little piggy went to Batley, this little piggy went to school;
This little piggy read stories, but this little piggy was banned;
And this little piggy cried all the way home.

In March 2003, Barbara Harris, headperson of Park Road Junior, Infant and Nursery School in Batley, Yorkshire, felt a shiver of fear run up her backbone. There, on the classroom shelves, was a copy of *The Three Little Pigs*. It must be, and was, banished instantly from the list of acceptable reading. Not because the under-sevens were being exposed to the ASBO-deserving behaviour of the Big Bad Wolf as he huffed and puffed until he had blown down the houses of the law-abiding piglets, but because the other protagonists in the age-old nursery story were – and probably Ms Harris forced the word out between clenched teeth – PIGS! Clinging tenaciously to half-remembered gossip, the worthy headperson knew she had to act at once. There was no time to consult. The story had to go, time-honoured or not.

Parents were predictably up in arms. 'I've never heard of anything so ridiculous . . . absurd . . . smacks of a fascist state . . .' and, inevitably, the favourite tautology: 'political correctness gone mad'. And then someone thought to ask the Muslim Council what it had to say on the matter. By now, the Council must be sick to death of non-Muslims presuming to act in their name and being left to pick up the pieces. On its behalf, Inayat Bunglawala said, 'This is bizarre – there is nothing to stop children reading about pigs. The ban is simply on the consumption of pork and pig products.' His colleague, religious leader Shaykh Ibrahim Mogra, expanded on his comments, explaining that 'there's no problem in talking about pigs, and pigs appearing in our *Three Little Pigs* stories. The Arabic word for pig is in the Koran text . . . Where the Koran mentions the prohibition of pork, it's for the consumption and the use of any part of the pig.'

Ms Harris remained unrepentant. 'All we are doing is trying hard . . . to ensure that all of our children are awarded the respect all human beings deserve.' Great stuff, but respect is a two-way process and, as Nick Seaton of the Campaign for Real Education commented: 'This will once again create a bad image of Muslims in the UK.' Alas, too late. Instead of the Big Bad Wolf being the one to end up in a cauldron of scalding water, it was the three little pigs who were turned into boiled bacon by Park Road School.

Ee bah gum, it's them pigs again!
In 2007 Honley Church of England school in Huddersfield was afflicted by a swine fever similar to that which caused problems just up the road in Batley in 2003. It planned a performance of Roald Dahl's *Three Little Pigs*, but got cold trotters when contacted by the organisers of the Kirklees Primary Music Festival, who insisted 'we have to be sensitive if we want to be multicultural'. The play therefore underwent a magical transformation, emerging as the *Three Little Puppies*. On this occasion it was Mohammed Imran from the local Hanfia Mosque, who was wheeled out to explain that Islam does not ban the mention of pigs, merely the eating of them – for which whole generations of pigs are undoubtedly grateful.

Bone Idle Is Best

Much merriment ensued in 2000 when a Staffordshire job centre rejected an ad from a local employer for a 'hard-working' and 'enthusiastic' worker. This, deemed the centre, was discriminatory – presumably against those who felt their human rights were invaded because they preferred indolence. In no time the story had gone the rounds of the country, and people all over Britain swore blind it had happened in their local public employment bureau (as we should properly be calling the job centre). And, come to think of it, perhaps they were all right. The then Education and Employment Minister, David Blunkett, was sufficiently credulous of the Staffordshire job centre's zeal in protecting the rights of the bone idle to weigh in with the observation that it discriminated against those with a disability because 'it is an insult to suggest that a disabled person cannot be reliable, hard-working and enthusiastic'.

One sceptical journalist took leave to doubt that the Staffordshire story had any truth in it. But a similar tale proved indisputable. In 2004 Beryl King, who runs two job agencies in Totton, Hampshire, was taken to task when she put forward an advertisement for 'warehouse packers who must be hard-working and reliable'. No way, she was told, could she be allowed to propose anything so alarming to the workshy. 'Has our world gone mad?' asked Beryl, before posing a rhetorical question: 'If I advertise for a typist am I discriminating against people who can't type?' There's only one answer to that. But she was on the rampage now and nobody could stop her as she built to her climax. 'How long before someone says you can't pay people for working because it discriminates against those on benefit who are paid for not working?' Shh, Beryl. For goodness' sake don't give them ideas.

At much the same time as Ms King was foolishly expecting co-operation from her local job centre, Pauline Millican was experiencing identical problems in Liverpool. She needed a receptionist for the family firm, Millican Opticians, so she placed one ad in a local newspaper and sent the same ad to the Huyton job centre. You won't need overly acute perception to guess by now that the latter was rejected because of the dreaded term 'hard-working' but, in a gesture to show their broad-mindedness, the job centre informed Ms Millican that she could keep the words in if they could say she insisted on it. So she insisted on it. As she said, 'I want my staff to be courteous, helpful, to arrive at work on time and to be prepared to lend a hand to whatever needs doing.' What happened? The job centre placed the ad but ignored Ms Millican's insistence and cut out the words anyway. Which made it all the more interesting that she received eight applications from the uncensored newspaper ad, but only two from the job centre that had eliminated the offensive words 'hard-working'.

It is only fair to inform our readers that having reached this point in the book we, the authors, are exhausted. The publishers are clearly expecting a level of hard work from us that discriminates against our human dignity. We feel that the general public should be expected to shoulder its social responsibilities towards us by paying the full price for this book even if we manage only to complete a quarter of it. Thank you for your co-operation.

Miserable workers required

In January 2003 the *Lancashire Evening Telegraph* reported that Travel Counsellors in Bolton had had their advertisement for a catering manager turned down by Job Centres Plus, a government employment agency. The travel agency was seeking 'a friendly person . . . with a flair for preparing fresh sandwiches, appealing salads and soups'. Was the problem that the term 'appealing' was sexist when applied to soups and salads? It might have been had Job Centres Plus read that far in the ad, but before they got there they had the heebie-jeebies because of the requirement for a 'friendly' person. The agency was told to drop 'the use of personality statements to avoid any possible discrimination'.

Love in a Cold Climate

We can all do our bit to reduce the threat of global warming, and local authorities are no exception. A number of them have made great contributions to eliminating the traditional warmth of personal relationships and reducing them to an icy chill. It would be unfair to say Rotherham set the ball rolling, but they were quicker off the mark than some. In 2002, the Director of Performance Management of the local health authority told nursing home Swinton Lodge that it must not use terms of endearment with its elderly residents. 'Love', 'dear', 'sweetheart' and 'darling' were forbidden – unless formal written permission had been given in advance. It's difficult to be funny about such a sad situation. Almost anyone who has spent time visiting people in an old folks' home understands that these common and long-standing terms of endearment help to reassure elderly people, who are often apprehensive at finding themselves dependent on others in residential care.

The following year, Bristol City Council instructed security staff to desist from calling women visitors 'love' or 'dear' and decreed 'madam' to be the only acceptable term. This followed a complaint from the city's Lib Dem leader, Barbara Janke, who would seem to have a highly developed sense of her own importance. 'Calling someone "love" is as Bristol as the docks,' fumed Tory councillor Richard Eddy.

Hull had no intention of being outdone by places like Rotherham and Bristol. Biding its time until 2005, it came up with an entire lexicon of incorrect language. By way of an hors d'oeuvre it consigned the terms 'elderly' and 'senior citizens' to the garbage can of history. These, according to Julie

Thomson, leader of the Equalities Unit, were demeaning. As she worked her way through the rich menu of the English language she became increasingly incensed, and by the time she got to correct modes of address for those of the female gender she was close to banning language altogether. 'Pet, luvvie, flower, love' – here she paused to gulp in oxygen – 'lass, sweetheart, darling, dear' were all of them abusive. The citizens of Hull must be made to learn that warmth and familiarity are evil, and cold formality must rule. Lib Dem councillor Carl Minns best summed up this flimflam. 'We are one of the worst-performing authorities in the country,' he said, 'and the fact that staff are more bothered about putting out lists like this instead of improving performance beggars belief.'

It's a shame that Hull's most famous son is no longer living. Philip Larkin would have had a high old time penning a biting poem to cut Ms Thomson down to size – provided she had left enough words standing for him to work with.

Darling, they'll go wild in Hull

For all we know, Hull's incorrigible Julie Thomson was inspired in her quest by the lead given in 2004 by English National Opera. To the sound of gloomy bass accompaniment it issued a document called 'Dignity at Work' in which employees were warned off 'darling', their age-old term of address. 'Luvvie, dear and sweetheart' were OK, so all was not entirely lost. Leaving aside the unlikelihood of changing such deeply ingrained habits, Ned Sherrin best summed things up: 'It all seems a trifle silly. Darling is a very convenient term if you can never remember who anyone is. It avoids a multitude of ambiguities.'

Potato Blight

Among the latest to be deeply affronted by a bad name call is the British potato. Had we met in the street, gripped you Ancient Mariner-like by the wrist and whispered the news you might well have shaken yourself free and hurried off looking apprehensively over your shoulder, but if you have read this far into the book you will no longer be surprised. Yes, it's true. In 2005, potatoes had had enough. They were up in arms, or rather tubers, and planning to demonstrate outside parliament and the offices of the *Oxford English Dictionary*.

What had caused this outbreak of spud rage? It seems that in 1993, the *Oxford English Dictionary* had included an entry for 'couch potato', a term that originated in the USA meaning 'a person who spends leisure time passively or idly sitting around'. In the years that followed, an underground revolution slowly took shape. Spuds everywhere lay passively and idly around on the ends of their tubers nurturing a sense of burning resentment. No matter their standing in British potato society, whether King Edwards or British Queens, Pentland Squires or Maris Pipers, a common purpose united them. By 2005 matters had grown to a head and the potatoes of Britain were ready to take their case to Kathryn Race, head of marketing at the British Potato Council.

She struggled enthusiastically on their behalf. 'We are trying to get rid of the image that potatoes are bad for you,' she explained to a wondering world as she unveiled plans for spud anarchy outside parliament and the publisher's offices. Plaintively, the editor of the *OED* protested that dictionaries did not make up the language, they 'just reflect the words that society uses'. This did nothing to assuage the potatoes' wrath. 'We want to use another term than couch potato because potatoes are inherently healthy,' said Kathryn Race before making the mistake that may have cost them their credibility.

The help was enlisted of 'celebrity chef' (a damning term if ever there was one) Antony Worrall Thompson. Licking his lips and salivating gently, he spoke movingly of the virtues of the potato. 'They are healthy, versatile, convenient and taste great too,' he enthused, forgetting the purpose for which he had been brought to the press conference. 'Indeed, life without potato is like a sandwich without a filling,' he added, making a lunge for the nearest kilo of Golden Wonders. So convincing was his exposition of the culinary virtues of the potato that before you could say Jersey Royals they were being boiled, sautéed and chipped almost as fast as you could dig them up. Thus depleted, the potatoes lost the will to fight, the sanctity of parliament remained unsullied, the *OED*'s offices were saved from spud-sacking and 'couch potato' remains inviolate in the dictionary.

Don't mention the cows

In 2004 the Welsh Development Agency wasted – whoops, spent – £150,000 drawing up a list of words not to be used when promoting the Principality as a place to do business. It was a rum concoction, plumbing the depths of mind-numbing irrelevance with the banning of 'maverick'. Why? Because Samuel Maverick was a nineteenth-century Texan rancher notorious for refusing to brand his cattle. Still not got it? Then you're not as on the ball as the WDA who spotted that the word maverick might trigger an association of ideas that could offend citizens of countries where the cow is considered a holy animal.

What a Load of Daleks

The *Collins English Dictionary* defines a Dalek as 'aggressive, mobile, and producing a rasping staccato speech', a description which, when one thinks about it, could apply to some of the hoodies you see hanging round town centres.

Daleks have been with us since the early 1960s and, as everyone who has ever watched *Dr Who* knows, they are ruthless, emotionless and they believe in the superiority of the Dalek race over all others. Which probably goes some way to explaining why while Americans are apt to say, 'Have a Nice Day', Australians 'G'day, mate' and we Brits 'How do you do?', the Daleks are best known for greeting everyone they see with: 'Ex-Ter-Mi-Nate, Ex-Ter-Mi-Nate!'

But not to worry, because as the Collins dictionary also mentions in its definition, the Daleks are 'fictional'. They're not real, just oversized pepper shakers on castors. Not that that prevented the BBFC (British Board of Film Classification) from slapping a 12 Certificate on a *Dr Who* DVD in 2005.

Now even though there are many middle-aged men – some of whom still live with their mothers – who have an unhealthy obsession with *Dr Who*, the programme is first and foremost for children. So it seems a bit strange that the BBFC should make a DVD of the series unavailable to millions of kids. Ah, but there was a good reason, as a spokeslady explained, and it was all because of that nasty doctor.

'We were concerned at the use of violence to resolve problems,' said the BBFC spokesauntie. 'However cross one might be with a Dalek, being cruel is not the way to deal with the issue. Some children might take it into the playground.'

What, the Dalek? If they've banned running and swings in playgrounds (see p. 153), are teachers going to turn a blind eye to a Dalek exterminating class 2C during morning break?

But back to the doctor, skulking in his Tardis while he plots retribution on the poor defenceless Daleks. 'The Doctor is a role model for young children but he takes out his anger on the Dalek,' said the BBFC. 'A good role model should not use torture to satisfy his desire for revenge. It is not an acceptable way to deal with the problems of power.' (We feel obliged to draw attention to the sexist use of the gender-inclining 'his' in this quotation – one hopes the BBFC took its spokeshumanoid to task for this monstrous aspersion.)

There are unconfirmed rumours that in the next series of *Dr Who* the Cybermen will act as intermediaries and effect a reconciliation between the Doctor and the Daleks in the Tardis. Steamy stuff! Expect an 18 classification for that.

You R-R-R having a laugh?
In 2005 Portway Junior School in Hampshire gave the classic fairy tales a makeover as part of their three Rs programme (Rights, Responsibilities and Respect, not the useless and woefully old-fashioned Reading, Riting and Rithmetic). With funding from the Department for Education, the school used *Cinderella* to explain to children the guiding principles of the United Nations Convention on the Rights of the Child. A reporter from the *Daily Telegraph*, who sat in on a lesson, described how the teacher asked if the Ugly Sisters had been nasty to Cinderella. Up shot a forest of hands, with one boy answering: 'They kept her in a cellar and made her work like a slave, which infringed Article 19 – the right to be protected from being hurt or badly treated.' You'll go far, my boy.

Wipe that Smile off Your Race

2003 wasn't the best of years for pub landlady Diane Prestidge. Two close friends had died and her husband had walked out on her, so she thought she would advertise for a new man to come into her life. Using one of the blackboards from her pub in Drybrook, Gloucestershire, Diane chalked a lonely hearts notice, taking her inspiration from the 1990s Hollywood film *Single White Female*, starring Bridget Fonda, and propped it up outside the Nelson Arms.

It read: 'Wanted: part-time single white male, 40–50. Must like cats. Must have a wicked sense of humour to cheer up overworked, underpaid, flu-ravaged, p★★★★d-off pub landlady. Previous applicants and ex-husbands need not reapply.'

The locals liked it and had a good laugh over their pints, but before Diane had a chance to vet any potential suitors she received a visit from a trio of female local councillors (they say bad things always come in threes) asking about the sign. Perhaps Diane, clearly a woman with a sense of humour, would have told them she wasn't that way inclined if she hadn't realised pretty quickly that they didn't find the sign funny. In fact, they belonged to Gloucester's Race Equality Council and they regarded the sign as rampant racism.

'I couldn't believe it,' stammered Dianne. 'When I realised that they were serious I had to shut the door on them. Otherwise I might not have been able to stay polite. I'm disgusted that taxpayers' money is being spent on investigating what is clearly a joke. It's not racist . . . [but] why shouldn't I want to meet a single white man at the moment? I've seen lonely hearts ads in papers looking for West Indians or other specific races.'

A spokesman for the Race Equality Council said: 'If a complaint is made then that is something we have to investigate and take seriously. I cannot say at this stage if we will be taking further action.'

Brazen cheek
In 2002, 33-year-old Susan Nickalls founded a new filmmaking company. She decided to call it 'Brazen Hussies' and sent the registration form to Companies House, whose business is to check that the name of a projected new company does not clash with an existing one. It could not resist the temptation to go interferingly po-faced. 'Degrading and demeaning,' it told Ms Nickalls. It 'pushed back the cause of women in today's society', it said, failing to spot the irony of a young woman doing the exact opposite. It refused to register her company. 'Names must not cause offence,' it continued. 'The system in Scotland is slightly different than in Wales and England.' In other words, saner. Susan Nickalls took the hint and simply registered her new company in Scotland.

Have It Your Way

What word links Afghanistan, Israel, America and the Park Royal outlet of Burger King? No conferring, now. Give up? The answer is 'Jihad'. No surprise for the first three but Park Royal in unexciting Northwest London?

It was in September 2005 that 27-year-old Rashad Akhtar from High Wycombe popped into the Burger King fast-food restaurant and left 'humiliated' after someone pointed out to him the chain's 'sacrilegious' ice-cream cones.

The design on the cone packaging showed a swirl of ice cream, or at least that's what everyone assumed but, in fact, as Akhtar told *Eastern Eye*: 'These people who have designed this think they can get away with this again and again . . . how can you say it is a spinning swirl? If you spin it one way to the right you are offending Muslims.'

Apparently, and we'll have to take Mr Akhtar's word for this, from one angle the swirl of ice cream looked similar – or at least a bit similar – to the word for Allah in Arabic script. 'This is my jihad,' thundered Mr Akhtar, who also wanted the designer sacked and Muslims to boycott the chain. In the face of such a threat Burger King ordered its managers to remove the offending item from sale.

Strangely, however, the *Scotsman* newspaper quoted a company spokesman (slogan: 'Have It Your Way') as insisting that: 'The design simply represents a spinning ice-cream cone.' So why scrap the cones? Evidently the collective backbone of Burger King's management bears a close similarity to that of the fish in their golden breaded fillets.

Piggy in the Middle

The pigs first realised they were bacon back in 1998 when Leicester Police confiscated a collection of seventeen miniature porcelain pigs from the front windowsill of Nancy Bennett's home, that happened to be in the same road as a local mosque. 'Muslims find pigs highly offensive,' explained police officer David Griffith, erroneously as it happens. 'That is why complaints were made.' Mrs Bennett avoided being stoned but she was threatened with prosecution, reported news agency Associated French Press, 'if she replaces the collection'.

In 2004 a row broke out in Derby over plans to replace the statue of the Florentine Boar in the city's Arboretum Park with one of a nineteenth-century architect. 'We should not have the boar because it is offensive to some of the groups in the area,' said councillor Suman Gupta, referring to Derby's Pakistani community. And yet, as we saw on p. 36, Muslim leaders and scholars have publicly confirmed that their religion has nothing against the poor old pig as a living animal. It is only the eating of it that is forbidden.

Nevertheless, many of our local councils continue to behave as though they know better than the minority they presume to act for. In 2005 Dudley Council in the West Midlands banned staff from displaying anything with pigs in their workspace, such as calendars, figurines, fluffy toys and even – as one woman discovered – a box of tissues featuring Winnie the Pooh and his curly-tailed accomplice, Piglet. A Muslim council worker had complained that he found such items offensive. Councillor Mahbubur Rahman backed the ban because it is about 'tolerance and acceptance of their beliefs'.

Again in 2005 a Lancashire newspaper revealed that both the Halifax and NatWest banks would no longer feature adverts containing images of piggy banks for fear, the paper reported, that they would upset Muslims. Both banks refuted the claims and it was never resolved who was telling porkies.

THE LIMP ARM OF THE LAW

The threat to life and limb of unseemly language and a reverential respect for the dignity and human rights of the criminal (or maybe it's a simple fear of lawyers) appear to have infected many of our police forces. To we the unthinking public, it frequently appears that the protection of the community and the pursuit of law-breakers have become laughably old-fashioned ideas.

Who Loves You, Jelly Baby?

The investigation dragged on for two years, the trial lasted eight days, the cost was estimated to be in the region of £250,000 and the jury took just 58 minutes to clear London Underground workers Carlo Rozza and Victor Cooney of biting the heads off black jelly babies in a racially intimidating manner.

The whole sorry saga began in January 2004 when Rozza walked into the staff room at Caledonian Road tube station to find Cooney and Daniel Jean-Marie having a bit of friendly workplace banter about jelly babies. Rozza asked Cooney for one from the packet and, when asked which colour, replied 'black'. Rozza told the court that Mr Jean-Marie became angry, stormed out of the room and told him to 'Fuck off'. 'We are talking about a bag of sweets, a bag of jelly babies, and three years later I'm in a court. Why?'

That was the question many people were asking, particularly as the pair had been cleared of racial harassment by an internal London Underground investigation in 2004. Nonetheless, Rozza and Cooney were questioned by police and Cooney was asked: 'Did you say anything about jelly babies? Anything about cutting their heads off? Anything about black or lime jelly babies that could have been misconstrued?' To each question he replied 'No', but still the case went to court.

Found 'Not guilty' in under an hour by the jury at Middlesex Guildhall Crown Court in November 2006, Mr Cooney said the verdict was a 'victory for common sense', although 'the trial has been a complete farce . . . the whole thing has been a disgrace. Two and a half years of my life has been wasted.'

Lollycoddled
Even in the days before the 'War on Terror' turned London into a city forever on a state of high alert, the Metropolitan Police had to deal with seemingly endless murders, robberies and muggings. Yet that didn't stop a group of female officers from taking time out to demand the removal of six ice-cream vending machines from their New Scotland Yard HQ in 2000. What they couldn't stomach was the 3D picture on the machines of a winking woman sucking an ice-lolly. The *Evening Standard* quoted a Met spokesman as saying: 'Since they [the machines] were installed, a number of staff commented on the suggestive nature of the large picture on the front. The style of the picture was recently brought to the attention of the Met's catering director who made the decision that it was not an appropriate image for police premises.'

The Plod Squad

Warden David Brennan was devastated when he arrived at the medieval church of Middleton in Rochdale, Greater Manchester, one March morning in 2005 to discover that vandals had smashed some of the stained-glass windows, among them a commemoration to the part played by Middleton archers in the Battle of Flodden in 1513.

Mr Brennan climbed one of the two twelve-foot ladders leaning against the Grade-1 listed building – whose wooden steeple was built in 1667 – and counted five broken windows, an act of desecration he called 'nonsensical'. He phoned the police to report the attack, expecting they would soon be round to assess the damage and file a report. Or so, in his unworldliness, he assumed.

Perhaps the warden had watched too many episodes of *Dixon of Dock Green* in his youth, or maybe he was just foolishly naive, but the moment Mr Brennan mentioned to the scene-of-crime officer that he would have to climb up on to the roof to take photographic evidence there was a sharp intake of breath. That would not be possible because no Plod in the photographic unit was 'ladder trained'.

'They said they weren't allowed to go on to the roof,' Mr Brennan explained. 'They didn't even come and have a look to see how safe it is . . . How is the Crown Prosecution Service able to present a case without photographic evidence? It is a farce. These safety laws are protecting criminals because forces are worried that officers who get injured carrying out their duty could sue them.'

As police forces in Britain often do these days, Greater Manchester Police sympathised with Mr Brennan before disclosing the impossibility of actually doing anything useful. 'The Health and Safety at Work Act (1974) states that employers are obliged to take all possible precautions to ensure the safety of their employees in the workplace,' they patiently explained. 'The varied roles of police staff make it difficult to prepare every individual person for all eventualities as they are often called upon to carry out a wide range of different tasks.

'Greater Manchester Police therefore train specific specialist teams on how to work safely in a variety of conditions and situations,' they continued, warming to their task. 'One of the situations [that] requires specific training is the use of ladders.' This is good advice because, as millions of DIY enthusiasts are aware, it is a daunting challenge to put one foot above another to climb a ladder. If only burglars and vandals were so safety conscious.

'Allo, 'allo, a low beam

In July 2006, Lucinda Fleming of Farnham had a letter published in the paper. Surrey Police had written to her, and presumably to hundreds of others, requiring information to be listed of 'identifiable hazards' should they ever need to enter her premises. A form was to be completed indicating slippery floors, ceiling beams, sprinkler systems, basement steps, ponds and the like. One hopes she will never have a burglary or worse. The time needed for the police to check her file and set about finding officers short enough to avoid beams, sure-footed on slippery floors, nimble on steps and able to swim will be substantial. But why go on. You've got the picture by now – and the thief has long since disappeared with it.

Don't Takeaway His Rights

It was a day of takeaways for Barry Chambers on 7 June 2006. First, the 27-year-old was one of a gang who took away a car from its owner shortly after midnight, only to be pursued by police from Cheltenham into Gloucester city centre. Eventually, the car was stopped and two men arrested but Chambers did a runner and shinned a drainpipe (without first obtaining written permission from the Health and Safety Executive) to take up position on the roof of a house in Midland Road.

Police tried to talk Chambers down but he was having none of it and at 8 a.m. started to throw bricks on the people below. An hour later a police negotiator was sent up in a hydraulic lift, to return a few minutes' later with a request from the wanted man for a drink. Shortly before 10 a.m. a can of cola was despatched to the roof, but Chambers was appalled to discover it had already been opened and refused it.

As the morning wore on and the summer sun grew hotter, Chambers' thirst not only increased but his tummy started to rumble. Initially he tried to take his mind off the discomfort by lobbing more bricks at the dozens of police by now laying siege to the house, but then he put in a request for a takeaway. Not any old takeaway, mind, it had to be a Kentucky Fried Chicken – a family-size bucket – with a two-litre bottle of cola. Oh, and could you throw in a packet of fags?

Down on the ground, David Dalton, the owner of a nearby guesthouse, assumed the police would tell him where he could stick his chicken. No chance. A police officer was soon trotting off to the local KFC. 'I couldn't believe it,' said

Dalton. 'When my son saw them sending up a KFC meal he said he'd like to climb up there to get a free one too. Surely the quickest way to get him down would be to starve him.'

Oh, Mr Dalton, how could you? That's not the way the Gloucestershire Constabulary operate, as a spokeswoman later explained. 'Although he was on the roof being a nuisance,' she said, 'we still have to look after his wellbeing and human rights.'

A 'nuisance' was one word to describe Chambers, although those local residents ordered to evacuate their homes – and the motorists who suffered as a result of all the roads that were closed off – probably plumped for a shorter word to describe the chicken-chomper. A spokesman for the Stagecoach bus company fumed: 'It was absolutely mad. This caused chaos on all the city-centre services.'

The siege continued throughout the afternoon – during which time one resident reported that a firefighter took Chambers 'tea and biscuits' (Jammie Dodgers, perhaps?) – and into the evening until eventually, at 9.37 p.m., Chambers decided he'd had enough and surrendered having caused an estimated £40,000 damage to cars and property. Later in the year he was sentenced to three and a half years.

The softly-softly approach caused uproar in the local and national press – with even a local Lib Dem councillor questioning the thinking behind the finger-lickin' good method – forcing the police to explain their strategy. 'The meal was part of the negotiation process and certain requests were made which we tried to fulfil because we wanted to work with him and persuade him to come down,' said a spokesperson. 'It was a hot day and it wouldn't have been in our interest if he had passed out through a lack of fluid and fell from the roof.' Then again, it was hardly in the police's best interests to engender the contempt of the dozens of local residents who'd been moved out of their houses for over fourteen hours.

Hardened criminal

Who says the police only go after soft targets these days? In February 2007 a bashful bobby in Cambridge was forced to get to grips with a four-foot penis – and an erect one at that. The penis belonged to eighteen-year-old history student John Knowles (I bet he wasn't short of a date at the summer ball) and caused deep offence because, according to a police spokesman, of its 'intricate' nature and its 'prominent position'. The penis, made of snow, soon disappeared of its own accord with the change of temperature. John was given an £80 fixed penalty for causing an offence, and the arresting officer was given an inferiority complex.

Wails and the Dragon

Landlady Angie Sayer thought she would celebrate St George's Day in 2006 with a bit of light-hearted fun in her pub, the New Inn, in Wedmore, Somerset. What about getting punters to pretend they were St George for the day, she thought, and charging them £1 for the chance to slay a dragon with three arrows.

She got hold of a children's bow-and-arrow set and then looked around for a picture of a dragon that would make a decent-sized target. In the end she settled for the red dragon found on the Welsh flag and fixed it to a board in the beer garden.

Angie's idea went down a storm with her locals, and adults and children lined up to try and down the dragon with an arrow. But one customer wasn't happy. Ms Sayer was stirring up racism against the Welsh by encouraging people to fire arrows at the dragon on their flag. So off he, or she, went squealing to the police, who once upon a time would've smiled sweetly at the old misery-guts and told him, or her, to run along home.

A few days later there was a knock at Ms Sayer's door (how long before they come knocking in the dead of night?) and two officers from the Avon and Somerset Police – who in 2006 failed to solve over 75 per cent of the crimes committed on their beat – informed her that they wished to interview her on suspicion of inciting racial hatred.

During the two-hour interview which followed, Ms Sayer told the police officers what she later told a newspaper, that 'people came dressed as knights from the Crusades' (careful,

Angie, dangerous word to use) 'and the kids loved shooting their little bows and arrows at the target. It was just a lovely day for everyone. It was never designed to hurt anyone, or cause any kind of upset. It was supposed to be a bit of a giggle.'

But the British police don't do 'giggles', and the two officers departed the pub with a warning that Ms Sayer could be charged under the Public Order Act 1986, which makes it illegal to provoke hatred of a racial group, the maximum penalty for which is seven years.

A spokesman for Avon and Somerset Police later confirmed that officers had visited the pub because 'we were made aware of an alleged hate crime'. Charges were never pressed, however, and the last word went to the unbowed Ms Sayer, who described the police action as 'lunacy', adding that 'people are too afraid to blink nowadays in case we offend someone'.

Here's to you, Mrs Robinson
In 2001 red-haired Anne Robinson let rip at the Welsh on the BBC comedy show *Room 101*. It was all harmless nonsense from the presenter of *Weakest Link*, living up to her reputation as a motormouth *par excellence*. 'I've never taken to them,' she roared, adding that they were 'irritating and annoying' and asking, 'What are they for?' She soon discovered what the North Wales Police Force was for when it launched an investigation into whether she'd committed a race crime. During the course of a £3,800 enquiry, which involved a superintendent, a detective chief inspector and two detective inspectors, Greg Dyke, then BBC director general, was questioned before it was decided there was 'insufficient evidence' to prosecute.

Cherie Trifle

How far has the madness spread? Right to the top, as the prime minister's wife discovered in September 2006 when she was a guest in Glasgow at the UK School Games. Cherie Blair was having her photo taken with a group of young sports stars when seventeen-year-old Miles Gandolfi, captain of the England U17 épée fencing team, put his fingers behind her head and made a pair of rabbit's ears. Cherie, despite being a human-rights lawyer, has a sense of humour and laughed, calling Gandolfi a 'cheeky boy' and pretending to give him a playful slap on the arm.

A pretend playful slap? No such thing these days, and within minutes the Games' organisers had called in the police following a discussion with officials from the Child Protection in Sport Unit (CPSU).

As six detectives scrutinised photos of the incident, Miles was interviewed by police and presumably offered counselling. 'I had no idea why the police wanted to speak to me,' he said later. 'I thought it was a joke. My reaction was just disbelief.'

Strathclyde Police later issued a statement saying that 'following further inquiries into an alleged incident said to have occurred at the UK School Games . . . it has now been established no incident took place. Police inquiries into the matter are now complete.'

Margaret Mitchell, the Conservative justice spokeswoman, echoed the views of the majority when she said, 'There are legitimate reasons why the CPSU was set up and this detracts from it. This was a non-incident and someone needs to look at the waste of police time.'

You're revving a laugh!

In September 2005 Ronnie Hutton, a mechanic from Stirling in Scotland, was charged with 'revving his car in a racist manner' after an off-duty chief inspector saw him testing the engine of his Lotus as a couple in Muslim dress walked past on the pavement. Hutton readily accepted he'd been revving his engine – a V8 twin turbo – and that 'it is noisy and frightening'. But he claimed it was only because he had a problem with the oil-pressure light that he was trying to fix. 'I would openly apologise to this couple,' he said. 'I am not a racist.' As journalists eagerly awaited the start of the trial, desperate to find out, in the words of the correspondent from *The Scotsman*, 'what exactly constitutes racist revving', prosecutors decided to drop the 'racist revving charge' and replace it with the more banal 'breach of the peace'.

Yob and Chips

In June 2006 it was widely reported in the media that Home Secretary John Reid wanted the British public to 'stop moaning' about yobbish antisocial behaviour and 'take action, it's your street, too'. It was all part of Tony Blair's Respect Task Force. As its official government website says: 'We want the public to take a stand against antisocial behaviour in their community.'

So that's exactly what Nicholas Tyers did in July 2006 when a teenager 'spat at a customer and smashed the window' of his fish and chip shop in Bridlington, East Yorkshire, causing £400 damage.

The yob ran off before Mr Tyers could nab him, but the next day he and his twenty-year-old son Lee, a Royal Marine Commando home on leave, spotted him and made a citizen's arrest.

'We went back to the house rather than the police station to call the police from there,' explained Mr Tyers. 'Nine times out of ten Bridlington police station is unmanned and you have to speak to someone on the telephone. We thought it best to call the police from home. When we got to the shop a police car was passing so we flagged him down and told them we had got the lad.'

Well done, the Tyers. The prime minister and his Respect Task Force will be proud of you. Who knows, you might even be in line for one of their Taking A Stand awards, to 'recognise people who have taken a stand against antisocial behaviour'.

Woah, not so fast! We're talking about the British police here. All it took was for the little tyke to complain that he hadn't been taken straight to the police station (they may look stupid, these thugs but, boy, do they know their 'rights') and suddenly Mr Tyers and his son were the ones being accused of kidnapping because it had taken six minutes to transport the boy in their car to the fish and chip shop.

'The police turned the tables on us,' said Mr Tyers. 'I was fingerprinted and had my picture taken and [was] treated like a criminal.'

The case was referred to the Crown Prosecution Service who decided to try the pair for kidnap, a crime that carries a maximum sentence of life imprisonment. So instead of deploying to Afghanistan with his elite unit – where every Allied soldier was needed in the fight against the Taliban – Lee Tyers had to wait for the trial to reach Hull Crown Court.

When it did, in January 2007, Judge John Dowse soon called a halt to the farce that had cost £60,000 to bring to court and ordered the jury to clear the pair. He said the Tyers had acted 'reasonably' and added: 'I began this case asking whether it was in the public interest, whether it should have been pressed, and the result is it has not been in the public interest. I raise the question of whether or not there are far more serious cases to bring?'

'I felt as if I was doing my public duty,' said Mr Tyers outside court. 'I have faced six months of hell waiting to prove my innocence. I have lost my faith in the judicial process.'

When the windows of his fish and chip shop were broken for a second time, Mr Tyers decided it would be best to pick up the telephone and inform the local station. Their response? 'All the police say when you call them,' complained Mr Tyers, 'is here is your crime number, claim off the insurance.'

Don't pin your hopes on the police

When Yusuf Nayir's takeaway restaurant was attacked by yobs late one night in 2003, the 41-year-old grabbed the first thing that came to hand – a rolling pin – and chased the hooligans down the road. One of the unfit thugs surrendered when he ran out of puff and allowed himself to be handed over to the police. But the moment they saw the rolling pin, the police threw Mr Nayir in the cells and charged him with carrying an offensive weapon. Fined £100 by Selby magistrates in North Yorkshire, Mr Nayir also had his rolling pin confiscated. Chief Inspector Andy Hirst, of Selby Police, said the incident was 'part of society we live in today . . . when people are faced with a threat against them they should leave it to us. If people do get involved and act in this way they are at risk of being arrested themselves.'

If the Helmet Fits, Don't Wear It

When Max Foster was woken early one morning in 2006 in Bath by the sound of his moped engine he rushed to the window to see three youths taking it in turns to race the bike up and down the road. He dialled 999 and two officers in a squad car arrived a few minutes later, just as the trio sped off.

Max dashed up to the police and asked them to 'follow that moped'. Oh no, sir, couldn't do that, sir. You see, if the three thieves 'haven't got a helmet on, we can't pursue them. We can't risk a lawsuit. We'd get sued if they fell off and hurt themselves.' Max at this point must have been wondering if he was having a bad dream. His £1,200 moped – his means of transport for getting to work each day – had just been nicked, the yobs were in the near vicinity but there was nothing the police could do. Apart from summoning up some courage, perhaps?

As Max told the BBC the following day: 'I can't believe it . . . because all the bike thieves know that [the police attitude], so that's what they do and they're laughing at the police.'

Inspector Tim House of Avon and Somerset Police sympathised with Mr Foster's predicament but reminded him that 'we must first consider the safety of the public at large, the time of day, number of people around, are there any pedestrians or young children playing nearby? The pursuit police make us consider all those options in sequence and then an officer in the force control room will decide on appropriate action.'

The police assured Max that an active search for the stolen moped was 'ongoing' but, despite five sightings of it being driven around Bath the following day, the bike had not been recovered by the end of the week.

On your bike

In March 2004 Merseyside Police called in the help of an American expert from the International Police Mountain Bike Association to teach its officers how to ride a bicycle. 'They will be taught to get on and off the bike and how best to do their job as a police officer while on a bike,' said a spokeswoman for the force, before adding the obligatory caveat about Health and Safety. 'It is incumbent on us as an employer to ensure officers are fully trained to enable them to do their job properly and safely.' Presumably, this included knowing how to mend a puncture, how to use your arm to indicate and how to do a wheelie to impress the Chief Constable.

Bad Golly

In March 2006 53-year-old Donald Reynolds was having lunch in a restaurant with his wife when his mobile rang. ''Allo, 'allo, 'allo,' said a voice at the other end, before identifying itself as an officer with the West Mercia Police Force.

It wanted to know how far away Mr Reynolds was from his hardware store in Bromyard, Herefordshire. Not too far, replied the shopkeeper. Has something happened? The police officer told him to come and open up his shop immediately.

Fearing that his shop may have been broken in to, Mr Reynolds hurried round and was met by the grave-looking policeman. 'When I got there he said, "I've come about the gollies, we've had a complaint they are causing offence".'

The courageous copper then single-handedly stormed Mr Reynolds' hundred-year-old hardware store – don't forget, he was unarmed – and arrested three golliwogs who were huddled together in the shop window in their black-and-white striped trousers and red jackets hatching another dastardly plot.

As the trio were led away (the local paper soon dubbed them the Bromyard Three), the lion-hearted police officer warned Mr Reynolds that he could well be charged under Section 5 of the Public Order Act, which outlaws the display of offensive material that 'might cause or is likely to lead to alarm, harassment or distress', the punishment for which is a £1,000 fine or quite possibly transportation to Van Diemen's Land.

'I can't really see what I have done wrong,' mumbled poor Mr Reynolds. 'It's just a traditional toy for my generation of people and the customers love them . . . Many people have told me they had gollies – I can't say golliwogs – when they were younger. It didn't even enter my mind that I might be committing a public-order offence by having them in the window.' Having taken a hundred golliwogs from a wholesaler a month earlier, Mr Reynolds only had a dozen left at the time of the police raid because 'they'd been selling like hot cakes'.

A spokesman for Worcester Racial Equality Council backed the police swoop, insisting that the sale of golliwogs would only 'lead to a worsening of race relations and this needs to be taken into account'.

For the next two weeks the Bromyard Three were interviewed by West Mercia Police but all they would reveal was that they came in three sizes, a twelve-inch model for £2.99, seventeen-inch for £4.99 and a two-foot version for £7.99. After consultation with the Crown Prosecution Service the police decided not to prosecute Mr Reynolds, although they said they would be sending a letter to the shopkeeper 'advising him about the sensitivity surrounding the controversial dolls'.

Conservative MP Andrew Rosindell wondered if the police shouldn't be 'out catching criminals and making our streets safe, rather than confiscating dolls. Public safety is of great concern to many people.'

A fortnight after the Bromyard Three were released, Demos, a government think-tank, released a study that stated that six out of ten muggings and 38 per cent of burglaries were never reported to the police because the public no longer had faith in them. The study added: 'The police were more likely to be rated as doing a good job by people who had no contact with them over the past year than those who had.'

To catch a thief . . . don't run

In May 2002 a policeman in West Yorkshire showed some of the spirit we used to routinely associate with the British police, pursuing a car thief on foot for half a mile until he got his man. But the prisoner complained that the policeman had given chase 'recklessly and oppressively, causing him to lose his footing and fall', damaging his designer jeans in the process. So instead of being congratulated the policeman – who described his experience anonymously in the Police Federation's magazine – was given a verbal warning for 'dangerous and careless chasing on foot'. 'It's too crazy for words,' muttered Chris Turton, chairman of the West Yorkshire Police Federation. 'I just couldn't believe it.'

Horsin' Around

There was a time when police officers had a sense of humour – it was a Wednesday afternoon in 1904 if the rumours are to be believed – but in the 21st century you crack a joke to the boys in blue at your peril, as 21-year-old Oxford University student Sam Brown found out in the summer of 2005.

Brown and a few mates left a nightclub in the City of Dreaming Spires in the early hours one morning and walked down a deserted street past two mounted policemen. 'Mate, you know your horse is gay?' Brown laughed to one of the bobbies. 'I hope you don't have a problem with that!' The pair of po-faced pony riders warned him not to repeat his offensive remark. When Brown did, not once, but twice more, the policemen informed him he was being arrested for a breach of the Public Order Act.

Brown didn't imagine they were being serious and walked away, at which point the mounted officers radioed for backup and trotted down Cornmarket Street in pursuit – think John Wayne as Rooster Cogburn in *True Grit* and you get the picture.

Brown was eventually corralled in Ship Street by the two mounted policemen and six constables on foot. One of Brown's friends, Matthew Williams, tried to intercede on his behalf by 'pointing out that "gay" was not a pejorative term, and that insulting a police animal was surely not an arrestable offence'.

Brown was taken to St Aldate's police station and after the arresting officers had looked up 'pejorative' in the dictionary, he was thrown in the clink for the night. He was released at seven o'clock the next morning and ordered to pay an £80 fine for 'causing harassment, alarm or distress' within three weeks.

Brown told his student magazine that he promised in future to 'hold back on gender-preference assumptions if they allow me to meet animals in the future', while his friend Williams – clearly too clever for his own good – said in the same publication that 'aside from the hilariousness of the event there's also a serious question; isn't it offensive to assume categorically the word "gay" is insulting? . . . I was offended that they (the police) assumed "gay" was being used as an insult.'

Thames Valley Police, not really knowing what Williams was on about, accused Brown of being 'abusive and acting in a drunken manner' and when he refused to pay the £80 fine they took him to court. It was only when the case opened at Oxford Magistrates' Court and the Crown prosecutors examined the details that they realised it was pointless to continue because 'there is not enough evidence to prove [Mr Brown's behaviour] was disorderly'.

The Thames Valley Police were disappointed with the outcome. 'He made homophobic comments that were deemed offensive to people passing by,' said a spokescreature of the incident that happened at 2 a.m. on a Monday morning – when nobody else was passing by – and involved a horse.

Can I Have My Ball Back?

It's not always easy to spot the potential criminal these days – the would-be suicide bomber, the ruthless mugger – particularly so on the London Underground during rush hour when great waves of humanity surge up and down the escalators.

And to all but the most trained eye Chris Hurd looked like any other city worker as he rode the underground after a hard day in the office in November 2006. The 28-year-old, an accountant for a major London firm, was dressed in a sober suit with sensible haircut to match as he stood on the escalator at Baker Street Station. But clutched in his hands was a bomb. No, hang on, that's wrong. Clutched in his hands was a ball. A cricket ball, if we're being precise.

'I took the ball to the office because I was getting more and more excited about the start of the Ashes,' explained Hurd, a decent leg-spin bowler for his local team, who like so many now-shattered Englishmen believed England might retain the Ashes against the Aussies down under. 'All day long, I was fiddling with it and throwing it into the air, which I do to strengthen my arm muscles for spin bowling.'

A little obsessive perhaps, but surely not a criminal offence. Then again . . .

'I was just holding the ball going up the escalator,' continued Hurd. 'There was a policewoman on the step below me and she was staring at the ball all the way up. As we got to the top, she tapped me on the shoulder and said she wanted a word. I wondered what on earth I had done.'

The maiden from the Met wasn't happy. She asked the armed and dangerous accountant if he was aware he was 'carrying a very hard object'. Hurd was stumped. Then he realised she was staring at his ball. 'Oh, this,' exclaimed Hurd. 'Yes, it's a cricket ball.'

'She told me I should not be carrying it in public because it was a potentially lethal weapon. I told her I was only carrying it because the Ashes were about to start and I was very excited.'

That went down about as well as umpire Darrell Hair in Pakistan. 'She confiscated the ball for most of our conversation, gave me a verbal warning and said she was being very lenient,' said Hurd, who had to wait patiently as the policewoman filled out a stop-and-search form before finally giving back his ball.

'How can a cricket ball be an offensive weapon?' muttered Hurd. 'I don't think it would be anyone's weapon of choice and all I was doing was holding it.' True, Chris, true. But look on the bright side. You're not Brazilian.

Come on you Spurs!

Premiership soccer team Spurs draws much of its support from the large Jewish population around its north London base in Tottenham. This support extends up the A10 into Hertfordshire. Each soccer team has a song for its fans to belt out at every opportunity, and *Yid Army* is Spurs'. But when eight teenage fans sang it during a boisterous farewell to a master at their school, Chauncy's in Ware, in March 2007, trouble in the shape of the fuzz was soon on the doorstep. The eight were arrested, spent ten hours in custody being fingerprinted, DNA'd and given the works. As the *Observer* commented: *Yid Army* 'is a weapon, ridiculing racists doubly because it dilutes intended spite . . . it binds all Spurs fans, Jewish or not. Take the goons seriously by banning *Yid Army* and you play into their hands.' And as the Headmaster added: 'Making criminals of misguided young people because you can must not be the future in England.'

Wanted: Human Rights for the Community

Perhaps it had something to do with the fact that British prisons are already at bursting point, overflowing with a record 80,000 inmates, or 'cons' to give them their tabloid title. But when two murderers did a runner from Sudbury Open Prison in late 2006 the local police didn't seem too eager to recapture them.

Jason Croft and Michael Nixon were both 28 and cut from the same cloth. Croft had killed a man with a knife and Nixon had battered a teenager to death with a concrete slab. Not the sort of people you want roaming the streets with time on their hands.

But Derbyshire Police were worried that if they released their photos the little lambs might burst into tears. Oh, bless. As a spokesperson for the force said, 'When making a decision to release photos, officers must take into account numerous factors including public interest and of course the Human Rights and Data Protection Acts. Photographs of named people in police possession are classed as data and their release is restricted by law. Guidance states that releasing a "wanted" photo should only happen in exceptional circumstances where the suspect may be a danger to the public.' One wonders what crime fits into Derbyshire Police's view of 'exceptional'. Anything to do with *Celebrity Big Brother*, perhaps?

Such was the uproar when the news broke that the Lord Chancellor, Lord Falconer of Thoroton, QC, weighed in to the row to prove that while Britain was on the brink of going mad, we were not quite there yet. 'Absolute nonsense,' he said of the decision not to release the wanted photos, adding, 'When you are dealing with two convicted murderers, both of whom have absconded, it is utterly obvious that there is no public interest arising out of the Human Rights Act which prevents publication.'

In the end it was the Greater Manchester force that cut through the cackle and published the photos of the two murderers, leaving Derbyshire Police free to chase chickens and arrest grannies for kidnapping footballs (see pp. 82–84).

Fuzzy behaviour
It seems police obsession with the inalienable rights of criminals is confined neither to daffy Derbyshire nor to convicted murderers. In December 2006 Isabel Kurtenbach, a jeweller in West London, was relieved of stock worth £2,000 by a woman claiming to be (a) wealthy, and (b) from one of the richest parts of the Arab world, viz Dubai. Pictures of the lady in question trying on the soon-to-be-vanished jewellery were captured with remarkable clarity on the shop's CCTV system. Other jewellers in the area recognised her at once as the same person who had hoofed it with expensive items on earlier occasions. That's as maybe, said the police, but pictures of her in flagrante delicto could not be issued because they might contravene the Human Rights Act. Before Mrs Kurtenbach could enquire what human rights she had in the matter, the helpful fuzz suggested she wait for the thief to strike again, and then perform a citizen's arrest. But what if she's on drugs and carrying a knife, asked Mrs K? The guardians of the law 'shrugged'. Only when the local jewellers threatened to take the matter to the press did New Scotland Yard spring into action. It sent four officers round to apologise.

Tattoo Much for the Police

The police don't accept any old riffraff these days. They have high standards that are designed to weed out undesirables, which presumably means people like Ivan Ivanovic. In 2006 the forty-year-old applied to become a police community support officer when he quit the British Army after 22 years of exemplary service. You might have thought the Cumbria Constabulary would be champing at the bit to have someone like Ivan in their ranks, an unflappable type who had served in Iraq and Kosovo and would be well equipped to protect the public in Britain's increasingly lawless towns.

As fit a forty-year-old as you're ever likely to see, Ivan assumed the medical would be a formality. But when the Cumbria Constabulary asked if he had any distinguishing marks, he replied that he had a tattoo of the Union Jack with the words 'British Army' underneath. Ivan thought nothing of it. Why should he, as 'the tattoo is a few inches long and below my left shoulder, so no one would see it'.

That wasn't the point, though, as Ivan discovered when his application was refused on the grounds that he had a 'lewd, offensive' tattoo that could be construed by some people as racist. 'I can't see why anyone would think that the flag of the country might be seen as racist,' said Ivan. 'It's crazy.'

Crazy, but not uncommon, as *The Times* showed in 2007 when it reported that a former Royal Marine commando had also been barred from joining the police force because he had a tattoo on his forearm of the Royal Marines Corps crest. What had particularly peeved the commando was the fact that his rejection came in the same month as another rejection made news headlines.

This time, however, it wasn't a tattoo but a touch that caused a bit of a kerfuffle. A Muslim woman police officer refused to shake hands at her passing-out parade with Sir Ian Blair, head of the Metropolitan Police Force. Apparently she took her stance against the most powerful police officer in the country because, according to the BBC, 'her faith prevented her touching a man other than her husband or a close relative'.

I've a bone to pick with you

In 2000 Clyde, a pointer dog with no previous convictions, had his collar felt by the West Yorkshire constabulary after he was accused of racism. Clyde was employed as a sniffer dog at Wakefield Prison and one British Asian visitor took exception to the number of times he was sniffed. 'Clyde should be pensioned off,' he fumed. 'Sniffer dogs should be impartial.' A prison service spokesman reacted angrily to the charge, saying, 'We totally reject allegations that any of our sniffer dogs are racist.' Nonetheless a report was compiled by the prison's race-relations officer and sent to the police, although charges weren't pressed. When invited to comment, Clyde sniffed the reporter's trousers before growling.

Rapid Over-Reaction Force

It's a dangerous world out there and, in our 21st-century risk-averse culture, who can blame the police for preferring to pursue people who aren't going to knock off their helmets?

There was the time in 2005 when 78 police officers took part in the operation to remove anti-war demonstrator Brian Haw and his placards from outside the Houses of Parliament. The operation cost £7,200 – quite a lot on bacon rolls and mugs of tea for the Magnificent 78, and £3,000 on overtime – and left many wondering whether the Metropolitan Police might have overreacted. 'I do think it brings the Met into a bit of disrepute,' said Liberal Democrat peer Lord Tope. 'Seventy-eight police officers arriving in the middle of the night to clear placards and chase mice. I really do think that it was huge overkill.' But Met boss Sir Ian Blair promised there would be 'no discretion' when it came to those who 'ignore the law'.

The following year the police's determination to root out hardened criminals was witnessed in Bedfordshire when 77-year-old Frank Cook, a farmer on his own land, fired a shotgun into the air to frighten off a dog that was threatening some of his lambs – as a farmer is fully entitled to do if his livestock are menaced by uncontrolled animals. A short while later Mr Cook was playing with his two young grandchildren in his garden when he heard the wail of sirens. 'I was standing out on the lawn with my grandchildren,' Mr Cook explained. 'To my utter astonishment, no fewer than six police cars drove up. Armed policemen stepped out of the front and stood with their guns at the ready.'

Not wanting to alarm his grandchildren, aged three and five, Mr Cook calmly told the policemen 'not to be silly and to send the armed men back into their cars and then I would talk to them'. At which point, 'one officer put an arm lock on me, frogmarched me to a car and pushed me in. They told me they were arresting me for criminal damage.'

For the next five hours Mr Cook was held in a police cell, while his fingerprints and a DNA swab were taken, and then he was released without charge. 'I cannot believe that something like this can happen in England,' said Mr Cook's MP, Nadine Dorries.

Then there was the case in 2003 when Derbyshire Police (you'll remember these are the intrepid protectors of the public who wouldn't publish a 'Wanted' poster for fear of hurting the feelings of two escaped murderers – see p. 78) had the tricky problem of assigning officers to two high-profile cases: one the brutal beating and robbery of a female riding instructor, the other involving the theft of chickens from a poultry processing plant owned by a prominent figure in the local community. In the end it was decided a solitary detective would look into the assault and battery while forty of her colleagues, including an undercover team, went chicken hunting.

Nine months later the riding instructor was murdered by the man who had ordered the initial beating, leaving the woman's mother to state: 'The police decided to investigate the missing chickens, possibly because it appeared more straightforward, rather than finding out who was targeting my daughter, and as a result she was murdered.'

You'd have hoped that Derbyshire Police might have learned a lesson from the chicken fiasco, but three years later they managed to outrage public opinion again. In the summer of 2006, 56-year-old Angela Hickling was bundled from her home in Heanor (in front of her teenage son), driven to the police station, interrogated, fingerprinted and obliged to give a DNA sample. Her crime? A neighbour claimed his son's football had landed in the Hicklings' garden and Angela was refusing to return it. In fact, she was unaware of any rogue football and when a team of policemen conducted a thorough search of the garden – and her home – they were unable to find the mystery ball.

After being questioned for an hour and a half about the missing ball (we've all met a football bore before, but that is ridiculous!) Angela was released and then informed two days later the investigation was being discontinued because of 'lack of evidence'.

In February 2007 *The Times* reported that the constable who had arrested Mrs Hickling had been 'reprimanded' by the Derbyshire Constabulary, which provoked her into making an official complaint to the Independent Police Complaints Commission. 'The officer's behaviour was too severe for me to let this go,' she told the newspaper, adding that the 'whole episode was a farce . . . why mess about over a football when there are burglars breaking into people's homes, people selling drugs and pensioners being mugged?'

The Derbyshire force's crime statistics for the period 2005–2006 revealed that of the more than 80,000 crimes committed on their patch, their detection rate was 25.8 per cent. A spokesperson said that obviously they were working hard to improve this figure and that 'the work of our officers in local neighbourhoods to create a link with the public to build trust, confidence and reassurance is vital'.

Big Brother is listening

In December 2005 author and broadcaster Lynette Burrows took part in a BBC radio discussion about child adoption. Burrows, well known for her views on children's rights and family values, said on air that she was against allowing homosexuals to adopt. The next day Mrs Burrows was contacted by a policewoman, who told her that a 'homophobic incident' had been reported against her. Burrows was 'astounded' and told the policewoman that 'this is a free country and we are allowed to express opinions on matters of public interest. She told me it was not a crime but that she had to record these incidents. They were leaning on me, letting me know that the police had an interest in my views. I think it is sinister and completely unacceptable.' Scotland Yard later confirmed that Fulham Police had investigated a complaint over the radio programme because homophobic, racist and domestic incidents were 'priority crimes'.

Holding Out for a Hero

In 2003 Amerjit Singh packed in his job as a legal executive to join the Cambridgeshire Police Force. The father of two wanted to make a difference to his community and, understandably, the Cambridgeshire Constabulary were pleased to have Amerjit, and his cousin. Not only were they fit and intelligent young men but they were also the force's first two Sikh police recruits. Hard evidence that their officers truly reflected the cosmopolitan nature of the county's population. 'I hope my joining will encourage others from Peterborough's large Asian community who may have any trepidation or fears about joining the police,' Amerjit said in one interview.

In September 2004 PC Singh – in his first year in the job and so a 'probationer' – and two other officers were called to a disturbance at a house in Peterborough. As they entered the building, the rookie policeman was confronted with an angry and agitated man who was threatening to jump from a second-floor window. PC Singh grabbed the man – despite taking a couple of blows in the process – and wrestled him away from the window and on to the ground whereupon he restrained him with a headlock.

At around this time the suicidal man's father turned up. Tearful hugs of gratitude all round, you might have thought, but not a bit of it. The dad was incensed at the way his son was being restrained, and made his feelings known in a formal complaint to Cambridgeshire Police.

They treated the gripe with the contempt it deserved and rejected the complaint, so the father appealed to the Independent Police Complaints Commission (IPCC). They studied the evidence, took into account that PC Singh – at no small risk to himself – had saved the man from probably committing suicide, and offered him words of advice. These pearls of wisdom, doubtless given by people who couldn't spell alacrity, let alone exhibit it, included the following: 'It is clear that an inappropriate and potentially dangerous hold was used.' In future Singh was told not to use a headlock but adhere to the guidelines approved by the Home Office. This admonishment was also added to PC Singh's record.

Although PC Singh was unable to comment on the absurd ruling, others were happy to do so on his behalf. His MP, Stewart Jackson, described the IPCC's findings as 'barking mad . . . we should be applauding the bravery and commitment of this young man rather than pillorying him', while David Sanders, a member of the Cambridgeshire Police Authority, wondered, 'Will a cop put himself out time after time just to find a complaint against his name at the end of it? If a bobby is out of order he should be disciplined. But the abuse of the system is sapping the morale of many good officers.'

The long and the short of it

Autumn 2006 saw a string of burglaries in the well-heeled towns of Knutsford, Alderley Edge and Wilmslow. At one point in the sequence, after a tip-off about an intended armed raid in Alderley Edge, police thought up the spiffing idea of leaving empty police cars in the street as a deterrent. When the three robbers turned up on cue, sporting two handguns, they simply walked past them and got on with their job. The police cars remained predictably immobile. Forced to think again, the police surpassed themselves. They advised shopkeepers each to keep a mobile phone and a tape measure to hand. The mobile was not for dialling 999, of course. Before you could hiss Health and Safety Executive (HSE), this might end in a chase that could contravene health and safety regulations. No, it was to take a picture of the robber (although one must doubt whether such a picture could be used without fear of damaging the criminals' human rights (see p. 78). To be even further on the safe side, while remaining as far away from the crime scene as possible, the police advised measuring the height of the persons who had just robbed you. To be sure they did not suggest asking the villains to stand still for a few moments while you ran a tape measure over them. Rather that you fix the measure to your doorframe so you could jot down their height as they fled the premises. This original scheme had one virtue. By freeing the police from the unpleasant business of preventing crime, it left them time to investigate misdemeanours such as flying the Union Jack in one's garden.

THE DISARMED SERVICES

What with health and safety to consider, never mind the odd lawyer and a dollop of political correctness, it's a recurring wonder that our services, whether armed or firefighting, are still able to do the job our taxes pay for. Don't despair. Throw into the mix the regular expenditure cuts by government, and the brave lads and lasses who provide these services will soon be as ineffective as the politicians, local and national, who scorn them . . . but at least they'll be ineffective in a politically correct manner.

Barmy Army

General Sir Charles Guthrie had the heart of a fearless soldier and the air of a family doctor. No ramrod back and army bark for Sir Charles; rather a man admired by the politicians for his intellect and insight; and an officer respected by his men for his leadership and bravery. It was no surprise, therefore, when the general was appointed Chief of the Defence Staff in 1997. Who better to be in charge of Britain's military than a man who had served his country in some of the world's most dangerous war zones without losing his smiling sang-froid? But Sir Charles was soon to discover that the bureaucratic minefields of Whitehall present their own unique challenges.

First up was the Ministry of Defence, fretting about the army's regimental sergeant majors. They explained to Sir Charles that all their incessant bellowing at recruits on the parade ground contravened health and safety regulations. Could they perhaps shout a little less loudly? Or, as novelist and former soldier Leslie Thomas wondered in a newspaper article, could it be arranged for the soldiers 'to wear earmuffs to soften the sergeant major's harsh words'? Allegedly, the general's curt response to the Ministry most definitely contravened health and safety guidelines on noise level.

But the forces of political correctness soon regrouped and launched another assault.

In 1999 a raft of what Guthrie called 'barmy ideas' was mooted in the name of political correctness by people whose experience of warfare had evidently been gleaned from watching repeats of *Dad's Army*. 'A New Army for a New

Millennium' seemed to be their slogan. There were calls to allow women to serve in front-line infantry regiments and for disabled peopled to join the armed forces. Look at Lord Nelson, they cried, he was disabled. At which point Sir Charles probably wished he was dodging the cannonballs on the deck of the *Victory* himself. His patience began to fray and he described their wittering as 'half-baked people talking about Nelson'. England's greatest sailor had lost an eye when he was a captain and an arm when he was an admiral, Guthrie pointed out, so that did not mean that the 'Royal Navy could recruit a seventeen-year-old midshipman with one leg and one eye'.

Guthrie was upbraided by human-rights organisation, Liberty, who informed him that 'the Armed Forces have a responsibility to ensure that they are equal opportunities employers, no matter what race, sex, sexual orientation or disability candidates may have'. And Lord Ashley of Stoke, chairman of the all-party Parliamentary Disablement Group, accused Guthrie of being 'besotted with the trench warfare of World War One'. Contrariwise, Simon Weston, the Welsh Guardsman so badly burned in the Falklands War, has a brain and a mouth that work in unison: 'War isn't a game. This isn't anti-disabled. It's just practical.'

General Guthrie's four-year appointment ended in 2001 and he stepped down to become Colonel Commandant of the SAS, an altogether more relaxed bunch than the pc brigade. Before leaving his post, however, he gave an interview in which he warned that 'if they introduce women into the SAS or blind people into the Coldstream Guards, if they put social engineering and equal opportunities in front of combat effectiveness, there is a real danger of damaging something that really works very well. I am absolutely convinced that some-times the rights of the individual are not as important as the team they are working for.' Then he paused, straightened his ramrod back, and labelled the people who advocate such things 'absolutely barking'.

Spaced-out minds
'I discovered the other day,' said General Guthrie in a newspaper interview in 1998, 'that somebody was advocating that an unmanned aerial reconnaissance vehicle, a UAV, should be called an uninhabited aerial vehicle.' Feminists were concerned that the morale of the British Army was being affected by such blatant sexism.

Best Breast Forward

Colonel Bob Stewart is one of Britain's war heroes for his outstanding leadership during the Bosnian conflict in the 1990s, and this despite the inadequacies of the outmoded, and sometimes inoperable, equipment his men had to fight with. He saw his mission as one to save lives, not destroy them, and to that end he was always prepared to bend or even flout the rules and his own orders, regarding the moral imperatives of the Geneva Convention as his highest authority. He slept in the same inhospitable surroundings as the men under his command, often without latrines or adequate supplies of water, but ensured that, no matter what, food always got through. So when Bob Stewart – now retired from the army, and a consultant on leadership, crisis management, motivation and security – speaks, you have to listen.

'This news is utterly grotesque,' he groaned in 2001. 'The "thin red line of heroes" that Kipling once wrote of is fast being replaced by the queue for the gender-reassignment counsellor.' Strong stuff. What exactly had so disturbed him? In four words, liposuction and breast enlargements. In April that year it was reported that twelve female soldiers had been given breast implants, four male soldiers had had sex-change operations and 'at least ten' had received liposuction to reduce the girth around their hips and stomach. The webbing was chafing them, you see, and naturally this caused them distress and not a little scratching.

We are unable to shed light on the breast implants, performed at a cost – to the taxpayer, naturally – of £2,500 a time. Perhaps they made it easier to rest the bosoms on the lip of the trench and get a steadier aim through the rifle sights? The only thing one can say with safety is that it was as well for the state of General Guthrie's health that he had, by now, retired as Chief of Defence.

Bob Stewart was in no mood to let go, however. What really upset him was that then, as now, the Ministry of Defence seemed so unable to find the money or the determination to ensure a proper infrastructure for the armed services. To take a single small example, in 1995 the army was still using a field radio dating from the 1950s and impatiently awaiting the new Bowman system, due for delivery that year. Seven years later it was still not ready.

Colonel Bob recalled a time in 1992–3 when 90 per cent of his fighting vehicles were out of action through lack of spares, and another when one of his patrols forty miles away came under heavy fire, but lost contact for eleven critical hours because the radio had broken down. Two months later, a brigadier came out to Bosnia and told him the MOD 'couldn't afford' a replacement radio system. 'I could not have realised that the top brass had higher priorities such as breast enhancements and liposuction,' said the frustrated colonel. 'Dare I ask,' he wrote later, 'how a female soldier who is so distressed by remarks about her appearance that she has to resort to implants, would cope under fire?' Steady on, Bob. You'll get the equalities and diversity mob all upset, which is far more dangerous than driving round Taliban-riddled Afghanistan in unarmoured Land Rovers.

Handbags at dawn

Captain Janet Kelly, an officer nurse in the British Army, is claiming substantial damages against a senior officer who called her a 'blonde thick bimbo'. The charge is one of sexual discrimination and is levelled against Lieutenant Colonel Jean Kennedy. How does one woman sexually discriminate against another woman? Don't ask us. This is Britain.

Flabbergasted Firefighters

Nanny is going to set you all a test. Is everybody sitting comfortably? Then I'll begin. Imagine you are living in Plymouth, your house catches fire and you ring the fire brigade. What is the most important thing the nice firepersons have to do? No, Dwayne, they don't put potatoes on the engine and whizz off to bake them for supper. Yes, Naomi? Get there as soon as possible to put the fire out? Oh, Naomi, what old-fashioned ideas you do have! Can nobody guess? Then I'll have to tell you. They carry out a risk assessment to make sure nobody gets hurt climbing on the fire engine, of course.

When the inhabitants of Plymouth heard, in 2006, that they were getting a spanking-new, three-storey fire station at Greenbank, costing £2.4 million, they may have believed for a few precious months that the service provided would be quicker and better than ever. That was before the Devon Fire and Rescue Authority slithered in. A pole, one for the sliding down of, was out. Far too dangerous, it said. Stairs were the only answer. 'There have been,' said Bernard Hughes, chairman of the aforesaid Authority, 'a number of injuries when firefighters have slipped on poles and damaged their ankles and knees.'

'Ludicrous,' countered the station officer, Ken Mulville. 'In more than thirty years I have seen one or two accidents with poles, compared with tens of accidents with people tripping on stairs while responding to accidents.' Having timed the relative response rates when pole-sliding or stair-tripping, he announced that it takes a second and a half to zip down a pole, and between fifteen and twenty seconds to gallop down two flights of stairs – depending, naturally, on the rate of downward gallop and the number of fallen bodies to be vaulted en route. 'Seconds can be critical when responding to a 999 call,' he added unnecessarily, since most of us can work out that those seconds could be the difference between life and death. The *Daily Telegraph* may have stumbled on the solution to the Devon Fire and Rescue Authority's dilemma. 'A Stannah stairlift would do the job nicely and in complete safety.'

Physician, heal thyself

Firemen arriving for work at their station in Arundel, West Sussex, one October morning in 2006 found it, and the engine within, blazing merrily. It took six appliances from towns round about to put it out, but by then it was too late. Despite the zeal of the fire service in ordering the rest of us to fit alarms and fire-retardant doors, it turned out that Arundel station had no fire alarm of its own. A shade careless, perhaps? Not really. As another of those unnamed spokespeople explained: 'A fire alarm is designed to save lives, whereas the building was unoccupied most of the time.' But not the twenty neighbouring properties, all of which had to be evacuated, as they were *not* unoccupied.

HMS Abject Victory

October 2005 saw the bicentenary celebrations of one of Britain's most critical victories in adversity, the Battle of Trafalgar. London's contribution to the celebrations was a re-enactment of Admiral Lord Nelson's waterborne funeral cortège from Greenwich to St Paul's. One year earlier a publicity photoshoot was arranged. An actor dressed as Nelson posed on the banks of the Thames before intending to board an RNLI lifeboat in order to sail up the river. Not so fast, muttered health and safety. You can only proceed with a life jacket over your Lord Nelson suit.

This latest piece of futility spawned a host of Internet musings on the outcome of Trafalgar had the Health and Safety Executive and today's politically correct society come into being two centuries ahead of time. In homage to the anonymous Internet authors, the following conversation might well have taken place aboard Nelson's flagship *Victory*, forcibly renamed HMS *Abject*:

'Send the following signal, Hardy. England expects that every man will do his duty. Got that?'

'Aye, aye, Admiral, though I fear I must make some slight adjustments. We're obliged to be an equal opportunities employer now, sir. Message will therefore read: England expects every person to do his or her duty regardless of race, gender, sexual orientation, religious persuasion or disability. I should add, sir, that only with the greatest difficulty was I allowed to keep the word "England" in the signal.'

'Good God, Hardy! Well, get someone up to the crow's nest at once to report on the position of the French.'

'I'm afraid that's impossible, my Lord. The crow's nest is closed – orders of Health and Safety. There's no harness there, you see, sir. They won't let anyone up there until there's full scaffolding round the mast. And while we're on the subject, sir, the rigging doesn't meet regulations and the crew are only allowed on it in hard hats. Oh, and before I forget, we have government-registered carpenters on board providing a barrier-free environment for the differently abled.'

'Differently abled? What kind of gobbledegook is that, Hardy? What does it mean?'

'With respect, sir, it refers to people such as yourself. You've only got one arm, one eye and . . . well, one of most things, my Lord, and it's to help you get around the ship.'

'Hardy, I've spent my life in the navy, never had a problem getting anywhere, including to be admiral, so don't give me all that rubbish.'

'Begging your pardon, sir, it's hardly rubbish, is it? I mean, ask yourself. Would you really have got the top job if it hadn't been for the quotas? It could be that it's only because the navy is short of men – I beg your pardon, persons – deficient in limbs and eyesight that you got fast-tracked up the ladder.'

'This is absurd, Hardy. I'm not allowed to know where the enemy is and now you're telling me I'm not fit for command. I've had enough. Order the cannon rolled out and primed.'

'Ah, now, sir, I'm afraid I have to tell you we can't have any shooting, sir. The men are afraid of being sued if they kill anyone – however accidentally. And we have the legal-aid johnnies on board touting for custom in case any of our chaps get hurt and can be persuaded to blame it on someone else. Such as you, sir, for giving them an order that, with careful hindsight, they decide might not have been in their own best interests. Especially if they can screw some taxpayers' money out of the deal. Sir.'

'Hardy, what on earth has got into you? This is war, Hardy. Our country is in grave danger of invasion. It's everyone's duty to get in among the French and blow them to pieces!'

'Oh, dear, dear, dear, sir. Do be careful what you say. These may be wooden walls, but they still have ears, and we have a Cultural Diversity Co-ordinator on board. He really won't like that sort of language at all.'

'I give up, Hardy. "Rum, sodomy and the lash," that's the navy I joined. But it's not worth wasting my time for this lot.'

'I don't know, Admiral. It's not that bad. I know corporal punishment is out, and rum's not allowed any more, of course. We can't have any antisocial binge drinking. But look on the bright side, sir. Sodomy's very fashionable these days.'

'Oh, very well, Hardy. What is there to lose? Come on and kiss me, baby.'

Don't mention the war

Nelson's flagship, Victory, is Portsmouth's principal tourist attraction, and is still a commissioned Royal Navy ship. But Portsmouth's bicentenary celebrations of the Battle of Trafalgar were not in the navy's hands but those of the Liberal Democrat Council. 'We're commemorating the death of our greatest seafaring hero, but the aim is not to celebrate his victory,' said Val van der Hoven, manager of the Trafalgar project, in October 2004. 'We don't want to go around like football fans shouting, "you lost, you lost".' Instead, the emphasis was on information about the diet of nineteenth-century sailors, recipes for ship's biscuits (virtually inedible in 1805, so unlikely to be a big winner these days) and so on – almost anything, in fact, except explaining why the 1805 victory was crucial to Britain's survival and subsequent growth in the nineteenth century.

When I Give the Order –
Trousers Down!

Aberdeen is not the warmest place in Britain. In winter the weather can often slip into the brass monkeys category. So one can only pity the lads in the Aberdeen University Officer Training Corps (a branch of the Territorial Army) since it would seem that twice a month, as they march to their training hall three streets away, they face the dilemma of stripping off halfway there, or taking a longer way round. What's up?

On the shorter route there is a mosque and, in his infinite wisdom, Training Major Nigel Canning decided (or received orders from above) in autumn 2006 that uniforms are out because 'some people might find them offensive'. Hostile remarks, it was claimed, have been made to the cadets by people at the mosque, and such a situation has to be 'nullified'. Therefore, no uniforms when in the vicinity of the mosque.

Naturally, the cadets were not best pleased at the prospect of having to slip from uniforms into civvies and back again every time they turned a street corner. Their relatives struck up the familiar chorus of 'political correctness gone mad' and promptly alerted the *Sunday Mirror*. That worthy organ did what the TA had evidently failed to do – it sought the opinions of the leading members of the mosque in question and, boy, did it get an earful!

Habib Malik, a community activist and a member of the mosque, laid it firmly on the line: 'This is not, and never has been, an issue for us. We've never complained about cadets marching past our mosque. Why would we? Most of us consider ourselves Scottish and see the army as being there to protect us. There is the odd idiot who bears a grudge against the army because of Iraq, but they're about one-in-a-million, and they most definitely do not represent us.'

Succinctly put. You can almost hear the exasperation in his voice. Once again, it's the faceless 'they' presuming to decide what is and what isn't in the best interests of a minority group. The one unusual thing on this occasion is that it wasn't a local council whose aim was so bad it shot itself in the foot, but the Territorial Army, who generally know how to handle a loaded weapon. As Habib Malik said, 'It gives people the wrong impression about Muslims. Something like this only puts barriers between the two communities, dividing us further. The army should talk to us before putting something like this forward, making it look like it's something we want. This is a big assumption to make on our behalf.'

So it's OK, lads. Keep those uniforms on – and if you've got long johns underneath, no one need ever know.

Harrods' defences hold out

Provided you have enough money you are welcome to shop at Harrods – as long as you are not a member of the armed services in the front line of defending this country's interests. In May 2007, BBC2's *The Incredible Battle of Trafalgar Square: Power to the People* secretly filmed six officers and men from the British Army seeking to enter Harrods, not en bloc but individually. None got through. All were barred by the brave commissionaires guarding the property of heroic owner Mohammed al-Fayed. The reason one commissionaire gave was that they 'might frighten the customers or (at the other end of the scale) confuse customers into thinking they could ask them the way!' Needless to say, Harrods was unwilling to be interviewed about this on the programme.

Rorke's Drift Wiped Out

'It is our policy to provide the widest range of plays and to encourage local writers,' said Peter Chegwyn, chairman of the Arts Panel of Hampshire County Council, in 1997. This bold policy found itself under siege almost immediately as local playwright-director Nick Scovell had his play, *For Valour*, run off the stage by the timidity of Portsmouth Arts Centre. *For Valour* got off on the wrong foot by being about the valiant defence of Rorke's Drift in 1879 by 137 British soldiers (all white, or pink, in those days) by roughly 4,000 Zulus (then, as now, unmistakably black, with maybe a hint of brown). 'The Centre has conceded there is nothing in the script that might be construed as racist,' said the author. 'The play gives the Zulus a voice, which the Michael Caine film (*Zulu*) did not. It is a celebration of valour on both sides.' This all sounds very splendid, so what caused the Centre's director, Nick Young, to boot it out so unceremoniously?

It's the cast, you see. The company, Dramatis Personae, is local like the author, and it is not a big, rich company like the Royal Shakespeare Company or the National Theatre. It has to do the best it can with what it's got, and the sad fact is it has no black actors, let alone Zulus, among its numbers – and no Welshmen either, which is almost as damning when you consider most of the British soldiers at Rorke's Drift were Welsh. The company's intention was to use their white actors, without any artificial blacking of faces, to play the protagonists on both sides and let the spoken lines of the script convey the humanity and impartiality of the play for themselves. In Nick Young's clouded view of the world, though, an all-white cast is 'insensitive'. It might offend 'multicultural users of the site'.

Could it be that Mr Young is being just a teeny bit patronising towards his multicultural users of the site? He is surely not suggesting they lack the intelligence and imagination to understand that, though the actors may be white, they are representing Zulus? If he went to the National Theatre in 2003 to see Adrian Lester's memorable performance in the title role of *Henry V* did he go home convinced that the warrior-king victor of Agincourt had really been black all along? Surely he couldn't be as simple as that? Perish the thought.

Health & Safety Executive 1, Burma Star Association 2
Funny place, Derbyshire. Not only are its police reluctant to catch escaped murderers (see pp. 78–9, 83–4), but its gauleiters (a.k.a. the local Health and Safety Executive) seem determined to place obstacles in the path of the well-intentioned. For years the Derby Branch of the Burma Star Association has set up a stall in the city's Eagle Centre to raise funds for World War II veterans, without whom the faceless HSE would not be here to strut its stuff. (Now there's a thought . . . but back to 21st-century reality.) The Eagle Centre has been having a facelift, and it seems the war veterans have been branded the unacceptable face of society. Why? They constitute a fire risk – or at least their stall has been so designated – and as Julie Ralphs from the Centre stated: 'We have really had to tighten up on our health and safety. We are having to keep all areas clear at the moment.' Quite right, too. Who wants people suing the council because they tripped over an unmentionable war veteran? But as Les Jones said on behalf of the Association: 'Other years we had no problems whatsoever, but this year I am a bit annoyed when they turned round and said we couldn't go there.' Luckily, a neighbouring indoor market and shop came to the rescue, and by giving the Association a welcome enabled them to have two stalls instead of the usual one.

RAF Veteran Downed by Killer Paint

Thanks to the quick thinking of the driver, 79-year-old pensioner Betty Andrews was saved from inflicting mayhem on a Cardiff bus and its occupants in September 2005. This dangerous old lady was attempting to board it when the ever-alert custodian of the vehicle spotted the rather undersized pot of paint she was carrying. 'Hop it,' he said, or words to that effect. 'You can't bring a highly dangerous substance like that on to my bus.' But it's only a can of paint. Dear, oh dear, what simple thinking! 'Paint,' as Cardiff Bus Company patiently explained later, 'is included in the UK-wide list of hazardous materials on public transport,' issued by God, otherwise known in these secular times as the Health and Safety Executive. Mrs Andrews was obliged to walk two miles home, eventually tottering over the doorstep in, as her son Peter described it, 'a hell of a state'. But fear not. 'The safety of passengers is our number-one priority,' said the bus company and sent Mrs Andrews a bunch of flowers.

But blow me down, seven months later Cardiff Bus was at it again. The flowers were obviously a PR ploy and not a reprimand to the driver for his callous treatment of an old age pensioner carrying a somewhat less than life-threatening substance. In April 2006, RAF veteran and retired painter-decorator Brian Heale popped out to run – or perhaps stagger would be a better word, as he is also in his seventies and was on the mend from a salmonella infection – an errand for a pal. He went to the DIY shop, a twenty-minute bus ride away, to buy a can of 'antique cream' emulsion for his friend. As he attempted to board a No. 9 bus for the return journey, he too was summarily ejected for callously ignoring the list of hazardous substances and putting lives at risk with a tin of antique cream emulsion.

In both cases Cardiff Bus remained unrepentant. On the paint issue it informed those bold enough to query the commandments of the HSE that 'two brand-new tins of paint were dropped by a passenger on a No. 61 bus . . . and it had to be taken out of service for extensive cleaning'. We begin to glimpse the fear that tins of paint engender in the trembling bosom of the bus company. They might have to spend money restoring their vehicles to immaculate virginity. Brian Heale may have been near the mark when he said, 'Next thing, you won't be able to take a wet umbrella on in case it drips water on the floor.'

Well, asked Mrs Andrews' son Peter, could they not at least communicate the list of things that could not be carried to people hoping to be among the elite few accepted as passengers? Oh no, said Cardiff Bus, with a dismissive wave of the hand: 'There is no benefit or gain to be had by putting posters up all over the place.' In other words, passengers are a barely tolerable nuisance whose transport needs rank beneath the importance of keeping our buses clean and tidy. If you live in Cardiff, the main thing to remember is that 'all volatile products need to be properly packaged and bagged when brought on to one of our vehicles'. Some might think human beings are fairly volatile substances. If you subscribe to that belief, be sure they are properly packaged and bagged before boarding a bus.

Oh, to be in England . . .

On 27th May 2007, the *Sunday Times* invited its readers to solve a multiple-choice conundrum. See if you can select which of the following four applicants to stay in Britain was refused residency because he was 'unable to demonstrate strong ties with Britain'. Is it –

(a) Mouloud Sihali, an Algerian illegal immigrant once of the Finsbury Park mosque where terrorist aspirations were fostered, and described in court as 'unprincipled and dishonest';

(b) 'AS', a Libyan illegal immigrant and Islamic extremist involved with a terrorist group in Milan. A court has agreed he is likely to try and kill again.

(c) Tul Bahadur Pun, a Nepalese Ghurkha, now aged 84 and needing medical treatment here for diabetes and a heart condition. He won the VC in 1944 when, fighting with the British Army, he took out a Japanese machine-gun post single-handed.

(d) Yonis Dirie, a Somali illegal immigrant, convicted of rape, and an armed robber and burglar to boot.

All those who picked (c), the Ghurka holder of the Victoria Cross, Britain's highest award for gallantry, go to the top of the class. You have an excellent future in modern Britain.

Bare-Shouldered Cheek

The Edwards family was excited, and who could blame them. A summer holiday in the South of France would be enough to put a smile on anyone's face . . . except, it would seem, those nice folk down at the Post Office.

When Mrs Edwards took her five-year-old daughter Hannah to the photo booth to have her picture taken for a passport photo there was the customary struggle with the revolving chair as she ensured her daughter was looking into the camera lens. Satisfied, she then inserted the money and told Hannah to say cheese.

The end result wasn't 100 per cent perfect, but do you know anyone who likes their passport photo? In Hannah's case the photo showed her face and the tops of her shoulder. Still, not a problem. Her face was visible and that's what matters in these precarious times when grim-faced airport officials make us stand in line like cattle while they empty the contents of children's knapsacks and force mothers to drink their baby's bottled milk.

Mrs Edwards took the photo to the post office in Yorkshire along with the completed passport forms. The counter clerk regarded the photo, winced, and gave one of those official sighs – the sort that conveys the level of your stupidity. We can't accept this, the assistant told Mrs Edwards, categorically not.

Mrs Edwards was baffled. Why not? I'm afraid your daughter's shoulders are exposed by the halterneck dress, and that would likely offend Muslim countries, the assistant explained, adding that she knew of two other cases of bare shoulders that had almost led to Jihad. 'I was incensed,' said

Hannah's mum, a Sheffield GP, well used to dealing with pains in the neck. 'I went back home and checked the form. Nowhere did it say anything about covering up shoulders . . . it's not as if anything else was showing, the dress she wore was sleeveless, but it has a high neck. I followed the instructions on the passport form to the letter and it was still rejected. It is just officialdom pandering to political correctness.'

Mrs Edwards spent the rest of the day having another set of photographs taken and chasing around to find another couple of 'responsible citizens' (who had known five-year-old Hannah for two years) to endorse them, the original signatories being at work.

The Post Office appeared anxious not to shoulder the blame – bare or otherwise – and issued a statement that said: 'Our offices have a Passport Office template which says what the photograph should and shouldn't be. Bare shoulders don't come into that at all. We can't see any instruction to that effect so all we can do is apologise to Mrs Edwards. It was clearly a mistake made by the clerk at the post office. It is the first time we have heard of such a rejection.'

Lethal safety pins

It's enough to make a veteran of the D-Day landings go weak at the knees. In November 2006, a friend of ours stopped to buy a Remembrance Day poppy at London's Victoria Station. Being encumbered with suitcases, he asked the seller if he could pin it on for him. No, was the reply, he couldn't. He could give him a safety pin, but health and safety regulations forbade him pinning it on in case of injury. Churchill, thou shouldst be living at this hour.

You Can't Be Too Careful

Needing a new passport in September 2006, recalls one of our two authors, I posed for the necessary photos, looking commendably grim, in a standard passport-photo machine. When I went to Haywards Heath Post Office with the requisite forms properly completed, the counter clerk studied the photos, tut-tutted, and went to find her supervisor. Clucking noises emerged from the background. The photos were rejected. It seemed the light was reflecting from my glasses and thus distorting my image, making it possible I was a potential terrorist lurking behind the glare.

'You must take them again in *our* machine,' I was instructed. I might have done, had the machine not displayed a handwritten notice, 'Out of Order', but this gave me time to study the photos. The bottom of one lens of my glasses, well below eye level, had a shadow of pale reflection. In an uncharitable view, it might have slightly obscured one square inch of my right cheek. I took the photo to another clerk at the far end of the long counter and asked her if she could see anything wrong with it. After subjecting it to suspicious examination, she could not. The application was despatched to the Passport Office and five days later I received my new passport. I have yet to be questioned, let alone detained, as a suspected terrorist on eight subsequent journeys in and out of the country – but there's still time.

I was luckier than Eliza, daughter of *Times*, *Spectator* and *Sunday Telegraph* columnist Ross Clark. In May 2006, her application was rejected by the Passport Office because 'the head is not upright in the photograph. It is either tilted to one

side, or tilted back or forward.' Mr Clark set about deter-
mining the 'lack of uprightness' with the aid of a protractor
and, measuring the extent to which Eliza's nose veered away
from the vertical, established that her head was tilted by eight
degrees – hardly enough to distort her true appearance, let
alone turn her into a desperado. It was unfortunate that, as
Eliza is mentally handicapped, getting her to pose at all in a
manner acceptable to the Passport Office (no smiling, no open
mouth, no looking sideways, etc.) was a twenty-minute task of
considerable difficulty.

Nor was this the Clark family's first problem in this department. Their son's passport photo was also rejected because 'the
poor chap's head was slightly too big'. A head must only cover
between 45 and 75 per cent of a passport photo, it seems,
otherwise you may be guilty of being taken for a terrorist or
other form of ne'er-do-well. The whole business would have
been slightly less ludicrous had it not coincided with the
accident-prone Home Office's admission that, in drawing up
the Identity Cards Bill, it had managed inadvertently to repeal
the law making it an offence to hold a false passport.

Up the pole

Come Remembrance Sunday 2006, members of Carshalton British Legion were dismayed to find they could not hoist the Union Jack on their 35-foot flagpole because a knot at the top had jammed the pulley. Not being spry enough to shin up and fix it themselves, they called the local fire brigade for help. Willingly, said the fireman who answered the phone. Two minutes' work. We'll be round. But he had reckoned without his station officer. No way, lads, he said. Health and safety regulations. No going up 35-foot ladders unless in an unavoidable emergency. Stan Graves, 84, a Burma Campaign veteran, thereupon threatened to climb the pole and get himself stuck at the top, but was saved the trouble when a local company, Orion Access Services, came to the rescue and sent a cherry picker on their staff to free the rope.

Relief No Longer at Hand

Time was when a war or international disaster saw British aid workers among the very first to arrive, roll up their sleeves and get to work bringing food, water and shelter to those whose lives were abruptly shorn of these vital, life-sustaining commodities. Now the risk-averse culture has struck, and when the short but vicious Israeli–Hizbollah conflict exploded in Lebanon in late summer 2006, the aid workers were left kicking their heels behind the lines. 'It never used to be this way,' lamented Dominic Nutt from Christian Aid. 'I lived for five weeks on the front line between the Taliban and the Northern Alliance, and all I had was a piece of paper which gave routes to the airport if trouble broke out.'

In Lebanon, by contrast, while aid agencies from Spain, Belgium and other Continental countries went straight to work with the shells falling uncomfortably close, British aid workers from Oxfam, Islamic Relief, Save the Children and Christian Aid had to wait for professional security officers to make detailed risk assessments. It came as no great surprise to any of them, given that they were there because of a war, that, by and large, and taking all things into consideration, the situation did appear to be what you might call a bit on the dodgy side. Marc André LaGrange, from Islamic Aid, reckoned that agencies should strike 'a sensible balance' between risk and need. In the past, it would have been up to the aid workers themselves to decide whether to take the risk. Many said they would have done and, given their past record, there is no reason to question them. Nor can one doubt that if, in Lebanon, they had been allowed to decide for themselves what was 'a sensible balance', most would have been in the front line, shoulder to shoulder with the Belgians and Spanish, doing what they had gone for – bring aid to suffering people.

Back in Britain, meanwhile, relief appeals were under way for the purchase of food and other necessary supplies. However, the aid workers on the spot, or more accurately behind the spot and therefore unable to see the problems first hand, were in no position to assess exactly what was required. This meant that the funds in the hands of their charities, and of government agencies, sat there unused. As Shaista Aziz of Oxfam said, risk assessment teams were of little value; what was needed was the ability to reconnoitre viable routes for aid trucks. Yes, yes, but really, you do make me cross; war-torn families can't seriously expect to take priority over a proper risk assessment. You must know that by now.

Don't let the lawyers hear you

In July 2006, according to *The Times*, a 'spokeswoman' for the army in Scotland announced new guidelines demonstrating its concern to protect soldiers. With immediate effect, drummers and bagpipers were banned from practising for more than 24 minutes a day if outside, and 15 minutes if inside. This follows a study carried out by the Army Medical Directorate's Environmental Health Team. In bygone battles, bagpipers led the charge to terrify the enemy. Now the terror is of being sued for hearing damage should lawyers manage to persuade a piper that it was not his choice to play the bagpipes, but the army's fault. Perhaps in future, we should conscript lawyers to lead the charge into battle. That should terrify the enemy. Failing that it might at least reduce the number of lawyers.

Earth Calling ODA

Women didn't have much fun in Afghanistan during the late 1990s when the Taliban ruled the country with their unique brand of oppressive intolerance. Religious police patrolled the streets beating any woman who dared display so much as a lock of hair or an inch of flesh, female education was outlawed and women were only allowed to work as doctors or nurses.

Still, where some saw doors closing, others, most notably the British Government's Overseas Development Administration, saw doors opening. They advertised in 1997 for a field manager to work in the war-shattered country, stating in the advert that women should apply as part of their 'policy of equal opportunities'. But wouldn't that be a little unwise, people wondered?

An ODA spokeswoman mulled it over before replying that 'to some extent applicants judge for themselves their suitability for the post, and it might be women look at the job and feel they don't want to apply'. Meanwhile Nicholas Winterton, Conservative MP for Macclesfield, shook his head in disbelief: 'Which planet is the ODA living on?'

Fight the Good Kite

It wasn't just women who suffered at the hands of the Taliban. They even banned kites. Kites! How can anyone get their knickers in a twist about a piece of plastic on the end of some string? You'll have to ask the Taliban or, failing that, Rossendale Council in Lancashire. In 2004 the good people of Sion Baptist Church in Rossendale decided to celebrate the end of the Taliban regime by staging a charity kite contest.

What better way to symbolise a new dawn for Afghanistan than with dozens of kites flying free in the sky? As the Reverend Ron Phillips – minister of the church – explained: 'The idea was to illustrate how lucky we are and how the people of Afghanistan have suffered . . . the competition was to be for the best design of kite and after the morning service we would see which kite would fly highest and for the longest.' Another great idea from his congregation, who had already raised several hundred pounds for the needy in Afghanistan through other events.

But it wasn't a great idea to the worthies of Rossendale Council, because in bureaucratic Britain there's no such thing as a fun day out flying kites. 'The council said it was necessary to obtain permission for the event beforehand,' exclaimed a perplexed Rev. Phillips, 'and, as it was a competition for which people had paid to enter, it required the authority taking out insurance against any possible claims for accidents or damage.'

Ah, so perhaps that's why the Taliban banned kites – they were worried about Taliban toddlers hurting themselves.

As one joyless council representative droned on about 'public liability' the Reverend Phillips, ever the gentleman, did his best not to lose his temper with the pettifogging nonsense of the whole thing, confessing that 'it seems surprising that you need permission for something as simple and harmless as kite-flying . . . we could not help but make the comparison between what the Taliban did and this.'

Dangerous Footpath

Delivering the post to the small community of Ardmore in the Scottish Highlands requires the postman to undertake a daily walk of one and a half miles along a footpath. For more than a century, hardy Scottish postmen have made the trip across the boulder-strewn, heather-clad braes, with wonderful views of the sea and the indented shoreline as reward. 'It's punishing and it's tiring, but I enjoyed it,' said George Mackay, who has walked the route for forty years to ensure the mail got through. Many people might even regard it as a privilege to lead such a life.

Now, despite a century of regular use by locals and their children as well as the postman, it seems this footpath has become a 'fundamentally dangerous' health hazard that could put lives at risk — or so the Royal Mail says. It produced a spokesman to explain (but as the media variously called the spokesman 'he' and 'she' perhaps we should call it a spokes-thingy to be on the safe side): 'The only factor that motivated Royal Mail's actions,' said the spokes-thingy, 'is concern for the health and safety of our people.' It went on to unfold a lurid tale of a relief postman suffering concussion from a fall as he traversed this dangerously well-trodden footpath in March 2005. All postal services to Ardmore were suspended two days later.

That was the Royal Mail's version of events, but it was not one that the locals recognised. The postman slipped, they said, continued with his round and did not even need to consult a doctor. So how come the Royal Mail knew he suffered concussion from a fall? Unworthy though it is even to think it, might a wee conspiracy theory be in order? After all, in the very same year Royal Mail suspended 700 services across the length and breadth of Britain on health and safety grounds, which, even allowing for the excessive zeal of the Health and Safety Executive, seems a suspiciously high number given the relatively undemanding task of slipping letters through letterboxes. Is there just the faintest of outside chances that in its efforts to cut costs and ready itself for privatisation the Royal Mail was looking for an excuse to drop the service to Ardmore? Perhaps that day it was even looking for a relief postman who was notoriously unsteady on his pins.

Nice Mr Osama

After 21 years of unblemished service as a prison officer, Colin Rose was sacked. Why? Two months after the lethal 9/11 attacks on New York in 2001, in which 3,000 people were murdered, he threw a bunch of keys into a tin chute. When a colleague commented on the force with which he had thrown them, he said, 'There's a photo of Osama bin Laden down there.' 'I took offence at the comment,' assistant governor Andrew Rogers said. 'If Asian visitors had heard the comment they might have taken offence too.' Two years later Colin Rose was compensated for wrongful dismissal by an industrial tribunal that described the assistant governor's actions as 'reprehensible'.

When the Chip Is Down

The youth of modern Britain are a feral lot, aren't they? If they're not roaming the streets late at night, they're busy drinking or mugging or having a bit of underage hanky-panky. Or feeding seagulls. Fourteen-year-old Jack Double, a gentle, hard-working lad, was strolling through Ipswich at the start of 2007 still basking in the warm glow of the certificate he had been awarded by his local council three weeks earlier for putting rubbish in a dustbin. 'I was walking along with a bag of chips on my lunch break when I bit into one and found it was really hard,' said Jack. 'The other half was green so I just threw it to a seagull.' Fortunately for the good folk of Ipswich, Jack's crime was witnessed by two sharp-eyed Ipswich Council Litter Enforcement Officers (surely only a matter of time before ITV make a drama series out of these boys). At great risk to their own safety, they tracked Jack back to his school and informed his teachers that they'd nabbed a felon. Jack was hauled before the beak and slapped with a £50 fine. Tough on Crime; Tough on the Causes of Crime.

'TIS THE SEASON TO BE MERRY

Nothing seems to infuriate some of our local councils more than the approach of a religious festival connected with the majority faith of this country. Christmas, being the most popular, is the most tempting of all the targets, though even secular excuses for enjoyment – if they have a traditional origin – are viewed with deep suspicion in some council chambers. Could this be because they threaten to lift the grey blanket of joyless conformity with which they would like to cover us all?

Only Global Warming Can Save Us

Is society as a whole at fault or are the parents to blame? In the old days snowmen were brought up to be respectful and obedient. Seen but not heard. But now? Now snowmen are out of control, an undisciplined rabble holding communities to ransom. Slap an ASBO on the lot of them or, failing that, melt them. That would certainly warm the cockles of Dr Tricia Cusack's heart, a lecturer in History of Art, Architecture and Design at Birmingham University.

Dr Cusack was so concerned by the increasingly confrontational behaviour of snowmen that in 2000 she wrote a fifteen-page academic paper entitled 'The Christmas Snowman: Carnival and Patriarchy'. In her devastating treatise, Dr Cusack exposed the image of the modern snowman, with his happy grin and roly-poly bonhomie, as nothing more than a sham. He was a bigot, she thundered; he was sexist, she raged; but worst of all, he was white.

Cusack warned that the snowman's 'cute front needs unpacking. Like Father Christmas, he is round, fat and smiling, suggesting overindulgence. The classic carnival figure is a fat, lusty eater and drinker.' Do not be fooled, wrote the good doctor, for the snowman 'presents an image, however jocular, of a masculine control of public space'.

Do you see snowmen in the kitchen cooking or in the living room ironing? Of course not, railed Cusack. 'The snowman's ritual location in the semi-public space of garden or field helps to substantiate an ideology upholding a gendered social/spatial system, marking women's proper sphere as the domestic/private, and men's as the commercial/public . . . his presence is a reminder of masculine dominance, order and surveillance.'

And in a rallying cry to the women of Britain, Europe and, indeed, the whole world (or at least those bits where it snows), the 21st century's Emmeline Pankhurst asked: 'Is it accidental, in view of the Western narrative of active masculine domination of nature/female, that out of virgin snow a male icon is built or erected?'

Cusack ridiculed the snowman's physique, 'his bulbous, overindulged body, phallic carrot-nose and black unindividualised eyes'. But feel no pity for snowmen because those unindividualised eyes would never shed a tear for Britain's ethnic minorities who 'find the central power relationship of Christmas threatening, not to speak of its whiteness – a white Christ, a white snowman'.

One or two misguided apologists tried to rebuild the snowman's crumbling reputation. Raymond Briggs, author of that disgracefully propogandist tract, *The Snowman*, pointed out that it would be tricky to build snowwomen because 'breasts and bottoms are difficult to sculpt using sloppy British snow'. And the SMP Brian Monteith, addressing the Scottish Parliament in January 2000, called upon 'children throughout Scotland to build as many snowmen as possible as a message of solidarity to Raymond Briggs'.

But such resistance appears futile and destined to fail in the long term. For Cusack is a fearless and tireless visionary, one who has been compared by some to William Wilberforce. Where he abolished slavery, Dr Cusack will demolish snowmen, or at the very least remove the carrot.

Out of the same mould

Martha Nussbaum, professor of Philosophy *and* Classics *and* Comparative Literature at Brown University, Rhode Island (where there would appear to be some kind of staff shortage), was invited to give the annual Gifford Lecture in Edinburgh. She announced on arrival that in addition to being the professor of almost everything at Brown University, she was also a herstorian.

I'm Dreaming of a Luminos Shine On

Throughout most of the twentieth century Hindus and Jews, Muslims, Sikhs and Buddhists in Britain have been content to get on with their own religious festivals and leave Christians and, for that matter, Zoroastrians, Taoists, Janists, Shintoists, Druids and Pagans, to get on with theirs. All anybody asked was mutual tolerance to do so. With the arrival of the nutty nineties this began to change. Slowly at first, but with accelerating momentum, town and city halls were taken over by men and women, or rather persons, whose knowledge of history hovered around zero, but who knew they wanted to rewrite it, whatever it was, in order to apologise for it. They began to cast about for something that carried the dual possibilities of requiring self-abasement from the majority and the opportunity to patronise the minorities, and with a flourish they came up – or down – with Christmas!

Birmingham was an early frontrunner. In 1995 the council dipped its collective toe in the water and ordered 'Christmas lights' to be referred to only as 'festive lights'. It is unlikely that anyone, other than council employees during office hours, took the slightest notice. In 1999, councillors in the North London borough of Camden banned Christmas. Just like that. Of course, they didn't really ban Christmas – how could they when it would mean abolishing the lucrative orgy of spending that fills councils' coffers through the business taxes on successful local shops and restaurants? No, they merely banned state schools in the borough from putting up decorations. In other words they were thoroughly hypocritical.

But the rot had set in, and in the parallel universe of council chambers up and down the land, Christmas was being thrown to the floor and given a good kicking. As the new millennium dawned the highest-profile bullies were Glasgow, Luton and – where else? – Birmingham, whose councillors show a tenacious propensity for making themselves look silly (see also p. 3). In 2001 Glasgow, determined not to be outdone by the other two, decided 'Shine On' was the perfect name to replace the disgraced Christmas. After admiring this stroke of genius for a few weeks, the persons inhabiting Glasgow City Chambers paused for some rare moments of sober reflection. Could they, without losing such dignity as remained to them, countenance seasonal greetings cards bearing slogans that *Viz* comics might have coveted, such as 'Here's wishing you a happy Shine On' or 'May your Shine On be the envy of the neighbours', above depictions of snow that could clearly not be white (racist) and must therefore be black (apparently not racist) or rainbow-coloured (hedging one's bets)? Worse, they might have to listen to the exuberant citizens of Glasgow belting out traditional ditties like 'On the first day of Shine On my true love sent to me . . .' So with a polite cough they backed away from 'Shine On' and settled for the fractionally less daft 'Winter Festival'. Birmingham, meantime, was – in what its councillors like to think of as their wisdom – coming up with Winterval, while down the M1 in Luton fevered brains – if you'll allow a word so inappropriate to the context – came up with 'Luminos'.

But why? In the name of Luminos Shining On Winterval, why? Now this is the really clever bit. Nanny will say this very carefully, children, to make sure you understand it. It is to ensure that no member of an ethnic community feels 'excluded'. There! You see? You hadn't thought of that, had you? No, and nor had the ethnic communities, most of whom have been living in a mainly Christian community for a very long time now and availing themselves without a second thought of whatever part of the Christmas festivities they wish. What the councils of Luton, Birmingham, Glasgow and places similarly afflicted have done is to proclaim to these same ethnic minorities that – after all these years – they too are to be allowed to indulge in the same orgy of overspending and overeating as everyone else. Now isn't that kind of them? And won't the ethnic communities be grateful to their city councils? No. They're too intelligent.

By November 2006 Muslims living in Britain had had more than enough of lunatic councils trying to airbrush Christian or other faiths out of people's consciousness. Islam teaches respect for other faiths, whatever a handful of fanatics may scream. 'The desire to secularise religious festivals is offensive to both of our communities,' said the chairman of the Christian Muslim Forum. It's vice-chairman, Dr Ataullah Siddiqui, added, 'Those who use the fact of religious pluralism as an excuse to de-Christianise British society provoke antagonism towards Muslims and others by foisting on them an anti-Christian agenda they do not hold . . . they get the blame for something they are not saying.'

Beardless wonders
In 1999, Telford Council replaced Father Christmas with Mother Christmas to 'recreate the Father Christmas figure in a more maternal image'. Officials said – but produced no evidence – that younger children were 'scared of a great big man with a great big beard'.

Peace on Earth, Goodwill to Few

With Christmas 2006 looming, Haringey Council in North London decided it was time to stamp out this Jesus nonsense once and for all. It informed the Polish and Eastern European Christian Family Centre (which has been running a toddlers' group since it was founded in 2002 by the Polish immigrant community – originally as the Polish Drop-in Centre), that the inclusion of the dreaded 'Christian' word in its new title would very likely mean the removal of its £7,000 per annum funding.

Debbie Biss, head of Haringey's Noel Park Children's Centre, through which the funding comes, demanded of Mrs Gosia Shannon that all activities 'will in future be strictly of a nonreligious nature'. She was, she said, 'concerned to learn that Gosia leads the singing of a song about loving Jesus in every session'. It was useless for Mrs Shannon to protest this was 'part of our Roman Catholic tradition in Poland'. Indeed she made matters worse by insisting that, at the Polish centre, they 'try to raise their children in a Christian way'. Clearly Mrs Shannon has not been in Britain long enough to realise that multiculturalism does not include the Christian culture in either its Protestant or Roman Catholic form.

She is learning the hard way. Her centre was told it must rewrite its constitution, promising to provide activities regardless of 'race, gender, culture, religion, sexual orientation, disability or means'. Luckily, the ensuing fuss forced a rethink. One assumes someone on Haringey Council awoke in a cold sweat one night, having had a nightmare that sooner or later, the council might be required to pass similar restrictions on local Hindus, Muslims and Jews, not to mention any Seventh Day Adventists, Plymouth Brethren or Jehovah's Witnesses in transit through the borough. What an uproar *that* would cause. And so it backtracked. 'The letter has been withdrawn immediately,' it confessed. 'It was not appropriate for this officer to be writing such a letter linking funding with the issues mentioned. We have invited this group . . . to meet a senior officer to discuss the funding.'

So it seems to be an all-too-rare case of common sense triumphing in the nick of time. Let's hope it lasts!

A Clear Case of Muddled Thinking

As the first mists of November rose from the Thames in 2005, Lambeth Council became the latest to decree that Christmas lights were henceforth to be known as 'celebrity' or 'festive' lights. But as this was Lambeth, long famed for its dotty behaviour, few outside the borough took much heed – except, perhaps, occasional Conservative-controlled councils. There were signs of unease among them. Surely they could take leave of their senses as decisively as anyone on the opposite wing? When Tory-run Waveney Council in Lowestoft began jumping up and down brandishing a report stating that funding for Christmas lights would not fit with 'core values of equality and diversity', it looked for a moment as if it was about to take leave of its senses in a way to make local left-wingers proud of it. But, truth to tell, the hearts of the councillors proved not really to be in it.

Council leader Mark Bee admitted that 'we do not live in an area of great cultural diversity'. Bee determined to clarify matters further. 'I consider the wording of the report unfortunate,' he buzzed, 'and I will be taking it up with the officer on Monday.' It seems it was no more than a simple matter of economics. The council intended to cut the grant for lights by 50 per cent in 2006, preparatory to scrapping it altogether in 2007. So Waveney is skint? Apparently not. 'If any communities came forward for funding we would deal with them in an equal way.' An ambiguous statement, admittedly, but hadn't he just told us that his was not an area of great cultural diversity, meaning, one assumes, that any demand for funding from another community was unlikely? Surely he couldn't be hiding behind economics to avoid looking like another craven council cowering under the threat of pc?

Down in Havant, Hampshire, meantime the Tory council was getting its knickers similarly twisted. The residents of Havant borough are 99.1 per cent white, making it probable that, whether active or passive followers of their faith, they are predominantly Christian. Never mind. Away with Christmas lights, and in with the 'Festival of Lights'. But just a minute. Where have we heard that before? Of course! Diwali, the Hindu festival of light that takes place every year in October/November (not, like Christmas, in December).

But if 99.1 per cent of the borough's residents are white and probably Christian, a bit of head-scratching suggests the maximum number of Hindu followers is hovering around the 0.9 per cent mark. One of them, Pushpar Sanderscorr, had a succinct view of the council's proposal to airbrush Christmas out of the town's calendar: 'It (Christmas) is not offensive, quite the opposite. We should celebrate all cultures, including Christian.' And from beyond Havant's borders, a spokesman for the Muslim Council of Britain put his finger even more firmly, if somewhat wearily, on the pulse: 'This sounds like a case of a local council taking it upon itself to decide what is offensive, rather than consult the community it serves. If the council took the trouble to ask local people what they thought, they would find that people of all faiths do not have a problem with us.' Could one put it better?

Can you conceive it?

Presumably to mark the seismic shift in values represented by the dawn of a new millennium, some primary schools – not yet required to abandon the Christmas nativity play – decided to replace the Three Kings with the Three Wise Women and, to show how gender-tolerant they were, to have a male Mary. The virgin birth is one thing, but this is truly miraculous.

The Meaning of Christmas
Eludes the Red Cross

In 2002, the Red Cross issued a directive from HQ. No Christmas. No advent calendars. No cards to be sold bearing any allusions to Jesus, whether grown up or still in the cradle, or to Mary. As for the Three Wise Men, they were deep in the relegation zone. After all, customers and staff might make comparisons with the folk in HQ. Frozen robins, on the other hand, got the thumbs up, as did squirrels scrabbling beneath the snow for the nuts they were sure they had buried somewhere near here and thankfully, despite Tricia Cusack's full-frontal attack (see p. 129), snowmen were left standing in the glacial temperature.

Most Red Cross shops ignored the ban in 2002, but by 2003 many of them had been forced into line. The reason, when finally prised from the organisation, baffled even acute brains normally adept at seeing logical connections. The Red Cross is an organisation dedicated to providing impartial medical aid and assistance in war zones, or in areas devastated by natural disasters. Its symbol, like its name, is a red cross. Its parallel, or sister, organisation in the Muslim world is the Red Crescent. One has as its symbol the Christian cross; the other has the Muslim crescent. Both religions preach and uphold the necessity of helping the sick and afflicted, and these two organisations aim to follow these tenets.

So why ban Christianity from its shops? Apparently because the Red Cross doesn't want to offend other faiths in case it is not seen as impartial when working in war zones. It is perfectly true that it has had problems in this respect, for example with Israel, and that there is a serious move afoot within the international community to adopt a new symbol, the Red Crystal. This still does not provide a logical reason for banishing Christianity from its British shops, but it does give rise to the suspicion that this is another patronising attempt to appease the Muslim minority by supposing that it would be hostile. One need only quote Inayat Bunglawala of the Muslim Council of Great Britain to appreciate the wrong-headedness of it all: 'This is political correctness gone too far. It's obviously well meaning but I'm afraid it will have the opposite effect and make people angry that they cannot be proud of their own faith.'

Bare legs are sinful

In the annual pantomime season, the slapstick-loving, knock-about Dame has traditionally been played by a man, and the Principal Boy by a woman. This, according to one very pc director, is only to enable men to look at the Principal Boy's legs. Despite legs being a useful commodity of which human beings are generally equipped with two each from birth, and which are not much of a novelty, this is not good enough for the director in question. He is insisting that the knockabout Dame must henceforth be a woman, and the Principal Boy must be a man. How does that help? Now all the women will be looking at the man's legs. I know. Let's ban pantomimes.

Christmas Comes But Once a Year – But in Some Places, Never

In December 2003 Rehana Nazir, multicultural services librarian at Buckinghamshire County Council, organised a party in one of High Wycombe's libraries to celebrate Eid, the Muslim festival that welcomes the end of the Ramadan fast. So far, so good.

A few days later, however, the very same library that hosted the Eid celebration was approached by Bridget Adams, a member of the choir of All Saints' church, to put up a poster advertising their annual carol service. 'Oh dear, oh dear,' said the library, or words of a similar nature. It seems the library that had just tidied away the dishes after an Eid party could not condone advertising a carol service – and not in that library alone, but in any of the other 33 libraries in the district under the control of the Tory council. By now you will not need to be a mind-reader to guess the reason. Indeed we can all join in the chorus, to the tune of 'O Come All Ye Faithful': It might offend non-Christians.

The council's policy stimulated the usual responses from the citizens of High Wycombe – 'barking mad', 'hypocritical', 'political correctness gone barmy', and even provoked one normally placid person into saying, 'I'm very surprised.' But perhaps the last word can be left to the measured Bridget Adams. 'I believe what they do at the library with Eid and Ramadan is right and very positive,' she said, before adding, not unreasonably, that she thought everyone should be allowed to advertise at the library.

> *Lord Chancellor Scrooge*
> In 1999, Derry Irvine who, in odd moments when he was not busy selecting hand-printed wallpaper for his offices, doubled up as Lord Chancellor, sent a memo to one thousand civil servants setting forth the jokes they may not tell at their Christmas party. It banned: stereotyped comments, jokes about women, men, ethnic minorities, sexual minorities and people with disabilities. His lordship was thereby safeguarded from jokes about his own disability – a lack of humour – but the party was presumably a quiet and dismal affair with so little left to talk about. Whitehall staff promptly dubbed the noble lord Scrooge, and may not have been displeased when the Woolsack was subsequently removed from beneath his posterior.

Father Christmas Gets a Gender Dressing-down

Father Christmas, or Santa Claus, is based on St Niklaus, or Nicholas, the saint of children. The fact that St Niklaus was undeniably a man is not good enough for the job centre in Liskeard, Cornwall, nor for their regional bosses in Exeter. As Christmas approached, and the residents of Liskeard realised it would not be banned, the manager of department store Trago Mills, Janet Curnow, sent an ad for a Father Christmas to the local job centre. The ad did not appear. Time passed, and Mrs Curnow received a phone call from Exeter explaining that she could not specify that a man was required for the job.

Obviously you spotted the flaw instantly, and even we only took a few seconds to do so. How can you ask a woman to be a father, whether of the Christmas or any other variety? But demonstrable fact is not a necessary ingredient of the pc world, and Mrs Curnow was required to write a letter explaining precisely why she felt she must have a man for the position. 'It needn't be a long letter,' the Exeter woman graciously allowed.

At this stage the owner of Trago Mills, Bruce Robinson, felt it was time to stand shoulder to shoulder with Mrs Curnow, and took the matter direct to the Supreme Being, otherwise known as the Department of Work and Pensions in Whitehall. He guaranteed complete impartiality in the selection of a Father Christmas, adding that the successful applicant, if female, need only have the following attributes: (i) a deep voice; (ii) whiskers; (iii) a big belly; and (iv) no readily discernible bosom. He could not resist adding that, in the event of a successful female applicant, he feared for the children of Liskeard who would, he felt reasonably confident, be terrified.

Faced with such a vision, the Supreme Being (otherwise known as . . . etc.) hastily backed down, muttering that every rule must have exceptions, and granting that Liskeard's Father Christmas could be one of them.

New Age carols

Some clergypersons in the 21st-century Church of England are so hypersensitive that gender-specific carols such as 'God Rest Ye Merry Gentlemen' and 'Good Christian Men Rejoice' have hit the bottom of the dustbin – the latter being doubly damned for upsetting both non-Christians and women. At this rate, 'Once in Royal David's City' will be blacklisted in case it needles trendy Islington republicans fearful of David Cameron's standing in the opinion polls; and don't be surprised if, come Easter, 'At the Lamb's High Feast We Sing' gets the chop for fear of giving vegetarians a giddy turn.

A Right Punch-up

For fifteen blameless years Reg Payn enjoyed himself as Bodmin's officially licensed puppeteer. It was a happy job, putting on his puppet shows and holding children rapt with something other than a TV screen or a games console.

Until the day in 2004 when Bodmin's Women's Rape and Sexual Abuse Centre decided that Mr Payn or, more specifically, his ever-popular Punch and Judy show, was contaminating the minds of Bodmin's little boys and girls.

The Centre began bombarding Mr Payn with leaflets explaining why Mr Punch attacking his wife with a string of sausages – and doesn't a crocodile make an appearance at some stage? – would only encourage the five-year-old boys sitting in the audience shouting 'He's behind you!' to grow up to be wife-beaters.

'They harassed the audience, accusing me of promoting domestic violence against women and threw leaflets at me,' Mr Payn told *The Times* newspaper, adding: 'Children of four and five know the difference between puppets and reality. I'm a father and a husband and I've no intention of promoting violent behaviour.'

Mr Payn pointed out that as well as being harmless slapstick that was first performed in England during the reign of Charles II, a Punch and Judy show was a tale of morality. When naughty Mr Punch lies to the policeman, the children are encouraged to shout out, 'You're fibbing, Mr Punch!'

But Maggie Parks, director of the abuse centre, was having none of it: 'It's appalling that children are encouraged to sit, watch and laugh at a baby's head being battered and a woman being beaten up with a stick when one in four women experience domestic violence.'

When Bodmin Council upheld the complaint and banned Punch and Judy from its parish, the press went wild. *The Western Daily News* printed photos of the councillors under the headline 'Show and Shame'. It wasn't long before a notice appeared on the council website, stating that 'contrary to recent press reports, Bodmin Town Council has *not* banned Punch & Judy', only asked Mr Payn to perform another puppet show.

The real losers, of course, were the kids who, unlike preceding generations of children, were denied the chance to laugh at Punch and Judy. Mind you, one supposes they could cheer themselves up by going home, switching on their games console and enjoying the thrills and spills of, for example, *Resident Evil 4* in which players find the corpse of a young woman skewered to a wall with a pitchfork. Good, clean fun compared with the filth of Punch and Judy.

Lyme Regis Suffers Some Eel-will

A characteristic of all oppressive regimes is that it only requires the word of one informant before the authorities take action. Group consensus is ignored. 'Twas ever thus. If, for example, a man in Occupied France was accused by his neighbour of working for the Resistance, the Gestapo didn't bother canvassing the opinion of the rest of the street to see if the neighbour was right, they just removed the accused. Which brings us seamlessly to the events in a Dorset fishing town in the summer of 2006.

For more than thirty years 'conger cuddling' has been an annual event in Lyme Regis. It wasn't the most sophisticated sport in the world – but then one could say that about football or fishing – and it was unlikely ever to be included in the Olympics. Yet it amused the townspeople and caused no harm to anyone. The reverse, indeed, because the proceeds of the event went to the RNLI (Royal National Lifeboat Institute).

For those unfamiliar with the sport, a team of nine players, or 'cuddlers', stand on six-inch-high wooden blocks laid out to form a triangle, while an opposing side of a similar number take it in turns to swing a five-foot, 25lb conger eel on the end of a rope, in the hope of knocking one of their opponents off his perch. Think skittles and you'll get the idea.

The most important detail, before we forget, is that the conger eel in question is dead before the game begins, having been accidentally caught in the waters off the Devon coast at an earlier time in the year and then frozen. Each eel is different, I suppose, but if we were eels and had the choice of being coated with jelly and eaten by Cockneys or tied to the end of ropes in the hope of toppling some bloke off a block, we'd opt for the latter every time.

But in 2006 someone denounced the conger cuddlers of Lyme Regis to the RNLI. The event was 'disrespectful' to dead eels, so they said, before threatening to film it and distribute the footage nationwide unless the RNLI pulled the plug.

And what, you may wonder, was the response of the RNLI? 'Stop wasting our time – we've got our work cut out with the business of saving lives at sea. Stop being silly?' Unfortunately not. Despite the fact that the RNLI stood to receive several hundred pounds from the tournament, they caved in to the blackmailer in the most craven manner and agreed that it was – that mealy-mouthed word again – 'inappropriate' to continue using a dead eel.

'We have been advised by the RNLI headquarters at Poole to abandon the conger cuddling event following a local complaint from animal-rights activists,' said Rob Michael, chairman of the Lyme Regis Lifeboat Guild. That infuriated Ken Whetlor, Mayor of Lyme Regis, who told the *Daily Telegraph*: 'The writer of that letter is a gutless troublemaker with nothing better to do than stop people enjoying an innocent event that helps to raise money to save lives. I cannot see how using a dead conger eel landed by a local fisherman is unethical.' It seems ironic that an organisation synonymous with courage on the water should prove so timid ashore.

SMALL
EXPECTATIONS

To be a good pc person requires indoctrination from birth. It is, moreover, of vital national importance that our youngsters know their human rights, such as the 'inappropriateness' of expending work and effort in the pursuit of excellence if they don't feel like it. Since a respectable proportion of our youth is also imbued with the idea of becoming rich and famous in the shortest possible time, whether as pop stars, ballet dancers or Alan Sugar's apprentice, one fears the disappointment that awaits many of them as they encounter the cutting edge of competition in later life.

How to Produce Olympic Champions

It's instructive to watch our politicians advocating the benefits of sport in schools as 2012, the year of the Olympics coming to Britain, looms on the horizon. These same politicians are among those responsible for selling off school playing fields, reducing physical education to (in some cases) a mere twelve hours a year in order to allow more time to achieve government-set targets in the three Rs, and for pushing such politically correct brainwaves as substituting 'group problem solving' exercises for traditional sports days. At the end of October 2006, Chancellor and would-be Premier Gordon Brown emerged full of a hitherto unsuspected zeal for sport, urging a national debate about 'taking sport and fitness more seriously in the fight to get Britain fit for the Olympics'. A nice thought, Gordon, but a pity it didn't strike you in your bath ten years or so earlier.

The political volte-face must be bewildering for poor Judith Wressel, head of Maney Hill Junior and Infants who, in May 2003, banned all competitive events because they are too stressful for children. The sack race, the egg-and-spoon race, the three-legged race – they all went. Taking part in traditional races can, she informed bemused parents, 'be difficult and often embarrassing for many children'. Instead, there was to be an 'activity-based event'. Not only that, but parents were to be banned from these 'ambitious organisational changes'. As Rob Busst, the father of two children at Maney Hill, said, 'Children do not become scarred for life if they lose the egg-and-spoon race. They all love being in the races and they love the fact that their parents are there to cheer them on.' But not, it seems, at Maney Hill.

Maney Hill is in good company, mind you. Woolpit Primary School in Suffolk suffers from a similar disease. Its sports day consisted of events like crawling under chairs, something that places them on distinctly dangerous ground, as one newspaper was quick to point out. What, it asked, if a fat child – or rather, oversized person of younger years – became wedged beneath a chair? Would this not constitute a clear case of discrimination against spherically challenged persons? If so, the European Court of Rights would have a thing or two to say about Woolpit Primary.

It seems unlikely that schools like Maney Hill or Woolpit Primary will be the source of tomorrow's sportsmen and women. Maybe it's just as well. Their unpreparedness for the hard work of achieving excellence might disappoint Gordon Brown.

Doh!

In April 2005, spin bowler Chris Schofield took Lancashire County Cricket Club to an industrial tribunal claiming unfair dismissal. In the previous season he had taken precisely one wicket, and his team had been relegated to the second division. This was no sudden loss of form. In the four seasons 2001–04 he had managed a grand total of 39 wickets at the high average cost of 42.2 runs each – not exactly match-winning stuff. Why, the tribunal demanded, had the club not boosted his confidence by playing him regularly in the first XI? As ex-international cricketer and journalist Derek Pringle said: 'The riposte is perhaps best left to Homer Simpson – "Doh!"'

Take Me Away, Mummy, It's Too Hard

When Jeffrey Taylor founded the National Dance Awards, sometimes referred to as the Oscars of British ballet, he had high hopes they would help to raise the standards of home-grown talent. For a while it looked as if he was winning. In 2004, Jonathan Cope won the top award for outstanding male dancer but both he and Britain's outstanding female ballet star, Darcey Bussell, were due to retire in 2006. In 2005, not a single British dancer was even nominated for a National Dance Award, almost entirely because none were good enough to be engaged by leading ballet companies in the UK. Instead, these organisations were looking abroad for their top dancers.

It has come to this, reckons Jeffrey Taylor, through a combination of an education system that discourages the pursuit of hard work and excellence, and health and safety restrictions. As a result, British ballet training has become 'a disgrace'. To give an example, teachers are no longer allowed to touch or manipulate the bodies of young dancers into the right positions. 'When I trained, teachers would be on their hands and knees forever pushing feet out and moving legs.' As Mr Taylor said, you are asking students to get into the most unnatural and often painful positions and hold them. There is no way you can describe what it's like. You have to show them and shove them into pushing the bottom forward, pulling the stomach in and the shoulders down and back. 'It seems OK in other countries,' he commented. Try that here, though, and the teacher is on a charge of sexual harassment quicker than Markova could do a pas de deux.

It's not just the unforgivable sin of actually touching someone; it's also the unwillingness to put in the effort that is having the damaging effect. 'There is no shortage of raw talent among the very young in this country, but it is being wasted because they are not trained rigorously.' Apparently, full-time ballet schools have given up trying to get girls to do daily pointe work – exercises on their toes – and only attempt it weekly 'because they (the girls) think it's too hard'. At St Petersburg's top school, the Vaganova Academy, by contrast, they work them to exhaustion because 'when the physical gives out, the true artist appears'. British schools keep their mouths shut because if Mummy doesn't like a teacher's criticism, she might take her wonder-child away and the school may lose its funding. It's no help to the student in the longer run because, when she falls well short of Darcey Bussell's standard, she will feel valueless. But never mind – Mummy can always send you to Canada to play hockey in the Seafair Minor Hockey Association (see p. 185) where achievement is the least of their concerns.

Scrambled egg

There was no egg-and-spoon race at Penshaw's Barnwell Primary School in Sunderland in 2006. Indeed, there was no sports day, because it was 'too competitive'. Does this mean Kathryn Linsley, Head of Physical Education, who announced the decision, might soon be out of a job? Allan from Motherwell emailed to comment, 'Perhaps they will stop teaching Maths too. I found that traumatic and threatening at school. Home economics can even be deadly.'

If in Doubt, Ban It

In February 2007 UNICEF issued a report on the wellbeing of children across 21 industrialised countries based on a study conducted between 2000 and 2003. The study examined forty indicators such as family relationships, health and poverty, and guess who came bottom, below the USA, Hungary, Greece, even lower than Belgium. Correct, Britain.

In the days that followed the publication of the report politicians, press and public wrung their hands and trotted out clichés like 'wake-up calls' and 'alarm bells'. Grand schemes were mooted concerning welfare, education and reducing juvenile crime, and how it was beholden on all of us to do our bit to improve the 'shameful' state of affairs.

Yet in the same month that UNICEF published the children's league table two incidents were reported in the British press – small, innocuous, localised incidents admittedly, but which nonetheless were painful examples of why being a child in politically correct Britain isn't much fun.

Devon Fire Brigade announced that children would no longer be able to play on their fire engines during demonstration days for fear, according to the *Daily Express*, of 'allegations of abuse'. 'Fire crews regularly visit schools and in the past children have been able to sit inside the engine, put on a helmet, hold the steering wheel and sound the siren,' explained the paper, but fire chiefs were now concerned that 'firefighters may be accused of touching children as they lift them up and down'.

Divisional officer Mike White told the *Express*: 'We are making sure our staff are protected from people making false allegations. We are not suggesting anything untoward has happened, it is just a sad indictment of the world we live in.'

A couple of weeks earlier the *Daily Mirror*, among others, reported that Burnham Grammar School in Buckinghamshire had banned kids from kicking a ball around in the playground at break time because it was too 'dangerous'.

Head teacher Cathy Long was quoted in the paper saying: 'It has become the latest thing to kick the ball at each other. A member of staff accidentally had a football kicked in her face and we have had a few kids having to see Matron because they have been whacked with a football. We have decided that other than during proper PE lessons, we are banning footballs.'

In the same week a committee of MPs published a report on the 'alarming' obesity epidemic among Britain's school-children – one primary school child in seven is now obese – and warned of 'possible serious health risks' unless something was done. Banning playground games of football probably wasn't what they had in mind.

Run for your rights
In 2006 a textbook distributed in the UK by Co-ordination Group Publications declared that school cross-country running could be a form of physical abuse. In a chapter headed 'Your Legal Rights' the book says: 'You have the right to be protected from emotional or physical abuse' and highlighted bullying and cross-country as two examples of what constitutes abuse. The Association for Physical Education described the book as 'nonsense', while others pointed out that the same could be said of all lessons. Exactly. Pythagoras and his Theorem still gives me unpleasant flashbacks.

A Walk on the White Side

It's hardly surprising that there's an obesity epidemic in Britain in the 21st century what with all the mixed messages coming out of government. One day they're telling us to turn off the TV and go and get some exercise, and the next they're criticising white people for cluttering up the Lake District with their backpacks and sturdy boots.

For years free guided treks were on offer in the National Park. Then, in January 2005, *The Times* revealed that they were facing the axe from the park authority as part of a strategy 'that hopes to win extra government and European Union funding . . . by meeting targets to attract more young, urban, black, Asian and disabled people'. Apparently the treks were a particular source of angst for the park authorities because most of the 30,000 walkers who took advantage of them shared the same colour skin – to wit white, or at best pink.

A park spokesman told the BBC: 'Our research shows that the majority who do use the walks are white, middle-class, middle-aged people. The government is encouraging National Parks to appeal to young people, to ethnic minorities and to people with disabilities. It is saying we ought to focus our activities on these kind of groups.'

As Terence Blacker commented wryly in the *Independent*, 'there were no specific plans as to how to attract their new market [but] the authority was taking an important first step by closing down facilities which catered to the inexcusably white, wrinkly and middle-class'. David Lyon, one of the 300 volunteer rangers in the Lake District National Park, wondered what the solution might be: 'We treat everyone the same on the walks, whatever their skin colour, age or social background. Stopping them seems incomprehensible. What are they going to do, bus in these people, or open an office in Manchester?'

The fact that wandering through the countryside is a purely personal choice, something that doesn't require skills or money, seems to have passed the government by in its desperate and patronising attempt to encourage people from ethnic minorities to trudge up to the Lake District when, frankly, many probably had far better things to do than pop blisters and eat soggy sandwiches. It was, as Terence Blacker said, just that the government was irked that 'the wrong type' of people were enjoying the Lake District and it wanted to change the situation with a spot of 'social engineering through funding'.

The ones that get away

A year after the government and its minions decided that rambling was altogether too white it was the turn of fishing to come in for a spot of social engineering. The *Sunday Telegraph* reported in March 2006 that the government was launching a campaign to encourage more people from ethnic minorities to take up fishing because, of four million regular fisherfolk, most were white and male. The Environment Agency produced a leaflet on 'Ten things you should know about angling'. Novice fishermen seeking tips on catching 20lb pike were instead informed that: 'Angling does not discriminate against gender, race, age or athletic ability', and that the 'government is interested in angling in the context of social inclusion in deprived urban areas'.

From Bard to Worse

Back in January 1994 (the madness has indeed been with us that long), an invitation was sent to Kingsmead Primary School in East London to go to the Royal Opera House and watch the Prokofiev ballet *Romeo and Juliet*. It was part of a Hackney Borough project, organised by the Hamlyn Foundation, to introduce children to high-quality culture at heavily subsidised rates – in the case of the Royal Opera it meant seats that normally sold for £50 a time were offered to head teacher Jane Brown for just £2. Bargain!

But not for Ms Brown. While other schools involved in the project snapped up the tickets and the kids struggled to contain their excitement at the prospect of an outing to the West End, she was turning down the offer because the Shakespeare tragedy was 'entirely about heterosexual love'. In addition, the *Evening Standard* reported, in the opinion of Ms Brown the play would not add to the cultural development of the pupils and she was of the view that 'until books, films and the theatre reflect all forms of sexuality, she would not be involving her pupils in heterosexual culture'.

Within hours of the story breaking Ms Brown was engulfed by such a storm of protest that even Prime Minister John Major launched a blistering attack in the Commons.

Gus John, Hackney's director of education and leisure, summoned Ms Brown to his office for crisis talks after he had first described her stance as a 'wretched and unwanted diversion from my more important duties'. When Ms Brown emerged from her dressing-down she told reporters, 'I am dismayed at the distress I have caused to parents, staff and pupils by the unwelcome media attention which has focused on the school. I only hope the opportunity to see a professional performance of *Romeo and Juliet* will arise again.'

But Ms Brown did have her supporters, with some applauding her move and saying that it was wrong to expose children to the violent scenes depicted in some Shakespearian plays. 'The effect would be the same as watching *The Terminator*,' explained Mark Lushington, the associate secretary of Hackney's teachers' association. 'The next day they would club together and say: "Remember what those Montagues did in the play last night? Let's do that too."'

The Hamlyn Foundation struggled to comprehend Ms Brown's attitude. 'It just seems so irresponsible,' said Catherine Graham-Harrison, the director. 'It's like a parody.'

A censor of perspective?

When Christopher Marlowe's masterpiece *Tamburlaine the Great* was staged at the Barbican in London in 2005, those familiar with the play were aggrieved to see one or two changes had been made to placate Muslim sensibilities. Not only was the burning of the Koran censored but so was a reference to the prophet Muhammad. Simon Reade, the artistic director, said the burning of the Koran 'would have unnecessarily raised the hackles of a significant proportion of one of the world's great religions'. Some of his peers disagreed. Terry Hands, who directed *Tamburlaine* for the Royal Shakespeare Company in 1992, said, 'I don't believe you should interfere with any classic for reasons of religious or political correctness.'

An Assault on Common Sense

One of the contradictions of Anglo-Saxon culture lies in our attitude towards children. A great many Americans, for example, see nothing wrong in beauty pageants for young girls barely out of nappies. We Brits think it's just a bit of 'harmless fun' to ogle female pop stars dressed up as sexy schoolgirls (the most recent example being that of Girls Aloud for the 2007 Red Nose Day), while supermarket chains sell push-up bras for the under-10s. In both countries one of the bestselling girls' dolls is the 'Bratz Doll', which comes dressed in miniskirt and fishnet stockings.

Yet the moment an adult exhibits the slightest degree of innocent affection towards a child the full weight of the law comes crashing down. This is exactly what happened in the summer of 2006 when 58-year-old vicar Alan Barrett paid a visit to the William MacGregor Primary School in Staffordshire, of which he was a governor.

As the Rev. Barrett told the *Guardian*, 'I had visited the school to help some pupils with their work and, at the end of the lesson, congratulated one girl who had been struggling.' This 'congratulation' took the form of a single brisk peck on the forehead – in front of the whole classroom – after she had come up with the right answer to a maths question.

The lesson ended, the school day finished and the Reverend Barrett returned home pleased that the pupils and staff seemed a happy and diligent bunch. But it appears the little girl went home and – one can only imagine – proudly told her mum that she had got a question right in front of the class and the Reverend Barrett had been so pleased he'd given her a wee kiss as a reward.

It wasn't long before, as the reverend told the *Guardian*, 'I'd become the subject of a police and social services investigation which examined my character, conduct and ministry'.

The reason? In the view of the girl's mother he had 'assaulted' her daughter with that kiss on the forehead. Staffordshire County Council 'initiated' a child-protection inquiry and the police and the diocese of Lichfield also began their own investigations into the alleged 'assault'.

None found that Reverend Barrett had any case to answer, although the Archdeacon of Lichfield's spokesperson said it was 'inappropriate' of him to have kissed the girl and issued the following statement: 'The conclusion that Mr Barrett had acted inappropriately is not a finding of guilt or negligence, but recognition that in today's climate, previously acceptable innocent behaviour is now subject to misunderstanding and suspicion.' The weary Rev. Barrett decided it would be best to resign as a governor of the school because 'giving a child a kiss of congratulations is inappropriate in this day and age'.

According to the *Guardian* the girl's mother 'was not satisfied with the investigation or the findings and continued to allege that Mr Barrett's kiss was an assault'. 'I am so disappointed with the way it has been handled,' she was quoted as saying, although fortunately she stopped short of calling for the reverend to be burned at the stake.

Don't Touch!

Fifty-six-year-old Olive Rack had been running a children's nursery school for over twenty years. One routine morning in spring 2005 at the Tresco House Day Nursery in Kettering, one of her two-year-old toddler charges whopped a baby on the head with a toy wooden brick. Mrs Rack took the girl by the hand, told her that was wrong, and led her over to sit on the 'naughty step' (as widely practised by mums following the success of *Supernanny*'s 'naughty chair' on our TV screens). As it happened, there were two early-learning advisors visiting at the time for a routine inspection. They said nothing then but, five weeks later, Mrs Rack was told by Ofsted that a complaint had been lodged, and shortly afterwards the police appeared on the doorstep. She was charged with common assault, with the threat of losing her home, her job and her reputation resting on the outcome. It was the beginning of a long and anxious fourteen months.

From July 2005 until September 2006, Mrs Rack was not allowed inside the nursery she ran, although she lived in the same building on the floor above. During that nerve-racking time, not a single mum removed her child from the nursery, and the mother of the toddler whom Mrs Rack was accused of assaulting made it very clear that she had no complaint. Indeed at the trial the little girl's mother gave evidence on Mrs Rack's behalf, telling the court that the inspector's version of events was 'highly exaggerated'. The magistrates dismissed the case, stating that Mrs Rack had behaved perfectly reasonably.

In the event, things turned out right but, as Olive Rack said after it was all over: 'Surely, common assault's got to be where there is an intent to harm, not just when you're touching a child or moving her away to protect another child? . . . Otherwise, how can you change a nappy? What do you do when you take a child for a walk and can't hold his hand – let him run in front of a car? There are too many do-gooders quoting the Human Rights Act at you.' One might argue with the term 'do-gooders' and suggest that, on the contrary, they are self-righteous, self-important do-badders – but that, of course, is a matter of opinion.

Hog roasted

England Test cricketer Matthew Hoggard received the Community Champion Award in 2007 for the time and care he devotes to coaching young kids and enthusing those deprived of outdoor sports facilities. A modest family man with a newly arrived baby, he confessed that finding the time was difficult. In terms of regrets he had only one: 'All these rules about not being able to touch the kids. You can't even arrange their hands on the bat. And then after the session they come up wanting to give you cuddles, [and] I'm there thinking 'Oh God, what can I do? It's a shame, all that.' Shame. The exact word.

Jack and Till

In January 2007 Jack Archer popped into his local Morrisons supermarket in York to buy a bottle of sherry. Well, perhaps 'popped' isn't the right word. After all, 87-year-old war veterans don't 'pop', do they, they 'shuffle'. However, Jack and his bottle eventually made it to the checkout and handed the girl some money. Are you over 21, she asked?

Jack laughed. Ah, that inimitable sense of British humour, still alive and kicking. 'But it then became pretty obvious she wasn't making a joke and actually meant it,' explained Jack. 'I was totally stumped so I just said, "I'm over eighty. Will that do?"' Not really, said the girl, have you got any proof?

Perhaps at this point Jack should have showed her one of his war wounds, but these days he'd probably be nicked for that. 'When I persisted that I really was well above the legal drinking age she let me have my sherry,' said Jack.

Naturally, Morrisons soon wheeled out the obligatory spokescreature to excuse their employee's staggering lack of initiative: 'We simply wish to make sure that we satisfy our moral and legal obligations with regard to the sale of alcohol,' it said, apparently managing to keep a straight face. 'As a member of the Retail Alcohol Standards Group, we take our responsibility with regard to selling alcohol very seriously and have procedures in place designed to ensure that we meet all legal requirements. Store staff are trained to be highly vigilant in the sale of alcohol and the detection of potential underage purchases.'

As soon as Mr Archer – who was awarded an MBE for his services to the city of York – left the shop he no doubt went straight down his local British Legion to brag to his pals that he had just been mistaken for a seventeen-year-old. 'I like to think of myself as a youthful 87-year-old,' he chuckled, 'but it would be a stretch to pass myself off as a teenager.'

The Terrible Twos

What is it about York? If shopkeepers aren't busy asking 87-year-olds for proof of age, they're banning two-year-olds from their premises. January is never the warmest month in England but in 2007 it was particularly nippy (if we are allowed to use such a naughty word) so when toddler Jay Cowper and his granddad popped down to the local store he was well wrapped up. No sooner had they entered than the shopkeeper ordered Jay – still getting used to this walking business – to remove his hood. Granddad laughed and said, 'He's only two and a half, I don't think he's going to rob you!' But the shopkeeper didn't find it funny. Either the hood goes, or the toddler does. At which point Granddad thought it best to take his custom elsewhere.

The unrepentant store later pointed out that their 'No Hoods' policy is well advertised and is to prevent troublesome teenagers from entering the shops. 'I can understand their point,' said Jay's grandmother, Brenda, 'because there are a lot of kids who cause trouble down there, but when it's a two-year-old it's a bit pathetic.' More than a bit, Brenda. More than a bit.

OUT AND ABOUT

If the UK is fast becoming the Unhinged Kingdom, does USA stand for the Unhinged States of America? Did they infect us with this pc nonsense, or did they catch it from us? Or is it the Anglo-Saxon world in general since, to the ill-concealed astonishment of more balanced – and apparently happier – countries in the continent of Europe, Australia and New Zealand are lolloping along in our sizeable footsteps? And we've barely started on the more far-out doings of the Health and Safety Executive, though rest assured, we will.

Giraffe's Privacy Invaded –
Animals Everywhere Outraged

In 2002, a giraffe in Washington Zoo clambered down the curtains. Close inspection found it to be as lifeless as *Monty Python's* parrot. Death comes to us all, even giraffes, but a reporter from the *Washington Post* wanted to examine the deceased quadruped's medical record. Whether the giraffe had left for another world in the middle of his paper's support-a-giraffe week, or whether he was an avid giraffeophile we do not know. Since that august paper was famed for the tenacity of its investigation of the Watergate scandal in the 1970s, it may have been hoping to relive past glories. Whatever the truth, Washington Zoo was not in compliant mood.

Instead of a good old-fashioned 'No dice, buster' when asked for the medical records, zoo director Lucy Spelman chose to elaborate. The zoo could not release the file on the giraffe because that would mean violating the privacy rights of animals. The vet–giraffe relationship, it appeared, was sacrosanct. How could any animal in a well-ordered zoo ever trust its keeper, never mind the curator, if snort, bellow or trumpet got out that any old human could lay hands on its medical history just by asking? Why, for example, should a python have to endure anxious enquiries about its slipped disc, or an elephant have to be distracted by questions about its earache?

Naturally the animal-rights world was only too ready to leap into the fray, and did so, only to run into a real problem. How could a human being speak on behalf of another species?

Would that be patronising to the beasts of the field, or arrogant beyond endurance? And how could you select the right human to speak with knowledge and accuracy on behalf of the animal in question? How could he or she be sure that the now-defunct giraffe would or wouldn't have wished its medical condition to be open to the scrutiny of the reading world – a world, incidentally, from which animals, being deficient in reading skills, are excluded? Far from keeping its terminal illness a secret, the giraffe may have wanted maximum publicity in order that giraffes as yet ungotten and unborn might benefit from better-informed medical care. It's enough to make a parrot want to pull its feathers out.

Scrabbling about for correct words
In 1994 Hasbro Inc, manufacturers of the word game Scrabble, and its subsidiary Milton Bradley, publishers of the *Official Scrabble Player's Dictionary*, caved in to the thought police and declared that a hundred or so words – described as racially or sexually repugnant – did not actually exist. Really naughty terms like 'lezzie' and 'darkie' had already been tripwired, so the world waited to see what words had been mere figments of their fevered imaginations. Trouble is, nobody was saying. So there are about a hundred words you can't use in tournaments, provided you can establish what they are.

Stop the World, I Want to Get Off

On 15 January 1999, David Howard (whose skin is the mottled pink colour that qualifies him to be described as 'white') called a meeting in his Washington DC office. Mr Howard was Head of Constituent Services, appointed by the new mayor, Anthony Williams (who is black). The job of the minute Constituent Services office was to provide emergency financial help to hard-up Washington residents, but Mr Howard had just been told that his budget was going to be about as small as his office – and it was soon to transpire that it would be infinitely smaller than the row shortly to break about his head.

There were only three people at Mr Howard's meeting, and he began by warning his colleagues that they had little cash to play with. 'I will have to be niggardly with this fund because it's not going to be a lot of money,' he said. One of his colleagues was black, and yes, you've guessed it. Almost instantly, word of Mr Howard's dastardly speech had flashed round Washington, then America and, before too much longer, the English-speaking world. 'He said the N-word,' screamed the media, metaphorically hopping from one foot to the other in glee at having a story they could spin out for days. Obviously, whoever first reported the episode did not have hearing so acute that it could detect a pin dropping at ten paces. Equally plainly, his or her high-school career had riven the English teaching staff with much pain and grief. And apart from all else, if Mr Howard had said what he was said to have said he would have made no sense at all.

Commentators of a more learned disposition turned to Wesbster's *New Collegiate Dictionary* to confirm what they suspected. 'Niggardly', it proclaimed with authority, is of Scandinavian origin, and means 'meanly covetous and stingy' or, in a word, 'miserly'. But by now it was too late. No matter that Mr Howard had used a three-syllable word meaning precisely what he intended to convey in the circumstances, the first two syllables sounded like the dreaded N-word, and therefore that's what he had said. He apologised and resigned, and Mr Williams accepted his resignation. The media, now seeing this as a cause célèbre in the heart of the nation's capital, turned on the mayor. 'What makes this the worst is that this guy essentially lost his job over something that wasn't even politically incorrect,' was typical of the criticism directed at Mr Williams. But he hadn't got where he was without knowing how to perform a U-turn in the face of enemy fire, and less than a fortnight after David Howard was said to have said what he hadn't said, the mayor announced a review of the incident, refusing to rule out the possibility of his reinstatement. By then the victim may well have been overheard humming, 'Stop the world, I want to get off.'

Professor Amy George, USA
'Come on, folks! This political correctness has gone too far. It's downright silly . . . As a black female college professor, I rightly encourage my students to freely engage in discussion of issues/topics that others might consider PC, and why not? We live in a democratic society, a free world that others envy. If we can't speak freely about issues, be they immigration, education standards, or other so-called "hot button" topics, then move to those countries where the leadership controls speech, movement, assembly, etc. Free speech must reign!'

BiGLeTS Strike a Blow for Depopulation

In February 2005, Jada Pinkett Smith, wife of actor Will Smith, dared to make a speech at Harvard University in which she announced that she had 'a devoted husband, loving children and a fabulous career'. On the face of it a cause for congratulation and, one would have thought, unexceptional as a statement of feminine achievement. But the world, at least in Boston, Massachusetts, has moved on if Jeff Jacoby of the *Boston Globe* is to be believed. Her disgraceful statement was so absurdly old-fashioned and behind the times that the BiGLeTS (Bisexual, Gay, Lesbian, Transgender and Supporters) on Harvard's worthy campus were outraged. They stamped their little hooves in anger as they searched for insults sufficiently venomous to hurl at poor Ms Smith. Finally they found the chink in her armour. She was denounced as 'extremely heteronormative'. Whatever it means, Ms Smith was so crushed she felt obliged to apologise as she fled the city.

The BiGLeTS were so pleased with themselves that they next targeted Mitt Romney, the Governor of Massachusetts, for announcing that every child 'has a right to a mother and a father'. What a thing to say! 'Hatemongering!' they screamed. How could anybody utter such 'brainless, fuzzy stuff', they demanded to know, without stopping to ask themselves how they would have got here without a mother and a father. And in case we hadn't yet got the message they warned us: 'The assault is not going to let up until the heteronormative deviants among us have been silenced!' As the *Boston Globe* commented, 'It would be laughable if the implications weren't so dire.'

Learn to include anybody – except Mum or Dad

If you thought Australians were robust, no-nonsense folk, think again. In 2006, Victoria's Department of Education and Training sanctioned the distribution to its schools of a teacher's manual written by lesbian activist Vicki Harding. 'Mummy' and 'Daddy' are condemned as intolerant, prejudiced terms to be jettisoned forthwith. When little Tommy or wee Katie is begging you for a bedtime story, he or she must henceforth address you as 'parent' or, failing that, 'guardian' to avoid offending any nearby homosexuals or lesbians loitering outside the nursery door. Furthermore, and to avoid any danger of growing up a disgusting heteronormative deviant, Ms Harding also advocates encouraging children as young as five to act out homosexual scenarios. It's certainly one way to halt the population explosion.

The Power of Imagination

On its internal flights within the United States, Southwest Airlines prefers bedlam to order and does not assign seats. As with, say, EasyJet in the UK, part of the fun of flying is the unholy tussle to scramble your way into a passable seat. On a 2002 flight, this routine was being played out as usual when 22-year-old attendant Jennifer Cundiff attempted to hurry things along with a light touch by calling out, 'Eenie, meenie, minie, moe; pick a seat, we gotta go.' Most passengers chuckled, order was restored, and the plane was able to taxi out for takeoff. Two of its passengers were seething, though, and it was no half-hearted seethe.

In February 2003, the two in question filed a case against the airline for unspecified compensatory and punitive damages. They were sisters, Louise Sawyer and Grace Fuller, they were black, and they were determined that the rhyme had been directed at them personally. 'It was like I was too dumb to find a seat,' complained Fuller, evidently unaware that passengers of varying shapes, sizes and colours were simultaneously scrambling for seats. Sawyer seemed more perturbed that some of the passengers had 'snickered', which made her 'feel alienated'. 'You may,' wrote one American journalist reporting this, 'be experiencing the first hint of a primal scream just now. You probably also understand without excessive mental strain that the attendant meant: "We're taking off. If you don't have a seat, pick one."'

The attendant in question was baffled by the whole thing. The rhyme Jennifer Cundiff had learned as a toddler went, 'Eenie, meenie, minie, moe; catch a tiger by its toe.' Indeed this was how the rhyme was recast as the Civil Rights movement got under way in 1950s' America, and few people below the age of about forty knew differently. But the words had once been less innocent, and a racist undertone lurked beneath the surface. Nonetheless, at the preliminary hearing the judge quickly dismissed any question of physical and emotional distress, but did allow a case to be brought against the airline for being racist and offensive. 'The trial will make good copy, so I mustn't complain,' wrote the same American journalist. 'When your livelihood depends on the consistent stupidity of human beings, one can only bask in today's unparalleled bounty.' Unlucky for him, then, that in March 2003, the airline won the case in short order, but the two sisters still managed the last word. They only lost because the jury was all white, they said.

Red rage

The self-absorbed now have something else to be on their guard against – their hair colour. An 'unspecified number' of red-haired men (which vagueness suggests less than half a dozen) complained after an ad for the gingery qualities of Corjuba Ginja rum was screened on New Zealand TV. In it, a redheaded student is rebuffed after thinking his teacher was becoming orgasmic about him rather than the drink she was caressing at the time. Twenty-one-year-old C Irwin complained that the ad was 'mocking people like myself in nasty fashion' and went on to allege that it 'will add to the atmosphere of denigration that currently exists towards red-headed males'. The NZ Advertising Standard Complaints Board decided the ad reinforced negative stereotypes and 'caused serious offence' to the aforesaid red-headed males.

Not So Peaceful Co-existence

Way back in 1887, when Native Americans were called Red Indians, despite being neither red nor Indian, and their menfolk were referred to as Braves, the 87,000 members of the Lumbee tribe petitioned the North Carolina Assembly to have a school founded just for them. To begin with it was called the Croatan Normal School. Successful from the start, it steadily expanded in numbers, range and achievement levels until, nearly seventy years ago, it graduated to the University of North Carolina-Pembroke School, proudly performing under its logo of an Indian, and with its sports teams nicknamed 'the Braves'.

One day towards the end of 2002, the Tribal Chairman of the Lumbees, Milton R Hunt, was enjoying a peaceful breakfast until he opened a letter by which, he said with masterly understatement, he was 'very surprised'. It was from the Minority Opportunities and Interests Committee of the National Collegiate Athletic Association and it ordered UNC-Pembroke to explain why it used the 'racially offensive' logo of an Indian, and the equally offensive nickname of the Braves on the athletics track. Mr Hunt barely had time to get over his choking fit and pick up the phone to his colleagues before scorn and outrage clogged the airwaves.

Athletics Director Dan Kenny was quickly out of the blocks. He dismissed the NCAA's intervention as wrongheaded. 'No other school was founded for Native Americans. We don't have to have you (the NCAA) tell us what's offensive.' Author and former pupil Bruce Barton reminded the NCAA that 'for a long time we were the only four-year university in the world for Native America. The name is very apropos.' The heavyweights took slightly longer to engage gear but, when they did, made every word count. Chancellor Dr Allen Meadors spoke of the school's rich heritage, and of how 'American Indians cherish having the Brave emblem since it honours their history and symbolises their integrity, courage and ability to overcome all odds'. Tribal Chairman Hunt, happily recovered from the initial shock, had a great deal to say on the subject, including some terse advice: 'The Lumbees don't want the NCAA to meddle. The logo and nickname are part of the university, and they would consider it an insult if they were changed. If the NCAA could have done a little investigation beforehand, they would have seen . . . that the Lumbee tribe supports them.' Alternatively, he could just have said – stop patronising us.

Breathe deeply before reading

Fifteen-year-old Andra Ferguson and her boyfriend Brandon Kivi, both students at Caney Creek High School in Texas, are asthmatics. One day in October 2003, KPRC-TV in Houston reported that Andra suffered an attack but had forgotten to bring her Albuterol inhaler. Brandon, who uses the identical inhaler, lent her his. 'It made a big difference,' said a grateful Andra. 'It saved my life.' (A big difference by any reckoning.) Brandon was promptly arrested, suspended from school and charged with delivering a dangerous drug, for which he faced expulsion and being sent to a detention centre.

US Constitution Apparently Invalid in New Hampshire!

When Hampton Academy Junior High held a Holiday Dance on 17 December 2004, seventh-grader Bryan Lafond decided to go as Santa Claus. Being America, his parents helped him dress in style and hired an outfit from Brooks, so there was no danger of his being mistaken for an undersized tramp with a dishcloth round his chin. His outfit evidently won much admiration from his friends but not, alas, from Principal Fred Muscara, ever alert for the inappropriate. Bryan's mother Leslie had not even had time to drive out of the car park after dropping him off before he was banging at the car windows. Mr Muscara, it seems, had told him his outfit was politically incorrect.

'It was a holiday party, not a Christmas party,' said the principal. 'This is a separation of church and state. We have a lot of students that go to Hampton Academy Junior High that have different religions. We have to be sensitive to that.'

As a matter of interest, the US Supreme Court has ruled – on more than one occasion – that Santa Claus is a secular symbol. That being so, dear old Santa should have been perfectly at home at a holiday party, but maybe Fred Muscara regards Hampton Academy Junior High as above and beyond the Supreme Court's decisions. As it was, he informed Brian that he was perfectly entitled to stay at the party but only if he stepped out of his costume, not something that greatly appealed to the lad as it meant he'd be dancing in his underpants for the evening.

The following Monday, Bryan's parents took the matter before the School Board. Why, they wanted to know, had Santa suddenly become anathema when, just two weeks earlier, the school had hosted a Parent Teacher Association breakfast with Santa? And why, they continued, had it not occurred to Mr Muscara that if Bryan was forced to disrobe, and if he was unwilling to risk being spurned by any girl who thought underpants were degrading in a dance partner, he would have to leave the school to go home for a change of clothes? Even in respectable New Haven, it is not wise for diminutive Santa Clauses to try thumbing lifts after dark, and in any case school rules forbade any pupil to leave the premises unless a parent is called. It was sheer good luck that Bryan's mother had not left the car park at the time. It seems that when Bryan returned to the school, the principal's greeting was: 'Are you trying to get me fired?' Bryan must have been sorely tempted to reply in the affirmative. As it was, a movement was soon under way with just that end in view.

Prime-time nipple alert
Although half the population has them, and babies couldn't do without them, many Americans clearly find the female nipple an inexcusable aberration. When Janet Jackson exposed one of her pair in a half-time concert during the 2004 Super Bowl, which gets astronomic ratings, a hefty chunk of the population bellowed in outrage, doubtless peering through its fingers as it did so. It comes as no surprise, therefore, that the previous year the Wyoming ski resort of Mary's Nipple, nestling below a mountain so shaped, has been officially de-nippled, and is now known just as Mary's. The new signs for the sanitised, if abbreviated, town name were delivered in April 2003.

Suspension for Big Winners

The state of Connecticut is among the smallest in the USA, but it sure is big when it comes to ensuring that the feelings of losing football teams are not wounded. The football committee of the Connecticut Interscholastic Athletic Conference, which governs all high-school sports, spent a couple of years discussing the matter before deciding to suspend coaches whose teams win by more than fifty points. This is called 'score management' and will, it is hoped, prevent 'incorrect' scores.

It seems the winning ways of New London High School triggered the move. In a single season they proved themselves to be so ruthlessly uncaring of the self-esteem of their teenage opponents that they recorded four wins of fifty points or more. A similar sensitivity has spread to the state of Iowa where, if a team gets to be 35 points ahead, time-outs are abolished and the clock is run continuously to bring the unseemly slaughter to an end as quickly as possible.

Nor is it just in Connecticut and Iowa that striving for excellence is being reined back. Over the border in Canada a hockey team of nine and ten-year-old boys called the Seafair Atom C Eagles was suspended in December 2004. This was not, as you could be forgiven for thinking, for having an unintelligible name, but because they refused to stop winning. 'The boys have been locked out and their play suspended indefinitely with threats that their entire season may be ended,' said Larry Mangotich, father of ten-year-old player, Lucas. Meantime, Len Cuthbert, President of the Seafair Minor Hockey Association, was explaining that they didn't want one team to be weak and another strong. The aim, he said, was that 'every team in every organisation wins and loses about the same number of games'. One dreads to think what might happen to hockey teams from the Seafair Association if they ever ventured to tour a sports-mad country like Australia.

It has been suggested that one reason European golfers are beating the United States by ever-increasing margins in the biennial Ryder Cup is because, with the exception of Tiger Woods and Phil Mickelson, American golfers have lost the appetite for winning tournaments. Appearance money is now so great that, we are told, more than a hundred golfers on the US circuit have become millionaires just by turning up and trundling round the course on the four consecutive days of a competition. As long as they avoid the cut at the end of the second round, they'll be in the money. It's not the greatest incentive for becoming as good as possible, but maybe they are early proponents of the idea that beating your opponents is not nice; or perhaps they are proving the old adage that winning is not the point, it's the taking part that counts. That said, spare a thought for the effect on the tender egos of those who fail to beat the cut and are eliminated at the end of the second day.

Don't ask me to take responsibility

In 2004, Boroondara Council, Melbourne, in cricket-mad Australia, decreed that batpersons were banned from hitting sixes on two of its grounds. A hundred clubs in the Eastern Cricket Association followed suit. One would think an individual walking round or along a sports ground would be aware that it was wise to watch the ball, and would take responsibility for their own wellbeing. But wherever one or more lawyers are gathered, you can be sure it will always be someone else's fault. As Rod Patterson of the ECA said, 'In this day and age we have a litigious society, and the council is concerned it may get sued if they allow cricket balls to come out of the park.'

Play Removed from Playtime

There are 137 schools in Broward County, Florida, and in 2005 running was banned in all of them. So were hand-pulled merry-go-rounds, teeter-totters (whatever they are) and swings – despite the National Program for Playground Safety stating that swings were safe for all age groups. Why this removal of play from playtime? Fear of legal action. According to Broward County's Safety Director, Jerry Graziose: 'We sometimes get a letter from an attorney before we even get an accident report from the school.' They certainly sue from the hip in Florida, though the *South Florida Sun Sentinel* reckons this is all part of a national trend. Growled Joe Frost, who runs the Play and Playgrounds Research Project at the University of Texas: 'Play is one of children's chief vehicles for development. Right now it looks like we're developing a nation of wimps.'

Is the fear of legal action justified, though? Mr Graziose said that in the preceding six years the county had paid out $561,000 in settlement of 189 claims for accidents in the playground and this, apparently, represents 5 per cent of the total for all kinds of injury claims in that period. Conversely, this means that 95 per cent of injury claims arose *outside* the playground. Observers worked out that, in the same six years, 1.35 million students had attended Broward County schools, and calculated that therefore only 0.01 per cent of them had been hurt sufficiently to make a claim. Did that justify depriving their children of the opportunity to learn about risk, such an essential skill for survival and success?

Ah, said some cynical Floridians, but if you let on that the amount paid out in playground accident claims is trivial, the queue to file a claim will stretch into Louisiana!

Little Red Riding Hood drunk and disorderly

Two California school districts banned the reading of 'Little Red Riding Hood' back in 1998. Could the wicked wolf's sharp teeth be giving the tiny tots nightmares? No, much worse than that. While you in your naivety thought Little RRH was being kind and thoughtful in taking her sick old granny some food and wine to keep her going, what she was really up to, the little wretch, was promoting underage alcohol abuse. These modern kids!

The World's Going to Potter

Unless you live under a rock – or haven't recovered from a nasty bang on the head during a lively game of Quidditch – you'll be aware that J K Rowling wrote the first Harry Potter book in an Edinburgh café while a single mum struggling to make ends meet. What you might not know, however, is that Harry, our bespectacled hero, is a sexist brute and that every one of the seven books is not only pagan but also 'phallocentric'.

Needless to say, the 'Potter is Potty' craze started in America. In 1999 the Board of Education in South Carolina discussed whether the books should be accessible to children after a mother said the goings-on at Hogwarts School for Wizards were full of a 'serious tone of death, hate, lack of respect and sheer evil' and various religious websites and publications condemned Harmless Harry, with one, the Freedom Village USA Ministry – why does that name scare us so much? – saying the Potter books disseminate 'witchcraft philosophy'.

Then in 2001 Dr Elizabeth Heilman of Purdue University, Indiana, addressed the American Educational Research Association conference in Seattle and accused J K of portraying girls as 'giggly, emotional and anti-intellectual' while boys were 'wiser, braver, more intelligent and fun'. The good doctor told her audience that Harry was forever coming to the rescue of his best friend Hermione Granger after she quailed in the face of danger.

The accusation sparked a transatlantic war of words with Sandra West, the chairwoman of the Headteachers Association in Glasgow, telling Dr Heilman she needed to lighten up.

'These books are certainly not sexist and to say so is complete nonsense,' she barked. 'Harry Potter novels are a terrific read and a great source of language . . . the most intelligent and brightest character in the whole book is Hermione and even in the sports teams the girls play a good role. I don't believe she is helpless, she has a great deal of ability and always manages to get out of tricky situations.'

But there was more than one American academic waiting to have a pop at Potter. Jack Zipes, a professor of German at the University of Minnesota, wrote a book called *The Troublesome Success of Children's Literature from Slovenly Peter to Harry Potter* in which he slated JK Rowling's creation for being 'sexist, tedious and grating'. Tedious and grating? With a book title like his? Pot, kettle and black spring to mind.

He then went on to say the books were part of a 'process by which we homogenise our children', adding that 'Rowling's books conventionally repeat much of the same sexist and white patriarchal biases of classical fairy tales.' In a subsequent interview Professor Zipes said he found the Potter books 'very eclectic, very conventional, and . . . really disturbing because of the focus on what I call "phallocentric power".' Call it what you like, Professor. Fortunately, more people are reading Harry Potter than are likely to read your work – by a factor of roughly 100,000:1 at a guess.

Shocking Pink

Pink, say psychologists, has a pacifying effect – but not on Erin Buzuvis and Jill Gaulding of the University of Iowa's law faculty. Quite what they were up to in the men's locker room of the university's (American) football team it may be better not to ask. Whatever it was, they emerged deeply traumatised and disturbed after finding the lockers in the visiting team's quarters were painted pink.

There is a reason for the colour. It was the brainchild of Iowa's head coach, Hayden Fry, who majored in psychology, and first decided to confront visiting teams with pink back in 1980. Fry figured that as pink is a pacifying colour it would be ideal for quietening the testosterone of the opposition so that by the time they got out on the pitch they would be as pussycats compared to his boys. Good thinking there, Hayden, and although we don't have a table of Iowa's results over the last quarter-century, they must be good or they'd have changed the colour by now.

They soon will, though, should Buzuvis and Gaulding ever have their way. They have decided that pink is to be the colour of oppressed women, lesbians and gays, and that their comfort and wellbeing are seriously compromised by the colour of the football lockers – despite the fact that women, oppressed or otherwise, and lesbians are unlikely ever to be in the locker room of the visiting men's football team. Irrelevant. 'The pink locker room is a subtle way of painting the words "sissy" and "girlie man" on the walls.' Possibly. So what? It seems to suggest Hayden Fry's original plan is still working. Alerted by the fuss, a visiting team from Colorado University spent the pre-match hour covering the walls with white paper in order not to see the pink, rather than discussing their match tactics. Once again, it seems Hayden had scored. And anyway, why should pink be the exclusive colour of OWLeGs (oppressed women, lesbians and gays)? The rest of the world is just as entitled to it. As one American reporter wrote: 'Buzuvis and Gaulding need to grow up and stop worrying about it. I would be tickled gay if they did.'

A rather stale idea

Amherst High School in New Hampshire (yes, it's that curious state again – see p. 183) has recently decided the hallowed term 'freshman', used across the country, is divisive. No sooner had the school had this clever thought than it was implemented. Overnight, freshmen ceased to exist and found themselves re-christened 'ninth-graders'. The school explained: 'This is 2005, and "man" or "men" no longer refers to all people.' Evidently they do not bother with dictionaries in New Hampshire schools. The authoritative *Webster's New Collegiate Dictionary* defines 'man' as 'a human being; the human race'. The school's time might be better spent on education.

G'night and Goodbye, Mate

'Pomposity gone mad', said former Australian Prime Minister Bob Hawke when he heard the news. He might have added 'mate' but didn't. 'Absurd and impractical', fumed the current Prime Minister John Howard. What had caused such high-level uproar? It seems that in August 2005, the head of a government department had been addressed as mate by one of the security guards keeping an eye on the parliament buildings in Canberra. Most Australians would feel a tad cold-shouldered if they were not saluted with this traditional form of Aussie greeting but not, it seems, this one. In no time he had caused a directive to be issued requiring the guards at Parliament House to address the inmates as Sir or Madam.

It was a pity he didn't stop to engage his brain, let alone brush up his knowledge of Australian history, before opening his mouth. Had he done so he might have predicted the storm of outrage that followed. 'Mateship' is as fundamental to Australian society as their flag is to Americans. In World War I the bravery of ANZAC troops on the Somme and at Gallipoli created a spirit of courage and mateship at a time when Australia viewed itself as a backwater, ashamed of its convict past. World World War II renewed that spirit and, from then on, the country has never looked back. The concept of mateship indicates egalitarian togetherness, and it is the glue that has bonded individuals into a successful whole.

The unfortunate departmental head was soon up the creek without a paddle as the tidal wave of protest broke. The *Sydney Daily Telegraph*'s 'ludicrous' was among the milder epithets as calls flooded in to radio chat shows, emails were fired off to

Members of Parliament and headline writers brushed up their biting monosyllabic wit. 'What's it feel like to be a pompous prick, mate?' might well have been among the greetings to the ill-advised head of that government department when next he crept back to his office.

Auf Wiedersehen, Pet

Anything Australia can do, Tynesiders can do better. In summer 2006, Newcastle City Council instructed its workers to desist from addressing women in the age-old Geordie style. 'Pet', 'hinny', 'dear', 'love', 'sweetheart' – all blacklisted, irrespective of the fact that affectionate daily greetings like 'Alreet, pet?' and 'Howay, hinny' are a normal part of Tyneside life. 'Totally bloody crackers. It's like they're trying to kill the Geordie language,' said one council employee. 'We're scared to talk to anyone now.' But surely abolishing warmth and affection is a small price to pay for achieving the 'dignity and respect' the council demands?

Wanted: Unisex Maximum-Security Wing

One night just before Easter 1996, Russell Williams walked into a crowded bar in Queensland, Australia, carrying a shotgun and shot dead Jo-Ann Leigh Brown, his ex-partner and mother of his two-year-old son. After a five-day personhunt he was captured and given a lengthy prison term, the first years of which he spent in a medium-security penitentiary. In 2003 he married a Cairns woman, who complained that her new husband had spent too long in medium security and should be moved to Lotus Glen near Cairns. In June 2005, though, he plotted a daring escape from Lotus Glen by helicopter that was only narrowly foiled and, not surprisingly, found himself heading to a maximum-security unit at the Arthur Gorrie Correctional Centre, designed for men rated violent, dangerous or at risk of escape.

Even Williams must have twigged he would have some difficulty convincing anyone that he should not be categorised under at least one of these headings, if not all three simultaneously, and fell to brooding on what trick he could spring next. Less than nine months after his failed escape bid, he demanded to be transferred to an open prison. This interesting proposal was, very understandably, declined. Then inspiration struck. Notwithstanding that he had proved terminal as far as poor Jo-Ann Leigh Brown was concerned, Williams declared that he and his fellow prisoners (who included murderers and serial rapists) were the victims of sexual discrimination on the grounds that the only inmates of the high-security unit were male.

Anyone accustomed to the no-nonsense fashion in which Australian sports teams brush off their opponents might have expected the average Aussie to roll around on the floor holding his or her sides at this novel suggestion, but Queensland's Anti-Discrimination Commission remained soberly upright. It required the State's Department of Corrective Services to set up a compulsory conciliation conference with Williams in March 2006. In vain did Judy Spence, the Minister for Corrective Services, point out that no maximum-security orders had been passed on any female prisoner because there had been no females requiring one. 'Prisoners are put into maximum-security units because they are the worst in the prison system,' she pointed out with apparently unanswerable logic. Unsurprisingly, the compulsory conciliation conference with Williams failed to reach a conclusion, leaving Williams free to take his 'case' to the Anti-Discrimination Tribunal. It would appear the only way out of the dilemma is to get Williams off everybody's back by transferring him to an open prison from where he can escape at leisure as often as he wishes, while keeping the Anti-Discrimination Commission happy by arbitrarily declaring a handful of female prisoners violent, dangerous or at risk of escape, and shoving them into the maximum-security unit. This would have the additional bonus of keeping the Commission and its lawyers in full employment for years ahead.

Queensland's Anti-Discrimination Tribunal scores again!
If you're determined to be a criminal, it pays to be banged up in Queensland. Sharif Mahommed is a child sex offender who was given an eight-year sentence in 2000. Being Muslim, Mahommed eats halal meat and, as the first Queensland prisoner ever to have this dietary need, it took some time to meet it. In the meantime he was given tinned halal meat, tinned beef and lamb, and vegetarian food. Freshly slaughtered halal meat did not come on stream until November 2003. For this he was awarded A$2,000 compensation.

The Handbag Haka

Dearie me! Who would have thought those great big hulks in black were nothing but cuddly softies underneath? On the eve of yet another titanic rugby clash between New Zealand's All Blacks and Australia's green and gold XV, Channel Seven's TV network poked a bit of fun in the direction of the Blacks, and it didn't go down at all well. Mind you, there's quite a bit of previous between the two neighbours, so it might have been predicted that hackles would rise to the vertical. The origins of the sensitivity may lie back in 1946 when the Aussie cricketers went to New Zealand to play the first ever Test Match between the countries (many years after the rest of the cricket world had accepted New Zealand as a Test side), but won so easily that on getting home they declared it null and void as a proper match. In 1980, New Zealand Premier Robert Muldoon added fuel to the fire of rivalry by announcing that the migration of New Zealanders to Australia at least had the benefit of raising the IQ of both countries.

The origins of the 2006 spat lay in a nightclub fight that May, when All Black captain Tana Umaga doused a disagreement between sixteen-stone clubmate Chris Masoe and another person by grabbing a woman's handbag and dotting Masoe over the head with it. Either the pain of the blow or the reprimand from his skipper caused Masoe to blub like a newborn. So two months later, when the All Blacks arrived in Australia for their rugby match, the temptation for Channel Seven was irresistible. Before the kickoff of every match they play, the All Blacks line up in front of their opposition and perform the Haka, based on a Maori war dance or greeting. Apologists for the Haka are various in their explanations of it, but when performed on the rugby pitch it is unquestionably designed to intimidate. Channel Seven, however, added a little something of their own to a recording of a haka. 'Australia is about to play the toughest team on the planet,' said the announcer, before cutting to the sight of three of the largest All Blacks swinging digitally superimposed women's handbags.

It goes without saying that the New Zealanders were less than amused. Where rugby is concerned they take themselves very seriously indeed. 'It's disrespectful and insensitive to Maori culture,' grumbled assistant coach Wayne Smith, a very mild reflection of the steam and outrage being generated back home. But Australians were too busy wiping the tears from their eyes and getting their breath back to pay much heed.

Tough gorgonzola, compagno

New Zealanders were feeling sensitive even before the Aussie handbag haka spoof. A few months earlier, international ad agency Leo Burnett devised a TV commercial for the new Fiat Idea featuring black-clad women performing an approximate imitation of an All Blacks pre-match haka around the car. The air was filled with the wailing of Kiwi diplomats. Either use genuine Maori men or a special haka for women, they implored. Otherwise you'll offend everyone – women, Maoris, All Blacks and anyone else left over. The Italians shrugged their shoulders, uncomprehending of these odd Anglo-Saxon sensibilities, and got on with broadcasting it.

Ernie, What Were You Starting?

There is a story that when, in 1930, the Middlesex cricket captain, R W V Robins was bowled at Lord's by Ernie Achong, a Trinidadian wrist-spinner of mixed Caribbean and Chinese descent, he exclaimed: 'Fancy being bowled by a Chinaman!' True or not, that incident is said to be the origin of the cricketing term 'chinaman', describing a left-arm bowler's ball that spins in one direction when the delivery action suggests the opposite. In 2000, it came under severe scrutiny from the United Cricket Board of South Africa as it pored over terminology that might cause offence in some corner or other. Then there was 'Chinese cut', an unintended shot that flies off the edge of the bat between the legs; someone, surely, must come out in goose pimples at the mere mention of it?

The members of the Board trooped off, metaphorically at least, to consult Goolam Bodi, an Indian-born spin bowler playing for the provincial side Gauteng. For good measure they also tried him out on 'coolie creeper' (a delivery, called a 'grubber' in Britain, that runs along the ground instead of bouncing). Mr Bodi considered the matter. 'Chinaman? That's the name given to the left-armer's wrist spin everywhere. Bowl it myself,' he summed up succinctly. So much for that, then. But, he added, 'coolie creeper does sound offensive to me'. Ah-ha. The UCB had scored! It rushed back to HQ and issued a proclamation. 'Coolie creeper' was banned and so – since Mr Bodi, being a bowler, evidently didn't spend enough time batting to have experience of it and therefore had nothing particular to say on the matter – was the 'Chinese cut'.

'A load of crap', said South Africa's international all-rounder Brian McMillan with even greater brevity than Goolam Bodi had managed. Unluckily for him, he had the disadvantage of being white, which outweighed his experience of cricket and its terminology around the world. Mr McMillan was required to apologise or be banned from playing so, despite the support of journalists who wondered aloud 'why such acute navel-gazing political correctness should unnecessarily attract worldwide attention', he did.

Thus emboldened, the UCB turned its attention to the term 'whitewash', universally applied to describe a series, in any sport, where one side wins every match. Even by UCB standards, this proved a challenge too far. Anyone who was ever at an international match in the Caribbean in the days when the mighty West Indian team was steamrollering another set of hapless cricketers visiting their islands, and heard their delighted supporters revelling in the 'blackwash', will realise this is picking sticky ground on which to fight. And English cricket fans who have never made it to the Caribbean will remember with dreadful clarity the blackwashing their side received when the West Indies were here in 1984 and won 5–0.

Poms abashed

In what must rank as one of Australian sport's most pointless gestures, and one blessedly certain of instant failure, cricket fans down under were instructed in the autumn of 2006 not to taunt visiting poms during the long-awaited England–Australia 2006–07 Ashes confrontation. Do not, ordered Cricket Australia, the sport's governing body, link the p-word with anything 'hurtful, racist, offensive or humiliating'. England's faithful cricket followers, the Barmy Army, must have hugged themselves with glee when they heard the edict. The traditional rivalry between the two sets of supporters is well over a century old and thrives on irreverent barbs and witticisms flashing back and forth before they all get together round a few tinnies. It would have been a heaven-sent platform for the poms to goad the diggers if only their cricketers had entered into the spirit of the thing. By getting thrashed 5–0, though, they handed the initiative straight back to the Aussies.

Colour Me Yellow

Unless he or she worked for Haringey Council or Medway Council (see pp. 29 & 32) an ordinary person might think a box of crayons unlikely to cause fainting fits among the endlessly twittering maiden aunts of the politically correct universe. An ordinary person would not be one who ever worked for Crayola, the American producer of crayons and coloured pencils, since its record of colour sensitivity has a long pedigree. In 1958 it eliminated Prussian Blue from its range because students were unfamiliar with Prussian history. Quite why one should require a detailed knowledge of Count von Bismarck's life, habits and inside-leg measurement before picking up a blue crayon may be considered strange, but no matter. Four years later they were at it again. This time Flesh was removed from the palette and renamed Peach because they had noticed, they said, that not everyone had the same skin colour. Very observant, and completely true, even if flesh is a different substance from skin and is pretty much the same colour by whatever skin hue it is covered.

Crayola then paused, drew breath and prepared to sail back into the fray in 1999. This time it was becoming extraordinarily agitated by its Indian Red crayons and pencils, having received feedback that some kids believed the name referred to the skin colour of Native Americans, once known as Red Indians. Although facts rarely trouble the pc brigade, it is at least instructive – and might have been to American school kids if Crayola had had the nerve to attempt it – to know that Indian Red derives its name from a pigment found in clay around the Indian subcontinent.

'If Americans have trouble figuring out that there's a whole country called India, and things relating to it are properly called Indian, that's their problem, not Crayola's,' wrote one newspaper at the time. 'Honestly. This is like accommodating the sensibilities of flat-earthers.'

Undeterred, Crayola ran a competition to think of a new name, promising a monster assortment of its products as a prize for the winner. There were some interesting suggestions. Coq au Vin, Brown Bubble, Pork-n-Beans, Meatball & Spaghetti and Cherry Mocha Scream betrayed the obsessions of an overweight nation with its food, and did not detain the judges long. They trembled a little longer over Red Rupture, Rupture Red, Ripest Red, Stoplight Red and Stop-Sign Red before deciding these were too – how could one put it – *red*. Finally, they settled with a sigh of relief on something that, at least in the short term, could surely cause no offence, real or imagined – Chestnut. But take no bets, and do not export to New Zealand. If redheads can take offence so easily (see p. 180) it may not be long before packs of lawyers seek out chestnut-haired folk and goad them into feeling insulted by the name of a coloured pencil.

Father creates a lather

In 2006, children's author Duncan Crosbie published *Titanic*, an account for nine to twelve-year-old children of a fictional family travelling on the doomed liner's 1912 maiden voyage. In it, the family meets various real people aboard, including Father Frank Browne who, carrying a recently invented portable camera, achieved fame as the only person to take a complete series of photographs of the liner before she sank. In the story, Father Browne agrees to photograph the fictional family. The American publishers demanded that for their edition, the wicked priest be defrocked and 'Father' removed from his name.

The Naked and the Dread

It's good to know it's not just Brits being driven mad by pc lunacy. The Kiwis are also going crackers, as Amanda Crozier discovered last year when she was dressing her sixteen-month-old daughter at the side of a public swimming pool in Christchurch, New Zealand, because the two family changing rooms were occupied.

Suddenly an attendant slithered up and asked her to refrain from what she was doing. Which was what exactly? Undressing your child in a public swimming area, she was told. 'You're kidding me, aren't you?' replied the mother of four. Oh no, said the attendant, and gave her a leaflet in which the management explained that there was a ban on child nudity to 'minimise the risks'.

After the story made the national press the manager of the pool felt obliged to elaborate. The *New Zealand Herald* reported her explanation that 'some swimmers were offended by child nudity and they were also worried about the risk of paedophiles photographing naked children'.

But Mrs Crozier wasn't having any of it. 'It's not very often I get cross, but I got terribly cross about that,' she said. 'It's a shame it has got to that degree really. They tell us they are looking after us, but really they are not because they are making it more difficult for us.'

Pool manager Ann Bergman said Mrs Crozier would have to like it or lump it because they wouldn't be changing their policy. Not only were some sensitive souls upset by a child momentarily in its birthday suit but, said Bergman, the ban was also 'in response to concerns about lurking paedophiles or people photographing naked children'. Perhaps if Ms Bergman insists on being so alarmist it would be more practical to ban cameras than nudity.

'That's today's changing society,' added Ms Bergman. 'We can no longer do what we [did] in yesteryear. It's not just in pools, it is life in general. We have to change with the times.' To which Judith Collins, a Kiwi politician evidently cut from stronger cloth than Ms Bergman, replied, 'Nonsense . . . how do they think babies are born? Do they think they come all dressed? Maybe they think there are paedophiles lurking around delivery rooms. People need to start thinking about what exactly they are saying here. Do they allow people to see each other undressed in the changing rooms?'

Wolves' howler

It was reported in December 2006 that Wolverhampton City Council was offering ethnic minority-only swimming sessions to the city's black and Asian residents. The *Evening Standard* quoted the council as saying the sessions were for swimmers with 'religious or cultural issues which would otherwise prevent them from taking part'. Not only were white swimmers excluded but special screens were erected around the pool for further segregation or, as the council would put it, privacy. A spokesman for the council enthused that 'it is one of the most ambitious schemes in the country and aims to tackle childhood obesity, engage the city's ethnic minority communities and work with children who fear water' – provided, of course, their skin colour is not 'inappropriate'.

HEALTH AND SAFETY IS BAD FOR YOU

In the beginning, the Health and Safety Executive's brief to ensure safety in the industrial workplace was commendable. But once the numbers start growing in a department with a mandate to meddle, the temptation to interfere with everything and everybody becomes irresistible. We have a secret suspicion the HSE will be satisfied only when every inhabitant of the Unhinged Kingdom is required to avoid accidents by living in bed – without pillows (banned), for fear of accidental suffocation if a proper risk assessment is not carried out before turning over.

Only Fools and Councils

You wonder what Del Boy and Rodders would have done if the Trading Standards Officer who marched up to Tony Spacey in Derby's Continental Market had ever dared show his face down Peckham way.

In 2005 Mr Spacey was doing a roaring trade selling honey and hive products from his stall when the officer demanded a word in his shell-like about his candles.

'I was absolutely dumbfounded when I was told this morning that I couldn't sell candles because they don't carry warnings that they could cause fire if used negligently,' said Mr Spacey. 'I thought that the whole intention of lighting a candle was to have a fire on the top.'

Tut-tut, Mr Spacey, a very simplistic view if you don't mind us saying, as Derbyshire Council pointed out in the statement they released to the press: 'These candles were sold without holders and could therefore be placed onto and burn down to an inflammable surface such as a table or television. Candles used in this way have sadly caused house fires and deaths and are therefore required to have labels explaining to consumers how to use them safely.'

Now if Del Boy could sell the idea of self-responsibility to 21st-century Britain, he really would be a millionaire by this time next year.

Postman Prat

In 2006 authorities in charge of a shopping precinct in Market Harborough, Leicestershire, ordered Postman Pat, his van and his cat to scram. The kiddies' musical ride had been on the pavement outside the precinct for years (30p a go), until the November day when someone, who would have been better employed polishing paper clips, decided that Pat had 'health and safety implications'. In fact, what they were worried about was that a shopper might fail to spot the large bright red van just as they might also fail to hear its irritating theme song, walk straight into it and sue the precinct, etc., etc.

No Room in the Inn . . . It's Been Closed Down by the HSE

Just imagine if the Health and Safety Executive had paid a visit to Bethlehem a couple of thousand years ago. They would have closed down that inn immediately because of 'overcrowding implications' and Mary and Joseph would have been reprimanded for the 'inappropriate' use of a manger. As for the Three Wise Men and their gifts . . . who gives frankincense as a present for a newborn baby? There's nothing wise about that, it's an 'aromatic hazard'.

One can only admire the dedication of our health-and-safety friends because they've certainly been making up for the 2,000 or so years that they were powerless. Take, for example, Chipping Sodbury Secondary School in Gloucestershire which, in December 2004, banned its pupils from wearing tinsel at the Christmas party for 'health and safety reasons'.

Deputy head teacher, Mel Jeffries, explained to the *Guardian* that: 'We want all our children to enjoy Christmas and have a good time, but at the same time make sure there are no accidents to spoil it. If tinsel is worn loosely around the neck it can be pulled tight and we don't want anything like that.' You don't want anything like school ties, you mean?

In 2005 Lee Sharrock, a business services manager, sent an email to the 400 staff working for a group of job centres in Greater Manchester, reminding them that it was very 'important that we pay attention to the health and safety implications' of Christmas decorations. To that end, continued Mr Sharrock (soon dubbed 'Scrooge' by the tabloid press), no decorations would be allowed to hang from ceilings in case someone fell off a chair while arranging them, and it was forbidden 'under any circumstances' to dangle paper chains from the walls. And if someone was brave enough to risk erecting a Christmas tree, they had a duty to ensure that all lights carried a twelve-month warranty. 'Decorations already put up, and which do not conform to the above criteria,' whined Mr Sharrock, 'must be removed immediately.'

In 2006 it was Santa himself who was shut down by the Wise Men (and women) of the HSE. For years, Father Christmas had taken time out from his busy schedule to appear in a charity procession in Leighton Buzzard, Bedfordshire, waving to the kids from a float as it moved through the town.

'Safety, Santa,' stormed the HSE, worried that he might fall from the float as the lorry that carried it moved at 5mph through Leighton Buzzard. The group that organised the charity event were told they had to insure the 'moving display' for £600 or the float wouldn't be allowed to float, but would have to remain static. 'Santa has been breaking the law by not being strapped into the vehicle,' Dave King, chairman of the local Round Table Association, told the *Daily Mail*.

In the same year the BBC reported that organisers of a Christmas party in the village of Embsay in the Yorkshire Dales were told that 'they must carry out a risk assessment of their mince pies – or their festivities will be cancelled'. Steve Dobson informed the BBC that he had written to the district council to ask if he could use the car park outside Embsay village hall and it replied saying that 'everything we do, from putting tinsel up to providing refreshments, has to be assessed. We have to consider the dangers involved, that someone might choke on their mince pie or have a nut allergy. I also understand that Santa may need a Criminal Records Bureau check.'

Is that a joke, Steve, that last bit? It's hard to know these days.

When the BBC asked the council to comment, the director of community services, Jonathan Kerr, said, 'We support these community events and we try to help local communities organise them and make sure they are as safe as possible.' And as joyless as possible.

Sink or swim

Little three-year-old Katie Bradford loves her trips to her local swimming pool in Exeter. All that splashing and sploshing – what fun! But on one occasion in 2006 she forgot her trusty rubber ring. Not to worry, said Katie's gran, Lyn, who was with her, there's a cupboard full of polystyrene floats by the pool, we'll borrow one of those. But when they asked the lean, lithe lifeguard to unlock his cupboard, he shook his head. 'Apparently if someone hurt themselves with a float we could sue,' Lyn raged to the *Western Morning News*. 'We didn't want to sue, we wanted a swim.' As Lyn began to tell her granddaughter that there would be no swim today, the helpful lifeguard interrupted and said there was no reason why the pair couldn't still go for a swim. Yes, that's right. The pool wouldn't let Katie swim with a float, but it would allow her to swim without one, even though she couldn't. 'It was an absolute farce,' said Lyn. 'We were told we couldn't have a float as it represented a health and safety issue. . . . [but] they seem to think that a non-swimmer using a float is more dangerous than not using one. The logic is completely barmy. Surely there's more likely to be an accident – if not a tragedy – if people are denied the most basic safety equipment.'

Health and Safety Cry Fowl

In the summer of 2006 Worcester auctioneer David Probert received a letter from the Health and Safety Executive – now a more frightening experience than having a brown Inland Revenue envelope drop on to your doormat (assuming you're still allowed to have a doormat, see p. 214) – telling him he was shouting too loudly.

'The letter said a complaint had been made about my auction and that I needed to fill in all these forms showing how much noise I made,' explained Mr Probert, who has been a livestock auctioneer for forty years. 'When I replied to the first letter telling them I wasn't going to assist their silly inquiries, I received a second more formal letter warning me of "further action".'

Even when faced with the threat of re-education, Mr Probert defied the Worcester HSE. He told the BBC, without shouting, that his twice-monthly auctions very rarely lasted more than two hours and that he found it hard to believe – as the HSE insisted – that his voice could reach the same decibel level (of 135dB) as 'standing within twenty-five metres of a jet aircraft'.

'I am continuing as I have for forty years on the premise that if I had damaged people's health there would be a lot of deaf people in Hereford,' said Mr Probert, who was curious to know if the HSE would be visiting the hundreds of other livestock auctions held over the UK. 'Are they really going to go round measuring everyone who makes a noise? It's the most stupid thing I've ever heard.'

But the HSE weren't going to take no for an answer, particularly if the 'no' might have exceeded the appropriate decibel level. They told Mr Probert they were 'duty bound to investigate' if his voice breached the noise threshold of 80 decibels (lowered from 85dB in April 2006). They also wanted to know how long staff at the Hereford Poultry Market were exposed to the fowl din because they were concerned that all the clucking and cock-a-doodle-doodling might be impairing their hearing.

'The whole thing is absolute nonsense,' added Mr Probert, 'a waste of time and money. It is such a shame that we have got to a stage where we are completely managed by rules and regulations.'

Stairway to Hell

Rugby World magazine reported in May 2007 that players at Devonport Services RFC in the south-west of England had to find a new way to get from their dressing room to the pitch after the HSE 'ruled that a flight of concrete steps under the stand, used for over 90 years, are too steep and narrow'. They were concerned a player might a) trip or b) suffer vertigo as he climbed the stairs onto the pitch. Apparently the HSE didn't voice their concerns about the physical nature of rugby, but surely it's only a matter of time before tackling, rucking, mauling and scrummaging come under their steely-eyed scrutiny, not to mention enjoyment.

Barmy Palmy

You could hardly call the Victorians a chilled-out bunch but compared to some of the people currently inhabiting our septic isle they now seem positively carefree.

It was during the reign of Victoria – when a trip to the seaside became fashionable – that Torbay (a 25-mile stretch of coastline in South Devon) was first decorated with palm trees in an attempt to make the English Riviera a touch more exotic.

For the next century or more the palm trees (*cordyline australis*, as Latin buffs will know) became as much a feature of Torquay as fish and chips and a downpour in June. So when in 2006 a main shopping street was redeveloped residents were a little surprised when instead of palm trees it was embellished with flowering pear trees.

Torquay's Chamber of Trade wrote to the council for an explanation, and got one from the Senior Urban Design and Landscape Officer. 'The palms need to be carefully and appropriately used,' he prattled. 'They can cause maintenance problems and, as they have very sharp leaves, need to be carefully used in the streetscapes, where they could cause injury to eyes/faces if inappropriately placed.'

The officer sympathised with the Chamber's concern but reminded them that 'it is usually not appropriate for palms to be placed in heavily pedestrian[ised] streets'.

The Senior Urban Design and Landscape Officer received the support of Colin Charlwood, a Liberal Democrat councillor, who told the *Guardian*: 'The truth is that, like everything else, health and safety regulations mean we have to be mindful that palm trees could be dangerous.'

Now with the bit between his teeth (a choking hazard, surely?), Mr Charlwood's musings assumed a positively surreal tinge. 'It is a little bit like keeping tigers,' he said, still referring to Torquay's palm trees. 'They are beautiful to look at but you wouldn't want them wandering the streets.'

Fortunately there were one or two people in Torquay willing to challenge such a vision. 'I cannot see palm trees as a serious health and safety risk,' harrumphed Torbay's mayor, Nick Bye, to the *Guardian*, 'unless you are in the Caribbean and a great big coconut falls on your head.' This, come to think of it, might explain Mr Charlwood's vivid imagination.

It's all gone pear-shaped

Hold on, Torquay, you might wish to rethink your policy of replacing palm trees with pear trees because, in October 2006, the BBC reported that Worcester City Council cordoned off a section of a public park after concerns that the fruit from two black pear trees (the fruit is part of the city's coat of arms) might fall on someone's head. According to the BBC, no one had actually been whacked on the bean by a pear but 'a city council spokesman said the precaution was cheaper than the potential legal cost if someone was hit on the head with a pear and sued'. The safety barriers were removed from Cripplegate Park once all the fruit had fallen to the ground. Hovering lawyers went home disgruntled.

Stepladder out of Line

You just know that any sentence that begins: 'The brigade is reviewing its stepladder policy' is likely to end with you wanting a stiff drink. Well, make it a double because in January 2007 several newspapers carried the story of the dedicated men and women of the Humberside Fire and Rescue Service who were told they were contravening Health and Safety Executive guidelines through the reckless use of stepladders.

As part of their fire-prevention campaign in 2006 the brigade's firefighters fitted, free of charge, around 15,000 smoke alarms in houses in the Hull and East Riding areas, making themselves more popular than ever with their general public.

One group to whom they did not endear themselves was the Health and Safety Executive. Possibly they were jealous that another organisation was interfering in their domain but, whatever the reason, they were not amused to hear that firefighters were using stepladders to install the ceiling smoke alarms – and not just teeny-weeny stepladders but ones that sometimes soared to a height of six feet. This was expressly prohibited by a HSE communiqué of 2005 concerning height regulations.

Sean Starbuck, regional chair of the Yorkshire and Humberside Fire Brigades Union, explained that the HSE 'told us not to use stepladders. It's not up to us to say that we are not going to use them. It's about legislation.' It leaves hanging in the air, though, the interesting question of how the smoke alarms are to be fitted without the use of stepladders. Scaffolding inside the living room, perhaps?

One Humberside firefighter, who wished to remain anonymous, fearing he would be dragged over hot coals (a definite contravention of health and safety regulations) if he was identified, told the *Daily Express*: 'Where will this end? Will we still be able to carry a rescued person down a ladder or enter a burning building without the HSE on our backs?'

Statistics from The Royal Society for the Prevention of Accidents were provided as proof of how dangerous stepladders can be. Apparently 40,000 people each year require some form of hospital treatment because of 'ladder-related' injuries. One suspects, however, that most of those unfortunates would, if given the choice, prefer a sprained ankle to third-degree burns or smoke suffocation.

All quiet on the playground front

If Susan Tuck, head teacher of Bracebridge Heath Primary School, Lincolnshire, devotes enough time to thinking it through she may come up with the perfect game for 21st-century schools – statues, a game requiring no sound and, on pain of being out, no movement. For the moment, in early 2007, she made do with eliminating from the playground tag and all games involving touching. She couldn't risk any banged heads after all. So, 'as I couldn't say to the boys that they couldn't play certain games and then allow the girls to go around linking arms', physical contact of any kind was put off limits. It was only to be expected that Lincolnshire Council would seat itself firmly on the fence and fail to provide any kind of lead, so it was left to the parents to express astonishment. As one said: 'I can't see it does much for children learning to play together.' But the Health and Safety Executive will be mighty proud of Ms Tuck.

Trip of a Lifetime

There was a time, a generation ago, when a 'tripping hazard' was how your parents warned you about the dangers of LSD. In the 21st century it's how Bristol City Council describe doormats.

In September 2006 they sent a letter to all tenants living in their 32,000 properties entitled 'Health and Safety Issues – Hazardous Mats'. The letter informed the council's inmates – sorry, tenants – that: 'During a routine Health and Safety inspection of the block, it was noted that loose mats were present in hallways/corridors outside of people's flats. These represent a "tripping hazard" and should be removed immediately. By all means have your own mats inside your front door but please do not leave them outside, creating a risk to others.'

The proclamation ended with an order that all mats were to be removed by 18 September and that 'any mat remaining in the hallways/corridors after this date will be removed and subsequently disposed of' – along with the occupants of the flat, if the tone of the letter was anything to go by.

Retired gardener Roger Perry told the *Daily Mail* the directive was 'absolutely ludicrous. The council says mats are a hazard – God only knows how. I've lived here thirteen years and never heard of any accidents. It's like Big Brother watching us.' Roger's neighbour, 82-year-old Albert Peacock, suggested that 'if the council are worried about people tripping, they should concentrate on mending the pavements'.

But Bristol City Council put their foot down (not on a mat, presumably) and insisted Mr Peacock and his ilk had to do as they were told. 'We know that asking people to remove mats is not popular,' said a spokeswhatsisname perceptively, 'but it is important that corridors in council properties are kept clear, as they are a means of escape from fire . . . mats are a trip hazard.' Oh, for the days of LSD . . .

Flower Power

In 2004 Suffolk County Council banned hanging baskets from Bury St Edmunds because of fears someone might get hurt. Not hurt, as in upset that the Purple Splendours aren't as blooming as they were last year, but hurt as in a hanging basket falls from a lamppost and gives a passer-by a nasty bump on the head. It didn't bother the council that for seventeen years the annual Bury In Bloom festival had passed off without a hanging basket acting 'inappropriately', to use one of the health and safety zealots' favourite words; nor that the Royal Horticultural Society stated that in forty years they had never heard of such an accident. Michael Ames, chairman of Bury In Bloom, told the BBC that the council was simply 'guarding their own backs over health and safety', while the council defended its decision on the grounds that: 'We have to be satisfied that the columns are strong and stable enough to take the weight.'

Bonfire of the Insanities

Guy Fawkes must be kicking himself that the HSE wasn't around in his day. Firstly, he and his pals would never have been allowed to stash all those barrels of gunpowder under Parliament, not unless they had undergone a training programme in how to lift heavy objects ('Bend your knees and keep your back straight, Mr Fawkes'). Secondly, there is no way King James would have been given permission to burn Guy on a bonfire without the HSE first carrying out a thorough risk assessment. As indeed they do with relish every Bonfire Night in the 21st century.

Such is the vigour with which the HSE and its co-conspirators go about their work that many groups are throwing in the towel (before it's banned as an 'aerial hazard'). In 2005, Test Valley Council in Hampshire told residents that instead of celebrating Guy Fawkes Night people should compost their garden waste.

The council's Environment Portfolio Holder (no, we don't know what it means, either) Tony Jackson, warned that 'Risks associated with bonfires shouldn't be underestimated', and his employees set out their advice in a booklet advising people that 'smoke from bonfires adds to the background levels of air pollution and exposure to smoke can be damaging to health, particularly for people with asthma, bronchitis or heart conditions. There is also safety to consider, not only of the bonfire spreading to surrounding fences and shrubs, but also the danger of smoke drifting over roads, which may cause a serious traffic hazard.'

The council's suggestion went down like . . . well, like Guy Fawkes in the House of Commons. One local resident told the

Daily Mail: 'Watching compost decompose, although it may be educational, is not half as exciting as fireworks.'

Then in 2006 Watford Borough Council announced: 'Due to a number of contributing factors we will not be having a bonfire this year. It takes significant staff resources to build and steward the fire, and reinstate the area afterwards. Once lit it is extremely difficult to put out, in case of overcrowding or crowd surges.' In place of the bonfire, Watford Council organised some professional fire performers to entertain the crowds. If, as one assumes, their performance required an HSE risk assessment, it may have been confined to the riveting spectacle of a Humberside firefighter erecting a stepladder (see p. 220).

Down in North Devon, Ilfracombe Rugby Club had given up having a bonfire night in 2002 because, in the words of club president Paul Crabb, 'we were expected to fill out form after form. The number of bits of paper you have to wade through to hold a bonfire is just insane. I thought the idea was to light a fire and have a laugh – but the council are all "risk assessment" and "liability". All the fun went out of it.'

Despite it all, in 2006 they decided to reinstate Guy Fawkes Night but with a virtual bonfire projected onto a sixteen-by-twelve-foot screen. They used heaters and a smoke machine for further effect, and broadcast the sound of crackling wood on a loudspeaker. 'We think we came up with an innovative solution to the health-and-safety nightmare,' said President Paul, 'even if it does sound a bit odd. It was certainly a lot simpler.'

'Goodness knows what our ancestors would think if they saw us all crowded around a picture of a bonfire instead of a real one,' local resident Clair Powell told the *Evening Standard*. 'They would probably think we were crazy.' Not you, Clair, just the HSE.

Silly Old Coo

Apparently in years gone by, or BPC as we know it (i.e. Before Political Correctness), the birth of a baby was an event to be celebrated. Nowadays, the moment the wee scamps are out in the world it's not milk being fed them, but their 'rights'. As every parent knows, it's the inalienable right of a newborn to belch/fart/cry when he or she wants. But now, according to the Calderdale Royal Hospital in Halifax, it's also every baby's right to be left in peace.

In September 2005 the hospital banned visitors from cooing at babies because, in the words of *The Times*, 'such behaviour infringes the newborn's human rights'. Debbie Lawson, neonatal manager at the Special Care Baby Unit, told the paper that: 'We know people have good intentions, and most people cannot resist cooing over new babies, but we need to respect the child. Cooing should be a thing of the past because these are little people with the same rights as you or me.'

To ram home the point a doll in a cot was displayed in the ward with a message attached asking people: 'What makes you think I want to be looked at?' What a warm and cheerful message to carry through life.

'Hopefully our message comes across loud and clear,' persisted Ms Lawson. 'The government has set a benchmark that every patient has a right to privacy and dignity, and we say that includes tiny babies as well.' Asked by *The Times* if the policy would be welcomed by the new mums, Lawson insisted she had her finger on the pulse of her patients' views. 'I can't imagine why any mother would complain. Most would be against strangers poking and prodding and asking questions.'

The reporter promptly set about testing Ms Lawson's thesis, only to be told by one new mum, Lynsey, that the rule was a 'ludicrous idea. If people did not ask me questions about my baby, I would be offended,' she added. 'I am so proud of Hannah and want to show her off, and I would imagine all new mums feel that way . . . babies love attention and I think it is cruel to ask visitors and parents to basically ignore them.' Another parent new to the baby game said, 'We wanted to talk about Annis all the time. She was our little miracle and we wanted everyone to know about her. It is flattering when people talk to you about your experiences.' About that finger on the pulse, Ms Lawson, you'd better call a doctor. We think you may have lost the patient.

Shock, horror! Minister outwits Health and Safety Executive!
In Westminster stands a building called Portcullis House that was raised at a cost to the taxpayer of £235 million. It houses MPs not just in comfort but in considerable style, and atop this magnificent edifice is a flagpole. It is possibly the most expensive flagpole in the land, but no flag fluttered in the breeze. Questions were asked, and asked again . . . and again. The flag, MPs were told, could not be flown because health and safety forbade it. There was no safe way off reaching this splendiferous flagpole, even were one willing then to run the hazard of climbing a ladder to unfurl the flag symbolising the might and glory of Her Majesty's Government. But there came a day in 2007 when the Leader of the House of Commons, Jack Straw, got tired of being asked about it. 'I insisted on inspecting this health and safety problem, though I was told it was too dangerous for me to do so,' he said. He discovered there were two bronze trapdoors that were unsecured and in danger of bigging one firmly on the head if care and circumspection were not exercised. And lo! He devised a solution so cunning that Health and Safety was cast into outer darkness and confusion . . . he fitted two hooks to hold the trapdoors open! And thus it came to pass that the Union Jack fluttered bravely over Portcullis House.

Accidents Don't Exist

In October 1999 Kulwant Sidhu, a 24-year-old police constable, was pursuing a villain across the roof of an industrial estate in Twickenham when a skylight gave way. PC Sidhu fell through the roof and died of his injuries. It was a tragic accident for a brave policeman upholding the very best traditions of the Metropolitan Police.

But, as the renowned columnist Simon Jenkins later explained in the *Evening Standard*, what followed was a crass and senseless witch-hunt. 'Whom to blame in this case?' asked Jenkins. 'Was the burglar prosecuted for causing the death? No. Was the policeman criticised, post mortem, for taking too great a risk in climbing over the roof? No. Was the maker of the skylight prosecuted for not using strong enough glass, or the local authority for inadequate lighting? None of these.'

In fact what happened was that the 'institutionally fanatical' Health and Safety Executive pointed the finger of blame at Lord Condon, Chief Commissioner of the Metropolitan Police in 1999, as well as the man who succeeded him, Sir John Stevens. But the HSE did more than just point, they dragged the two men to the Old Bailey, where they were tried on a charge of criminal negligence.

You see in the minds, tiny as they are, of the HSE, Lord Condon and Sir John were responsible for the death of PC Sidhu as they had failed in their duty of care. For three weeks in 2003 the trial dragged on, while outside on the streets of London, the Met, minus their leader, were doing their best to protect the capital from a terror attack.

The pair were cleared of the charges in a case that cost £1 million in lawyers' fees (although, looking on the bright side, it will help to restock their wine cellars) and a further £2 million as the Met prepared its defence. And the whole farrago left Judge Justice Crane in a dark mood: 'It seems to me the time and money might have been much better spent,' he seethed, 'particularly in the dangerous times in which we now live . . . the HSE should look carefully at whether the decision to prosecute in the first place in this case was a wise and sensible decision.'

Justice Crane was particularly perplexed, as indeed we all were, as to why the HSE had pressed the prosecution when, in the aftermath of PC Sidhu's death, the Met had changed and tightened its safety procedures concerning the pursuit of suspected criminals. Was it, wrote Jenkins, because the HSE was after a 'spectacular scalp'?

Outside the Old Bailey a relieved Lord Condon said that 'had this case succeeded, it would have begun a paralysis in British policing'. Had the Met lost the case, reported the *Daily Telegraph*, it had 'planned to instruct its officers not to climb above head height'.

The HSE remained defiant, however, with their QC saying that the accident 'could and should have been avoided . . . it is far better some minor villain escapes across a roof than a police officer is killed'.

The last word belongs to Sir John who, as he left the court where once he had been commended for his bravery as a policeman, told reporters: 'This prosecution has clearly demonstrated a fundamental lack of understanding of the unique nature of policing by those in positions of responsibility in the HSE.'

An Act of Man

It seems the HSE never learn, and fortunately for all of us Simon Jenkins won't let them forget the fact. Three years after they failed in their attempt to convict Sir John Stevens and Lord Condon of criminal negligence, the Health and Safety Executive turned their attention to the National Trust after another tragic accident.

On New Year's Day 2005 a fierce wind suddenly tore through Dunham Massey, a spectacular park in Cheshire owned by the National Trust. One of the centuries-old beech trees toppled over in the gale, crashing against another close by which, in turn, fell on top of an eight-year-old boy. It was a horrific incident, but it was an accident. Yet, as Jenkins wrote in the *Guardian* in November 2006: 'What used to be called an Act of God has, since the invention of the HSE, been redefined as an act of man. There is no longer any such thing as an accident, or lawyers would starve.'

The police, working this time *with* the HSE, arrested and cautioned the property manager for possible manslaughter. A year later, however, the police dropped the charges for lack of evidence – but not the HSE. It wants to see the NT banged up for criminal negligence under the Health and Safety at Work Act. 'The crime, presumably, is neglectful ownership of any tree that might fall over in a high wind,' said Jenkins. 'The case has traumatised the National Trust and its park staff nationwide. They are responsible for six million trees under which millions of human beings wander daily. Should they chop down every old tree, or only some, or close all treed areas to the public? Nobody knows.'

Where it will all end, we can only guess. Will the HSE (the 'storm trooper of health and safety fascism' to quote a Jenkins' phrase) ever realise that by pursuing such absurd prosecutions they only undermine their genuinely worthwhile work in trying to reduce the more than two hundred deaths caused from industrial accidents each year? Or will they press on, diluting every remotely risky activity until, in the words of Tony Blair in 2006, we end up 'having a wholly disproportionate attitude to the risks we should expect to run as a normal part of life'.

In at the deep end

Old swimming mates Kenny Robinson (66) and Alan Treece (64) barely thought twice when they dived in, as they had for the past twenty years, to begin one of their regular swims together at Erith Leisure Centre in Kent. But, this being 2006 (August, to be exact), they surfaced to find two policemen waiting to arrest them. They had, it seems, flouted the new health and safety rule that banned diving. Mr Treece was less than amused, and protested loudly. Two hours later, therefore, more police arrived at his home, arrested him and carted him off for four hours' worth of fingerprinting, DNA samples, mug shots and acquaintance with the inside of a cell – all the imposing paraphernalia associated with the arrest of real criminals in the days before health and safety regulations forbade the police to chase and arrest them. And Mr Treece's fate? An £80 fixed penalty under the Public Order Act. If the HSE don't get you, the Public Order Act will.

The Latex Ranger

It's one of the telephone calls parents fear most, that from your child's school saying there's been an accident. So when Julie Scott answered the phone in 2006 and heard one of her nine-year-old daughter's teachers at the other end her heart sank. Tragedy had unfolded during playtime and now little Emily, sweet, smiling Emily, was being cared for by staff at Uphill Primary School in Somerset.

Bracing herself for the worst — a broken arm or a gashed head maybe — Mrs Scott asked what had befallen her daughter. She's nicked her finger, she was told. I beg your pardon? Yes, Emily had nicked her finger when she was unzipping her coat — the way kids sometimes do. There were a couple of spots of blood and it would be for the best if they put a plaster on the dodgy digit.

Yes, that was fine by her, replied a relieved Mrs Scott. Not so fast. It wasn't fine by Uphill Primary School. They had recently banned all plasters on health and safety grounds, just in case any of the children were allergic to latex. Not that Emily had any problems with latex, but that was beside the point. As a teacher explained, they could only dab the finger with a paper towel. It was up to Mummy to come in and apply the plaster, which she did, as well as leaving a box of plasters close at hand 'in case of further mishaps'. Nine out of ten women of working age have a job these days. Are they expected to drop everything because a teacher can't or won't apply a plaster or a bandage?

Emily's dad, Kevan, a chap who sounds as if his head's screwed on the right way, was not happy when his wife told him about the plaster disaster. 'If they're worried about being sued, I'd suggest there are more people who might sue for not putting a plaster on a bleeding cut, than are allergic to latex . . . she just had a little cut where the fingernail meets the skin. Would she have been taken to hospital if nobody had been at home to answer the call?'

A spokesman for North Somerset Council issued a rambling statement, saying, 'We provide broad guidelines for first aid in schools and there is no mention of using plasters . . . it is down to the school to use its judgement about whether it is appropriate to use plasters or not. This case highlights that we perhaps need to reissue guidelines to schools to clarify the issue.' Heavens above! We'd forgotten how boring school could be.

The Magic Roundabout

Some have said the BBC has dumbed down in recent years, but we thought they were referring to the programmes rather than the intelligence of the staff. Evidently not. The Corporation emailed eight hundred of its Birmingham staff advising them how to get through the new revolving doors. For especially challenged employees the email contained thoughtfully prepared matchstick diagrams to show the Beeb's finest broadcasters how to master the doors. The email – entitled 'Revolving Security Door User Instructions' (wasn't that the title of a *Monty Python* sketch?) – explained that 'to enter the secure space move directly into the revolving door compartment. The door will start automatically. One person per compartment. Keep hands, feet and bags away from the edges of the door.' When asked to comment a BBC spokesperson replied: 'We are keeping in line with the Health and Safety at Work Act.' Of course!

The Bacon Slayer

St George might have been able to slay a dragon, but he would have been no match for the Health and Safety Executive of 2006. England's patron saint didn't stand a chance; it was all over by breakfast time. Actually, it was all over before breakfast had even been served.

The village of Bromham in Wiltshire decided to celebrate England's national day with a full English breakfast: bacon, eggs, sausage, the works! And, in the process, it intended to raise a few hundred quid for the local primary school. But then the HSE emerged from its den breathing fire (at 'appropriate' temperatures within the guidelines for such activity).

'I was astonished to discover that we had to adhere to health and safety regulations to cook people breakfast,' Peter Wallis, chairman of the school's parents and teachers association, told the *Wiltshire Gazette*. 'We have to provide evidence that whoever is handling the food has been trained to do so . . . this is just plain daft. These breakfasts have been going on for many years and we've never poisoned anyone.' Mr Wallis failed to understand that it is a dangerous and complicated business to open a packet of bacon, remove a few slices and place them under a grill.

The local council, however, told Mr Wallis that the breakfast could continue, just as long as they didn't serve eggs – forbidden because no one at the event had been properly trained in the preparation of protein-based foods – or use anything that contained cheese or milk as the organisers of the breakfast didn't have the right facilities to chill and store these products. 'We spoke to other schools in the area,' said Mr

Wallis, 'and decided that because people were not properly qualified in food preparation we had to cancel the event.'

We can tell Mr Wallis from personal experience that he missed a trick by failing to realise the point of smothering these worthy local activities in wet blankets. It is to make money for the local council. You too can become a certified food-preparer on payment of £45, for which you will receive a set of self-administered, multiple-choice questions, accompanied by a little booklet from which to deduce the right answers. The questions include such gems as: 'What would you do if you saw a mouse in your kitchen? Would you (a) scream and run out of the kitchen? (b) ignore it and carry on cooking? or (c) . . .' etc. But by now I think you get the drift.

ITN does its bit for global warming

The BBC is not alone in showing an excess of care for its employees, even if it is mixed with an excessive belief in their inability to think for themselves. In 2006, *The Times* quoted an email sent to ITN staff on 3 July cautioning that, given the warm, sunny weather, 'do please ensure that you . . . wear suitable clothing, apply sun cream . . . and drink plenty of water to keep hydrated. In addition, try to take breaks out of the sun. Following these few simple points should help avoid excess heat effects.' Judging from the quality of ITN's summer output, it didn't help.

Don't Let Them Eat Cake

In the summer of 2006 Elaine Richards baked a cake for an elderly friend at a day centre in north Devon, a heart-warming gesture, particularly as we're frequently being told that Britain's elderly are shamefully neglected.

But when Mrs Richards arrived at the Age Concern centre in Barnstaple she was informed that she would have to have her cake and eat it herself – there was no way it would be allowed inside. 'I thought they were pulling my leg until I realised they were being deadly serious,' Mrs Richards told the BBC.

When she asked why her cake – made with flour and free-range eggs – was refused admittance to the centre, Mrs Richards was told that they only allowed residents to eat those bought in shops. So she went to the supermarket and compared their cake ingredients to her own (for which she had won prizes in the past). The shop's 'was full of artificial dyes and all sorts of things, which made it even more ridiculous'.

The Regional Director of Age Concern reassured Mrs Richards it was not a slight on her baking abilities, but that as 'the average age of residents is eighty-five, they have many disabilities and some of them are diabetic and our policy is to keep them as well and safe as possible. We are just trying to be responsible and bought cake is a responsible line we have adopted.'

When Mrs Richards heard she 'just laughed . . . I thought it was so stupid'. Stupid, Mrs Richards . . . Health and Safety? Oh, behave.

A Nation of Smiley's People

In 1947–8, food rationing was climbing towards its peak. The Labour government of the day employed a small army of spies to move incognito among the people and report on any shopkeeper or member of the public that appeared to be circumventing the rationing laws, and it also openly encouraged people to inform on each other. As Mark Roodhouse of the University of York has commented: 'British society . . . was almost at breakdown. There was a strong emphasis on enforcement, almost like a new Gestapo.' It is neither an exaggeration nor manipulation of the facts to say that Britain flirted w ith a brand of government perilously close to Stalinism, albeit without the executions. Public resentment reached such a pitch that the government was driven out of office in the 1950 and 1951 elections.

In 2007 another Labour government, one that already had British citizens under close surveillance through a significantly greater number of CCTV cameras than in any other country in the world, tore a leaf out of its predecessor's book. In February 2007, a month or two ahead of the prohibition of smoking in any enclosed space, it announced it was making £29.5 million available to local councils to train staff to police the ban in bars, restaurants and shops. In plain language, government-paid snoops and narks were, as the BBC reported, 'to enter premises undercover, to sit among drinkers and even to photograph and film people'. They would be free to give on-the-spot fines of £50 to individuals and to instigate court action against premises on which law-breakers were found, with the prospect of a £2,500 fine for the business concerned.

£29.5 million could fund considerable, and much-needed, improvements in care for the elderly. Alternatively, it could make a more than helpful contribution to restoring the pensions that thousands of people have lost thanks, the courts have judged, to government carelessness. Such positive ideas are evidently less important to our control-obsessed rulers than tracking down any smokers who may choose to flout the law.

The £29.5 million set aside for this purpose will, it must be presumed, pay for many hundreds, if not thousands, of informers. It is said that in London alone there will be 'several hundred' such people. All this in a country that, however loudly pressure groups protest against proposed laws of which they disapprove before they are introduced, has a remarkable record of abiding by laws once they are on the statute book. Indeed, a recurring British complaint is the speed with which we implement unhelpful EU legislation while several of our European partners turn a blind eye to it if they deem their best interests threatened. Scotland showed how unnecessary this unpleasant army of informers is. It introduced similar anti-smoking legislation in spring 2006 and, very properly, left it to the police to enforce as they would any other law. In the first ten months of the ban there had been only eleven fixed-penalty notices issued to premises.

The smoking snoopers would be bad enough were they the only example of the direction in which our society is being subverted, but they represent a trend rather than an isolated case. With effect from June 2007, four thousand government inspectors were given the legal right to inspect our homes with forcible entry if necessary and assess what improvements have been made to them and whether they enjoy a good view. Not only are we required to contribute to the cost of a further millstone of civil service bureaucracy by paying them £200 for such forcible entry, but their findings will be used to justify increases in council tax on individual homes. The idea that an Englishman's home is his castle is thus destroyed at a stroke. And this is still not the end. The government is proposing to develop the society of narks and informers further by asking local residents to spy on motorists passing through their area and report them if they suspect them of exceeding the speed limit.

It is immaterial whether or not you are a driver or a smoker, and whether or not you deplore speeding at all times or support a ban on smoking. The burning issue is this: once the concept of introducing paid informers into society is accepted, what will be next? How long will it be before the role of these people is expanded to report on, let us say, 'inappropriate language', to 'the authorities'? Or to sniff out an 'inappropriate' use of colours, 'inappropriate' physical contact, or any of the other 'inappropriate' issues that have raised their heads in the pages of this book? Will we be able to trust our friends and acquaintances, the people we mix with in pubs and clubs, reading groups and sporting activities? Or will we, like the people in Orwell's *1984*, shuffle around, our eyes glued to the ground ahead of us, looking to neither left nor right, fearful of being denounced?

In the Spanish Paradors, the country-wide chain of hotels owned by the government, a policy statement in Spanish, English and German is placed on every table in a clear rigid holder. 'Courtesy of Choice,' it reads, 'reflects the centuries-old philosophy that acknowledges differences while allowing them to exist together in harmony. Courtesy of Choice accommodates the preferences of individuals by offering both smoking and non-smoking areas in the spirit of conviviality and mutual respect.'

You will have assumed by now we are heavy smokers. This is not the case, and one of us does not even drive a car. What we are is committed believers in John Stuart Mill's deservedly celebrated sentence quoted at the beginning of this book: 'Mankind are greater gainers by suffering each other to live as seems good to themselves, than by compelling each to live as seems good to the rest.' In recent decades it has been not merely sad, but alarming, to watch the erosion of tolerance and trust in Britain in the face of what has been labelled 'political correctness'; and to countenance, with the connivance of the insurance industry, the stultifying intrusion into community life of the Health and Safety Executive as its acolytes go far beyond their original brief of ensuring the safety of the industrial workplace. The question is whether we will sit back passively while the situation slips beyond redemption or, by determined and persistent protest at such patronising bullying, demand its reversal.

THE CASE OF THE
HAUNTED
HORRORS

ANTHONY READ

Illustrated by
DAVID FRANKLAND

WALKER
BOOKS

For Elliot and Oliver, Jack and Miranda

This is a work of fiction. Names, characters, places and
incidents are either the product of the author's imagination
or, if real, are used fictitiously.

First published 2009 by Walker Books Ltd
87 Vauxhall Walk, London SE11 5HJ

2 4 6 8 10 9 7 5 3 1

Text © 2009 Anthony Read
Illustrations © 2009 David Frankland

The right of Anthony Read and David Frankland to be identified as author
and illustrator respectively of this work has been asserted by them in
accordance with the Copyright, Designs and Patents Act 1988

This book has been typeset in Garamond Book

Printed and bound in Great Britain by Clays Ltd, St Ives plc

British Library Cataloguing in Publication Data:
a catalogue record for this book is available from the British Library

ISBN 978-1-4063-0343-8

www.walker.co.uk

CONTENTS

A jagged flash of lightning tore open the
night sky over Baker Street. For a moment
it was as though someone had switched on a
giant floodlight, lighting up the buildings below
– then, just as suddenly, it was gone and everything was even darker than before. The lightning
was followed almost immediately by a crash of
thunder that sounded like a thousand cannons
being fired at once.

"Blimey, that was a close 'un!" exclaimed
Sarge. The old soldier usually counted the seconds between flash and thunder, to tell how far
away the lightning was – five seconds for every
mile, he reckoned. This time there had been no
gap, which meant it must be right overhead.
He looked anxiously around, to see if anything
had been struck. Then, hanging on tightly with

his one good hand to the pitcher of beer he was carrying home from the pub, he hurried back to the Baker Street Bazaar.

As he pushed through the wrought-iron gates and hurried into his lodge, the deep rumble of the thunder echoed overhead like a roll of drums. Strangely, though, there was no sign of rain. Another lightning flash and a bang as loud as a volley from all the guns of the Royal Artillery made him jump so hard that some of the beer slopped over the edge of the jug and splashed onto the floor.

"My oath!" he cried. "It's enough to waken the dead."

Sarge put the pitcher carefully down on the table and reached for a cloth to wipe up the spilt beer. As he straightened, he glanced out of the door and along the Bazaar to Madame Dupont's waxworks exhibition – and froze. There was a dim light moving behind one of the windows.

"Hello," he said to himself. "What's goin' on? Looks like somebody's in there!"

Tucking a truncheon under the stump of his amputated left arm, he lifted a bunch of keys from their hook on the wall, picked up his bull's-eye lantern and set off to investigate.

The waxworks gallery was always a bit spooky at night. Standing in their shadowy alcoves around the wall, the wax figures often looked as though they might be coming to life. But Sarge was used to this, and it did not worry him. He shone his lantern around the room in case an intruder was hiding among the models. There was no one. Then he heard a sound – the quiet, stealthy sound of someone moving. It came not from the main exhibition, but from the side room that Madame Dupont had recently turned into the Dungeon of Horrors.

Sarge was not a nervous man, nor was he very imaginative. But he didn't like going into the Dungeon, particularly at night and on his own. True to its name, this gallery was full of horrors: lifelike – or perhaps death-like – wax figures of murderers and their victims splashed with gore; unspeakable monsters and deformed creatures so revolting they made your stomach turn. It was so scary that Madame Dupont had offered a prize of the princely sum of five pounds to anyone who would spend a whole night alone in there. So far, no one had dared to take up the challenge. Could it be, Sarge wondered, that somebody was doing so now? Or was there a more sinister explanation?

Seeing light seeping through the crack under the heavy oak door to the Dungeon, Sarge summoned up his courage, took a deep breath and gave the door a cautious push. It creaked loudly as it opened – a sound effect that Madame Dupont had installed especially to make people nervous. Inside the room, someone or something moved. The beam from Sarge's bull's-eye lantern swept over the wax models, picking out a headless corpse, a grinning skull and finally the agonized face of the murder victim in Madame Dupont's latest tableau. Next to it stood the figure of another man, his face lit eerily from below. And it was the same face.

Sarge let out a yell and screwed his eyes tight shut. When he opened them again, there was no one there. Only a thin wisp of smoke hung in the air. The figure had disappeared.

Seeing a Ghost

The morning dawned bright and sunny, with no sign of the previous night's electric storm. The Baker Street Boys were cheerful as they left HQ, their secret cellar home, for another day on the streets of London. Rosie, the little flower girl, filled her tray with posies for the ladies and buttonholes for the gentlemen, and set off to sell them on bustling Baker Street. Shiner headed for Paddington railway station carrying a green wooden box holding his boot polishes, brushes and cloths. Queenie started on her round of shops – grocers, greengrocers, butchers, bakers – looking for yesterday's leftovers to beg or buy cheaply from friendly shopkeepers to turn into one of her tasty stews. Everything seemed like a very normal, ordinary morning – until Wiggins,

Beaver, Gertie and Sparrow strolled up to the Baker Street Bazaar.

As they approached the entrance gates, they were surprised to see a small crowd of people on the pavement outside. Most of them were the owners of the little shops that lined the inside of the Bazaar, plus a couple of coachmen whose carriages were parked inside. At the front was the unmistakable figure of Madame Dupont, wearing a vivid purple cloak over an equally bright red satin dress. The tall green ostrich feathers in her hat swayed backwards and forwards as she pushed and tugged at the heavy iron gates and shouted for Sarge to open them.

Being an old soldier, Sarge was usually up and about long before anybody else. It was unheard of for him not to be "on parade", as he always put it, bright and early. But on this morning there was no sign of him, and the big gates were still firmly locked.

As the four Boys arrived from one direction, PC Higgins appeared from the other.

"'Ello, 'ello!" the burly policeman called out. "What's goin' on here, then?"

"Ah, officer," Madame Dupont greeted him. "We are locked out. Locked out of our own businesses. It's a disgrace!"

"That's not like Sergeant Scroggs," said PC Higgins, pushing back his helmet.

"D'you think something's happened to him?" Wiggins asked.

"Could have."

"But there's no way we can find out without getting in," said Madame Dupont impatiently. "And the keys are in his lodge."

"That's soon fixed," said Wiggins. "Gertie here could be over that gate in two shakes of a dog's tail. Climb anything, she can."

"Is that right?" PC Higgins looked suspiciously at the tousle-haired girl in boys' clothes.

"Sure and haven't I been cloimbin' trees since I was knee-high to a grasshopper?" Gertie told him with a cheeky Irish grin. "Shall I show you?"

"Go on, then," grunted the policeman.

"And just get a move on," Madame Dupont snapped. "We're sick of having to wait here like ninnies."

Wiggins and Beaver gave Gertie a leg-up, and

in no time at all she had hopped over the gate and down the other side, run to the lodge and knocked on the door. When there was no answer, she lifted the latch and opened it.

"The keys should be hanging up just inside," Wiggins called to her. "The one for the gates is the biggest."

Gertie stepped in and reached for the key, then let out a shriek.

"What is it?" Wiggins asked as she came tumbling out of the door, clutching the key and looking pale. "What's up?"

"It's … it's Sarge…" she cried. "I think … I think he's dead!"

There was a gasp from the little crowd. Gertie's hands were shaking so much that she couldn't get the big key into the keyhole, so Wiggins reached through the bars and took it from her.

"What's he look like?" he asked as he unlocked the gate from the outside.

"He's stretched out on the floor, all stiff and still."

"Everybody stay where you are," PC Higgins ordered. "This is a job for the police." He pushed through the gates and went into the lodge, placing his large boots very carefully so as not to disturb any possible evidence. The others watched breathlessly and waited for him to emerge, which he did very shortly.

"Well?" demanded Madame Dupont. "Is he dead?"

"Dead *drunk*," PC Higgins replied, holding up an empty bottle. "What you might describe, ma'am, as paralytic."

"Drunk on duty!" Madame Dupont declared, trembling with indignation. "It's a disgrace! The man's clearly not to be trusted. I shall see to it that he is dismissed from his post and never works again."

"That's for you to decide, ma'am. It's not a police matter."

"Poor old Sarge," said Beaver. "Ain't there nothin' we can do for him?"

"Only one thing you can do, lad," the policeman replied. "Make him as comfortable as you can and let him sleep it off. Now, if you'll excuse me, folks, I shall return to *my* duties." And after touching his helmet in a salute to Madame

Dupont and the others, he turned away and plodded off down the street.

From round the corner came the sound of one of the little German bands that could regularly be seen and heard on London's streets, and soon afterwards the four musicians appeared, wearing military-style uniforms and playing a jolly oom-pah tune as they marched slowly along the pavement. Their leader paused to give the policeman a smart salute and held out his collecting box as he passed them, but PC Higgins kept his hands firmly behind his back.

The Boys just about managed to lift Sarge from the floor and onto his bed. He mumbled something in his sleep about a dead man walking, but he didn't wake up and they decided to do what the policeman had suggested and leave him where he was.

"Can't understand it," said Wiggins. "I know Sarge likes a glass of beer or two, but I ain't never seen him blotto. Not even a bit tipsy."

"P'raps somethin' upset him," said Sparrow.

"You mean he was like drownin' his sorrows, ain't that what people say?" asked Beaver.

"My da used to do that sometimes," said Gertie, "when he was thinkin' about my poor ma and how much he missed her."

"P'raps Sarge was missin' his arm," said Sparrow. "Or his days in the army, with all his mates."

Later in the day, when they went back, the four Boys found Sarge awake and nursing a bad headache – and they discovered that the reason he had drunk a whole bottle of spirits was something quite different from what they had thought.

"I seen a ghost," he told them. "In the Dungeon of Horrors. It was that chap what murdered his wife and done hisself in. Madame's latest tableau."

The Boys stared at him, open-mouthed.

"You mean the waxwork come to life?" Beaver asked.

"No! It weren't the waxwork – it were *him*," Sarge groaned, holding his throbbing head. "Standin' right next to it. Large as life and no mistake."

"But he's dead ... ain't he?" asked Sparrow.

"And buried," Sarge asserted. "And if he hadn't done hisself in, they'd have hanged him for murder anyhow."

"So you reckon you seen his ghost?" said

Wiggins, thinking hard. "What exac'ly was he doing when you spied him?"

"Doin'? He weren't doing nothin'. Just stood there, starin' at me, like *he* was the one what'd seen a ghost."

"I see. Then what?"

"Then he vanished. Like in a puff of smoke."

"Cor," Sparrow breathed. "No wonder you wanted a drink."

"Trouble is, when I'd had one drink I wanted another. And my jug was empty."

"You didn't get like that on one jug of beer, though," said Wiggins.

"No – I always keeps a bottle of brandy in the cupboard, in case of emergencies. Like if a lady or gent was to come over all faint."

"And this was an emergency?"

"Well, it ain't every day a chap sees a real live ghost, is it?"

"Or even a dead one," Sparrow joked, then quickly shut up as the others glared at him.

"Well, live or dead, he's done for me," Sarge moaned. "Madame Dupont says as soon as Lord Holdhurst comes back next week she'll get him to sack me. I'll have no job and no home."

"She can't do that!" Beaver protested.

"She says I must've been seein' things 'cos I was drunk. But I weren't drunk when I seen that ghost. Only afterwards. I swear!"

"We believe you, Sarge," Wiggins told him.

"Yeah, but will His Lordship?"

"We'll tell him," said Sparrow. "He knows us from when we saved Ravi and the Ranjipur Ruby."

"It's no good. He won't listen to you."

"Then we'll find somebody he *will* listen to," said Wiggins. "Don't you fret – just leave it to the Baker Street Boys."

Billy opened the door of 221b Baker Street and looked down his snub nose at the four Boys standing on the step.

"Oh, it's you," he sneered. "What d'you want?"

"Hello, Billy. That's a fine way to welcome your old mates what saved your bacon after them Chinamen pinched Mrs Hudson's valuable ornament," Wiggins said cheerfully. "I see it's back in its rightful place," he added, pointing at the jade dragon standing on the hall table.

The pageboy turned to look at it, and nodded.

"Yeah, well, thanks," he said grudgingly. "Mrs H was pleased about that. Now, what can I do for you? Mr Holmes ain't here. He's away on a case."

"Like he always is," chuckled Wiggins. "But it ain't him we're after. We want to see Dr Watson."

"Then you're in luck. 'Cos he's just got back from his rounds. I'll see if he's at home."

"What you talkin' about?" said Gertie. "You just said he was."

"What I said was, he's in the house. Being 'at home' means he's prepared to receive visitors. That's how it's done in polite society," Billy sniffed.

"Never mind all that," said Wiggins. "Just go and tell him we're here and we gotta talk to him about something, and it can't wait."

Billy trotted off upstairs and returned a moment later to usher them up to the rooms Dr Watson shared with Sherlock Holmes.

"Now, then, my young friends," the doctor greeted them. "What is it you want to see me about that's so urgent?"

"It's Sarge," Wiggins blurted out.

"Sarge?" The doctor looked puzzled. "Oh, you mean Sergeant Scroggs?"

"He's in trouble. Big trouble. And we thought, seeing as you told us how he saved your life on the Khyber, you'd want to help him."

"Indeed I would, if it's within my power. Tell me what this trouble is."

"They're gonna sack him and throw him out of his home," Sparrow blurted out.

"All because he seen a ghost," added Gertie.

"But if he hadn't seen the ghost, he wouldn't have needed a drink," Beaver joined in, his words tumbling out helter-skelter, "and if his beer hadn't all gone he wouldn't have needed the brandy what he kept in case of emergencies, and if he hadn't—"

"Wait, wait!" cried Dr Watson, holding up his hands to silence them. "You're making my head spin. One at a time, if you please."

"Right," Wiggins said, taking command. "You three be quiet and leave this to me. It's like this, Doctor. When we went round the Bazaar this morning, we see Madame Dupont and all the shop-keepers and coachmen standing outside the gates, what was locked 'cos Sarge was still asleep. Only he wasn't just asleep, he was spark out. Sozzled."

"Ah, he was inebriated."

"Eh?"

"Drunk."

"That's right. Like you say, Doctor. Inebrified."

"A very serious offence for a soldier, being drunk on duty."

"Yeah, we know that. But he had good reason."

"He'd seen a ghost, you say?"

"That's right. In the Dungeon of Horrors last night. The ghost of the bloke what murdered his wife then topped hisself."

The doctor nodded. "I can understand a man needing to fortify himself after an experience like that. He might well find such an apparition somewhat unnerving."

"Exac'ly. Only Madame Dupont don't see it like that. She reckons he must have been drunk already and that's why he was imagining things."

"And we know he wasn't," Gertie burst in, unable to contain herself any longer. "He's not like that, is Sarge. He never gets drunk and he never tells lies."

Dr Watson stroked his chin thoughtfully. "I quite agree – it's not like the Sergeant Scroggs I know."

"If he had been drunk, he'd have owned up and took his medicine," Sparrow declared. "It's not right. We gotta help him."

"Very well," said Dr Watson. "I shall see what I can do. Perhaps I could have a word with Lord Holdhurst. I believe his family owns the Bazaar."

"We tried that already," said Wiggins. "We went round his house, but they said he was on his estate in Scotland till next week."

"So we got till then to sort it out," Gertie said, brightening up.

"We better had," said Beaver. "'Cos if we don't, when Lord H gets back he'll give poor old Sarge the boot."

Dr Watson agreed to go and see Sarge and also to talk to Madame Dupont and the shopkeepers. When he spoke to his old comrade, however, Sarge was adamant that he really had seen a ghost and that he had not got drunk until afterwards. Dr Watson gave him a thorough examination but could find nothing wrong, apart from a bad hangover. Knowing Sarge to be honest and trustworthy, the doctor believed him. But although he did his best to persuade Madame Dupont and the others, they refused to budge. The businessmen (and women) of the Bazaar were determined to report Sarge to Lord Holdhurst and demand that he be sacked. They could not trust a drunken man to guard their premises, they said – especially one who claimed to see ghosts.

Gathered in HQ that evening, the Boys were depressed and downhearted. Not even the fact that Queenie had managed to find some tasty scrag-end of mutton to go into her stew could raise their spirits. The idea that their friend was about to lose both his job and his home was too much to bear.

"If only there was *somethin'* we could do to help him," wailed Rosie.

The others nodded glumly, then after a moment's silence Wiggins suddenly perked up. "Hang on," he said. "P'raps there is!"

"What?" asked Beaver.

"Well," Wiggins began, "they all say Sarge *imag-*

ined seeing that ghost 'cos he was drunk, right?"

"Right," said Queenie. "'Cos they don't believe there is a ghost."

"But what if somebody else – somebody what was stone-cold sober – was to go in there at night and see it?"

The other Boys stared at Wiggins in admiration. Then doubt crept in as light dawned.

"You don't mean…?" Rosie began.

"Us?" Shiner concluded. "Oh, no. Ain't no way I'm gonna spend the night in that dungeon with no spook."

"You don't have to," said Wiggins. "It wouldn't do for all of us to go. That might scare the ghost off."

"Yeah, I dare say it would," said Gertie, sounding relieved.

"But there'd have to be more than one, or nobody'd believe us. So that's me and somebody else…"

There was a pause, then Beaver bravely volunteered. "Me," he said. "I'll come with you."

"Good lad. Come on, let's get round there now."

In the Dungeon

"You wouldn't catch me spendin' the night in there, not for all the tea in China," Sarge told Wiggins and Beaver as he unlocked the door to Madame Dupont's waxwork museum. "You're very brave lads, and I appreciate what you're doin'."

"We couldn't just let 'em kick you out and do nothin', could we," said Beaver.

"There's a good many as would," replied Sarge. "Maybe I should come in with you…"

"No, you shouldn't," Wiggins said firmly. "If we're gonna prove there really *is* a ghost in there, and not just in your imagination, we gotta be able to say we seen it for ourselves, without you. Right?"

"I suppose so. But you take care. I'd never

forgive myself if anythin' happened to you."

"Don't worry," Wiggins told him. "It's only an old ghost, ain't it? Anyway, there's two of us. We'll look out for each other. Right, Beav?"

"Right," said Beaver, trying to sound confident, but the word came out as a squeak. He cleared his throat noisily.

"Come on, then," said Wiggins, pretending not to notice. He checked his trusty bull's-eye lantern and stepped through the door. Beaver followed, sticking close to him.

Inside, Madame Dupont's Red Indian brave stood guard, threatening them with his toma-hawk. The Boys were not afraid; they had seen him too many times before. But the main hall was dim and full of shadows, and the flickering of the gas jets, which had been turned down low for the night, caused some of the waxwork figures to look as though they might be moving. This made both Boys nervous, but they pressed on boldly towards the heavy barred doors of the Dungeon, wondering what horrors it would hold.

"That door could do with a spot of oil," observed Beaver as it creaked open.

"It's s'posed to sound like that," Wiggins replied.

"It made me jump."

"That's the idea."

"Oh, yeah. See what you mean."

The gas lamps here had been turned down so low that it was very dark indeed, with big patches of shadow in which nothing could be seen and anything could be lurking. The Boys had never been inside the Dungeon before, and they looked around open-mouthed as the beam of Wiggins's lantern picked out macabre scenes from the blackness.

They gasped at the gruesome sight of an old, rotten gibbet, from which dangled the skeletal body of a dead highwayman in a metal cage, its flesh long decayed away, its bones covered with the tattered remnants of clothing, its blackened teeth bared in a ghastly grimace beneath the empty eye sockets. They trembled at an ancient Egyptian mummy, swathed in bandages, which looked as though it were about to sit up in its painted sarcophagus. They shuddered at the sight of a Tudor executioner, his face half hidden by a black mask, holding aloft the head of a queen, which he had just severed from her body with his bloodied axe.

Further back, the light from the lantern glistened on the blade of a guillotine from the French Revolution, about to fall on the neck of a hapless aristocrat. And in another corner a medieval torturer lowered a red-hot poker towards a half-naked man stretched on a rack, his face twisted in a soundless scream.

Some of the scenes were from more recent times. The infamous Jack the Ripper, shown slashing a young woman with a long knife, had committed several murders in the East End barely ten years earlier and was still feared in the area. But the newest tableau was of a crime that had taken place only a few months ago, and which was still fresh in people's minds. It showed a man in his mid-thirties about to shoot himself with a revolver after murdering his wife and child – and it was *his* ghost that Sarge had seen the night before.

The scene was very realistic – Madame Dupont had bought up all the things that had been in the man's study, where the murders had been committed, and she had recreated every detail with the help of photographs taken by the police at the time. Prints of the photos were displayed alongside the tableau, to show everyone how clever she had been. Wiggins and Beaver stared at them, and felt a fluttering in their stomachs at the thought that while all the characters in the scene were just wax models, these black-and-white pictures were of actual dead people.

"Urgh! Gruesome," said Beaver. He turned back to the figure of the man with the revolver. "D'you think that's really what happened?"

"I dare say," Wiggins answered.

"But what if it wasn't? What if that's why the geezer come back?"

"How d'you mean?"

"P'raps he wanted to tell people what *really* happened. I mean, if everybody says he done it, when really he didn't, he wouldn't be able to rest easy, would he?"

"You mean he'd want to come back from beyond the grave to set things straight, like?"

"Exac'ly. Wouldn't you?"

Wiggins thought about this for a moment, then grinned. "Well," he said, "if he comes back again tonight you can ask him."

Beaver wasn't too sure that he'd want to speak to a ghost – or even that he'd dare to. So he said nothing, and the two Boys crouched down in a corner, out of sight behind the guillotine and the doomed French aristocrat. Wiggins closed the cover of his lantern and they waited, nervously, in the darkness. It was deathly quiet. Even the tiny squeak of a mouse and the skittering of its feet on the floorboards seemed to echo around the Dungeon like the noise of stampeding cattle. And when the clock in the main gallery struck the hour, it sounded to the Boys like Big Ben itself. Wiggins counted the chimes under his breath – ten, eleven ... twelve.

"Midnight," he whispered to Beaver. "Watch out now. This is when ghosts walk."

Right on cue, they heard a faint noise outside. The sound of a muffled footstep. Wiggins held his breath. Beaver clenched his teeth to stop them chattering. Then came an eerie creak.

"That's funny," murmured Wiggins. "I didn't

think ghosts needed to open doors. I thought they walked right through 'em."

He raised his head very carefully and watched as a dark shape materialized in the doorway. It moved across the Dungeon and stopped by the new tableau. There was the scrape and flare of a match being struck, and then a softer light as a lantern was lit. The Boys could now see that it was held by a tall man, who began inspecting objects in the make-believe room, starting with a leather-bound book that lay on the desk. When he half turned, Wiggins saw that his face was indeed that of the murderer in the tableau, but ghostly pale. Unable to help himself, Wiggins let out a gasp.

The man spun round, raising his lantern higher. "Who's there?" he called sharply.

The two Boys stayed still as statues – or wax-works. They stopped breathing. They didn't even blink. But it was too late. The man knew they were there.

"Come out and show yourself, whoever you are!" he barked. "I warn you – I am armed."

Reluctantly, cautiously, the two Boys stood up. The man stared at them. They stared back at him.

He was tall, well-built and dark-haired, and wearing a long black coat.

"Children!" he exclaimed. "What on earth are you doing here?"

"'Ere, who you calling children?" Wiggins said boldly. "And come to that, what on earth are *you* doing here?"

"You ain't no ghost!" Beaver exclaimed.

"Why should I be a ghost?"

"'Cos … 'cos…" Beaver pointed a trembling finger at the waxwork figure.

The man looked at it, puzzled. Then his face cleared. "Ah," he said. "You thought I was…?"

"And we weren't the only ones," said Wiggins. "Our friend Sarge did as well. It *was* you he seen last night, wasn't it?"

"Sarge? Oh, you mean the commissionaire. Yes, I'm afraid it was. I'm sorry if I gave him a fright."

"You did more'n that," Wiggins said. "You cost him his job."

"In that case, I am truly, truly sorry."

Beaver stared at the man with deep hostility. "So you should be," he said. "And where's your gun?"

"I beg your pardon?"

"You said you was armed."

"So I did. I was lying."

"Why? Don't you know it's wrong to tell lies?"

The man shrugged.

Wiggins smiled. "You was scared, wasn't you?"

"I confess I was. And that's the truth."

"What of? It ain't ghosts, is it?"

"No." He gave Wiggins a sharp look. "You're a very astute young chap. And very bold, too. Who are you?"

"My name is Wiggins. Arnold Wiggins. Captain of the Baker Street Boys. And Beaver here is my lieutenant."

"And what do they do, your Baker Street Boys?"

"We're special assistants to Mr Sherlock Holmes, the famous consulting detective."

"Sherlock Holmes! The very man I need."

"Well, he ain't around right now. So you'll have to make do with us."

You? The man gave a hollow laugh. "What could you do? A bunch of street urchins and ragamuffins?"

"You'd be surprised what we can do," Wiggins replied loftily.

"Yes, I'm sure I would. How many of you are there?"

"Seven."

"But we got lots and lots of friends," Beaver interjected. "And we can go everywhere. Nobody notices us, 'cos they don't think we're worth botherin' with."

"They think we're just a bunch of street urchins and ragamuffins," added Wiggins with a sly grin.

The man paused, thinking hard. Then he shook his head. "I don't think so," he said at last. "It would be far too dangerous."

"Never mind that," said Beaver. "We're used to danger. Fenian terrorists, Black Hand gang assassins, Indian thugs, Chinese triads. We seen 'em all off."

"Course," Wiggins continued, "we could just tell Madame Dupont and the police how you broke in here in the middle of the night, like a burglar…"

"You could. But who'd believe you? A bunch of street urchins…"

"Madame Dupont would. And PC Higgins – he knows us. And Inspector Lestrade of Scotland Yard. And then there's Mr Holmes…"

"Enough, enough! Very well, you may help me. But there is one condition. You must not breathe a word of this to anyone – not Madame and certainly not your police friends – until the matter is settled. Do you agree?"

"Hold on," said Wiggins. "We ain't agreed to take the case yet. We don't know who you are, or what it's all about. Right, Beav?"

"Right." Beaver stared suspiciously at the man, and then indicated the wax model. "For a start, if you ain't him, who are you?"

"My name is Selwyn Murray. He was my twin brother, Alwyn."

"Twins! No wonder you look exac'ly the same."

"Not exactly. We are – were – what they call mirror twins. Everything was the same, but the other way round. I have a mole on my left cheek, for instance, Alwyn had one on his right, and so on. I am right-handed, Alwyn was left-handed."

"Oh, I get you," said Beaver. "Just like lookin' at yourself in a mirror."

"Precisely."

"Well, in that case," said Wiggins, shining his lantern on the wax figure once again, "Madame D got it wrong. Look, he's got the gun in his *right* hand."

"A natural mistake, you might think."

"Yeah – 'cept it weren't her mistake."

"How d'you mean?" asked Beaver, puzzled.

Selwyn Murray looked acutely at Wiggins. "Go on," he said.

Wiggins moved over to the photographs and tapped one of them meaningfully. "Look at this picture, where he's shot hisself and he's lying 'cross the desk, dead."

"Do I have to?" Beaver asked with a little groan.

"See where the gun is?"

"Oh, yeah – it's by his right hand!"

"Exac'ly! If he'd shot hisself, he'd have used his left hand, and that's where the gun would have dropped."

"Hmm. You're a clever lad to have spotted

that," said Selwyn Murray. "Maybe you will be able to help me after all."

"Course we will. It's plain to me that there's been some jiggery-pokery going on here."

"That's precisely what I believe. Someone arranged this so that the world would think my poor brother killed his wife and child, then took his own life."

"You mean somebody else murdered them all?" gasped Beaver.

Murray nodded grimly.

"Why'd they do that?" Wiggins asked him.

"Because," he said, "they thought Alwyn was me."

Sarge opened the door of his lodge cautiously and peered out through the narrow crack.

"It's us," whispered Wiggins. "Beaver and me."

"Are you all right?" Sarge opened the door wider, then stopped as he glimpsed a shadowy figure behind them in the darkness. "Who's that?"

"We found your ghost. Only it ain't his ghost, it's his twin."

"What you talking about?"

"Let us in, quick, and I'll tell you."

Sarge stood back and watched suspiciously as the dark-haired man followed the two Boys into the lodge. And although he had been warned, he still caught his breath as the light fell on Selwyn Murray's face.

"It's him!" he exclaimed. "He's the one I saw."

"That's right, Sarge," said Wiggins. "This is Mr Selwyn Murray, twin brother of Mr Alwyn Murray, deceased. He ain't no ghost."

"So you wasn't drunk," added Beaver.

"Not at first, anyway," Wiggins said with a grin.

"Well, I'm blowed." Sarge puffed out his cheeks and collapsed into a chair.

"I believe I owe you an apology, Sergeant." Murray bowed his head to him. "I am very sorry to have caused you so much trouble."

"*Trouble?* You scared me half out of my mind last night!"

"I really didn't mean to. And I shall do everything in my power to make things right again."

"Hmph," Sarge snorted. "That's somethin', I suppose. What was you doin' in there anyhow?"

"Visiting my brother – and looking for clues to his death."

"Couldn't you have done that durin' openin' hours, like any normal person, 'stead of creepin' about in the middle of the night pretendin' to be a ghost? All you had to do was come and ask."

Murray shook his head. "I might have been seen."

"You *was* – by me. And a real nasty turn you give me, I can tell you!"

"There are people who want me dead. At the moment they cannot be sure that I am back in London, but I know they will be watching for me, waiting to kill me as they killed my brother."

"But your brother done hisself in," Sarge said. "After he'd killed his missus and their poor little girl."

"No, he didn't," Wiggins said.

"How d'you know that?"

"'Cos he was a mirror twin," Beaver explained. "So everythin' was the other way round, only they didn't know that, so they put the gun in his wrong hand, and Madame Dupont didn't know that either, so she copied the photos and…"

"Steady on!" Sarge cried, utterly confused. "Hold your horses. You've lost me."

"Perhaps it would be better if I were to explain," said Murray.

"I wish you would."

"My brother did not kill himself, or his wife and child. They were all brutally murdered."

"Whatever would anybody want to do that for?" Sarge asked, shocked.

"Because they thought he was me."

"You mean whoever it was wanted to kill *you*? Why?"

"Because I know too much."

Sarge shook his head in bewilderment. "I'd better put the kettle on," he said. "I think I'm goin' to need a strong cup of tea."

DANGLING THE BAIT

Sarge filled his kettle with water and put it on his little gas ring to heat up. While they waited for it to boil, Murray began his story.

"First," he said to Sarge, "I must swear you to secrecy. Unless anything happens to me, you must tell no one about this – or about me. These boys have already agreed. I am only telling you because I have caused you so much trouble already and I want you to know why. I will do all I can to put things right, but you will have to be patient."

"I suppose I can wait till Lord Holdhurst gets back next week," Sarge replied grudgingly. "That's when I'll get the sack."

"I won't let that happen, I promise."

"All right, then. Your secret's safe with me – till next week."

"Good. Because it is not just my life that is in danger, but the security of our country."

When he heard that, Sarge stood to attention and raised his hand in a smart salute. "I'm an old soldier, sir," he said. "You can rely on me to do my patriotic duty."

"And us," said Beaver, copying him.

"Hang on," Wiggins interrupted. "Your brother was killed months ago. If it's that important, how come it's took you so long to do anything about it?"

"I have only just found out. I've been away – far away – and out of touch."

"Why? Where've you been?"

Murray hesitated, a troubled expression on his face. "I can't tell you that," he said.

Wiggins looked steadily at him, then slowly shook his head. "Well, if you don't trust us," he said, "I don't see how we can help you."

"It's not that I don't trust you. But if I told you, it might put your lives in danger. I don't know if I'm prepared to take that responsibility."

"We don't mind a bit of danger, do we Beav?"

"Er, no," said Beaver, sounding a bit less sure,

but ready as always to follow wherever Wiggins led. "We're used to it."

"Very well. I have been in a Russian prison camp."

"Cor!" exclaimed Beaver. "What was you doin' in Russia? You a spy or somethin'?"

"Something like that," Murray admitted. "I was trying to recover some secret plans that had been stolen from the British Admiralty."

"And the Russkis caught you?"

"Yes. Someone betrayed me."

"You was lucky they didn't shoot you," said Sarge. "That's what they usually do to spies, ain't it?"

"I suppose they thought I might be of more use to them alive than dead. So they locked me away in the frozen wastes of Siberia. I managed to escape, but I was a thousand miles from anywhere and being hunted by the secret police. It's taken me months to make my way home."

"And when you got here, you discovered that your brother was dead," said Beaver. "That must have been terrible."

"Yes, it was," said Murray, biting his lip at

the memory. "It was a terrible blow, made even worse by knowing that it should have been me."

"But if you was working for the government, why don't you go to the police?" Wiggins asked.

Murray gave a bitter laugh. "Because that would let them know that I am alive and back in this country. It was someone from our government who betrayed me to the Russians."

"A traitor!" Wiggins exclaimed.

"That's what I discovered in Russia – that there is a traitor high up in the British Admiralty. And I know that he and his associates want me dead before I can unmask him. They will stop at nothing to prevent me from doing so."

"Do you know who the traitor is?" asked Beaver.

"Not for sure. I suspect two or three people, but until I have proof, I daren't show myself. If I were wrong, I would have alerted the real villain – and then I'd be done for."

"There must be somebody you can trust," said Sarge.

"No," said Murray despondently, his shoulders sagging. "Whoever I go to may turn out to be the traitor, or somebody in league with him. There is no one."

"Hang on," Wiggins said, "there *is* somebody. You got the Baker Street Boys."

Murray lifted his head and smiled. "So I have," he agreed.

"I told you we'll help you. Now, first things first – where are you staying?"

"I've taken a room in a cheap lodging house not far from here, somewhere they wouldn't think of looking."

"But they might – and somebody might spot you coming and going. That won't do. We gotta keep you out of sight while we get to work. And it's gotta be somewhere where we can report back to you without nobody noticing us."

"What about HQ?" suggested Beaver. "He could have my bed. I don't mind."

"You're a good lad, Beav," Wiggins told him, "but I don't think he'd be very comfortable. I got a better idea."

"What's that?"

"You got an empty shop at the far end of the Bazaar, ain't you, Sarge?"

The commissionaire nodded enthusiastically – he was starting to enjoy this real-life spy adventure.

"That's right," he said. "We haven't been able to find a new tenant since old Mrs Pettigrew died. She used to sell ribbons and embroidery threads and such. The windows are boarded up, so nobody can see in. It'd make a perfect hideout."

"That sounds splendid," said Murray. "I could camp out there and no one would know."

"There's even a few bits of furniture," added Sarge. "Old Ma P had a couch in the back room so she could lie down when she felt poorly, which she often did. You'll be right as rain, sir. The lads could bring you provisions, and I'd be here on sentry duty."

"Excellent. Couldn't be better." Murray's eyes sparkled with fresh life and he straightened his back, cheered by the prospect of doing something positive. "We must start planning our campaign immediately."

It was already getting light by the time Wiggins and Beaver got back to HQ. They woke up the other Boys, who tumbled out of their beds and crowded around them, eager to know what had happened.

"Did you see it?" Rosie asked eagerly. "Did you see the ghost?"

"Well, we did and we didn't..." Wiggins replied.

"That's plain silly," scoffed Shiner. "Don't you know?"

"Yes, we do," Beaver retorted. "We did see what Sarge *thought* was a ghost ..."

"...only it wasn't," Wiggins continued. "It was a real live geezer, what looks exac'ly like the dead bloke in the waxworks,"

"On account of him being his twin mirror," added Beaver.

"His what?" asked Queenie. "I ain't never heard of anybody bein' a lookin'-glass."

"His mirror-twin brother," Wiggins corrected, going on to explain what it meant and how it proved that Alwyn had been murdered. Then he told them the whole story, and how and why Selwyn was in danger. "But we're gonna help him," he concluded. "We're gonna catch the traitor and the murderer."

"Sounds dangerous," observed Shiner.

"That's never stopped us afore," Sparrow said scornfully. "Sounds excitin' to me."

"And me," Gertie agreed. "An excitin' adventure. Can't wait."

"Half a mo'," said Queenie. "What about poor old Sarge? Ain't we supposed to be gettin' him his job back?"

"We will," Wiggins assured her. "Soon as it's safe for Mr Murray to show hisself."

"Anyway," Beaver added, "Sarge knows all about it. He's in on it too."

"I s'pose that's all right, then. So, what do we have to do?"

Wiggins took off his billycock hat and produced two envelopes from inside it. He smoothed them out and laid them carefully down on the table. Above the name and address on each of them were written the words PRIVATE AND CONFIDENTIAL in bold letters.

"First thing we gotta do is deliver these," he said.

"What are they?" Rosie asked.

"Bait."

"You mean like on a fishin' line?" said Gertie.

"Exac'ly," grinned Wiggins. "And we're gonna catch a big fish. Mr Murray reckons the traitor's one of two men, but he don't know which one. So he's wrote these letters as bait. Now we gotta dangle the bait and see which of 'em takes it."

"Then what do we do?" asked Shiner.

"We keep an eye on him, and report everything we see to Mr Murray at the Bazaar. He'll tell us what to do next."

After they had eaten a hurried breakfast, Wiggins divided the Boys into two groups of three – Queenie, Shiner and Gertie in one; Beaver, Rosie and Sparrow in the other. He read out the two names and addresses on the envelopes and told each group which one to watch. The two houses were in different districts, though not too far apart, and both were in fairly easy walking distance from Baker Street.

"Shouldn't be too hard," he said. "All you gotta do is wait for your man to come out, then track him."

"Yeah, but how will we know who to track?" Queenie asked. "I mean, we don't know what either of 'em looks like."

"That's right," agreed Beaver. "I mean, if some other geezer comes out of the house first, we might follow him and that'd be no good 'cos he'd be the wrong geezer – and if we was to do that, then the geezer we was supposed to be followin' would come out later and we wouldn't be there to follow him, 'cos we'd be busy followin'—"

"Right! Right," Wiggins interrupted him. "Good point. But I've already thought of that."

He paused, thinking hurriedly while the others watched him and waited for him to go on.

"Well?" Shiner prompted suspiciously.

"Well, what we do is this…" Wiggins replied slowly. Then his face cleared and he went on confidently, as though he had known the answer all along. "When we gets to each house, I go up to the front door and ring the bell. Then when somebody opens it, I say I got a message for the bloke whose name's on the envelope and I gotta give it to him personal. I say I been told it's urgent and I'm not to hand it to nobody else.

And when they fetch him to the door, I get him to come right out onto the doorstep so you can have a good gander at him."

"But that means he'll get a good gander at you," said Beaver. "And if he gets a good gander at you, he'll know you and if—"

"Don't matter," said Wiggins, quickly cutting him off. "He won't have seen the rest of you, and you'll be the ones following him."

"Cor." Sparrow gazed at Wiggins admiringly. "That's brilliant. You think of everythin', don't you."

"I try. Now come on, let's get going!"

The first address was in a quiet street in Mayfair, the most expensive area in all London. While the others stood back, trying to look as though they were nothing to do with him, Wiggins walked up to the shiny black front door and pulled the highly polished brass bell handle.

"I got a letter for Sir Charles White," he told the manservant who opened the door.

The man regarded him with disdain and said nothing but held out a white-gloved hand.

Wiggins shook his head and told him he had strict instructions not to give the letter to anyone but Sir Charles in person. The man glared at Wiggins through hard, pale eyes set deep under a heavy brow. He was a big, burly man who towered over the leader of the Baker Street Boys, and for a moment Wiggins thought he might seize the letter. He stepped back out of reach.

"Wait there," the man rasped, and he disappeared back into the house, closing the door carefully behind him to make sure Wiggins didn't follow.

It was a full two minutes before the manservant opened the door again. He stood holding it for a distinguished-looking gentleman in a black frock-coat and grey striped trousers, who inspected Wiggins carefully.

"I understand you have something for me," he said.

"Are you Sir Charles White?" Wiggins asked him, stepping back from the doorway.

"I am he."

"Can you prove it?"

"Don't be impertinent, boy! Hand it over."

"Only, the bloke what give it to me made me promise I wouldn't give it to nobody except Sir Charles White."

"Hmm. Who is this 'bloke', may I ask?"

"I dunno, guv. Foreign-looking geezer. He come up to me in the street and give me a bob to bring this to you. That's all I know about him."

"Gave you a shilling, eh? An expensive delivery when he could have popped it in a post box for a penny."

"Yes, guv. Must be something special, eh?"

"We shall see. Give the boy sixpence, will you, Fredericks?" He stepped out of the door to take the letter from Wiggins's hand as the servant scowled and delved into his pocket to find a coin. "Thank you. You can run along now."

Happy that the Boys had had a good look at Sir Charles, Wiggins posted Beaver, Rosie and Sparrow on watch and left with the others for the next address.

This turned out to be a much smaller house, in a shabby road on the other side of busy Oxford Street. The familiar cheerful oom-pahs of a

German band greeted the Boys, and Gertie pointed as the musicians approached.

"Sure and isn't that the band that was playin' outside the Bazaar when we found Sarge?" she asked.

"You're right," Wiggins replied. "They do get around, don't they!"

He took the second envelope out of his hat, checked the address and pointed to a front door across the street. The brown paint was beginning to peel, the brass doorknocker was dull for want of polish, and the whole house looked slightly neglected.

"What a mess," Queenie sniffed, remembering her time at Mountjoy House. "Mrs Ford would never stand for that – she'd have the servants on to it in no time."

"You gonna show 'em how it's done, sis?" Shiner teased her.

"You could apply for the housekeeper's job, now you're an expert," Gertie joined in.

"We'll have less of your cheek, if you don't mind," retorted Queenie, giving her a playful cuff around the ear.

Wiggins began to cross the road to the house, but he was barely halfway there when the door opened and a man came out, blinking at the morning light through steel-rimmed glasses. Although, like Sir Charles, he was dressed in the black coat and striped trousers of a government official, there was something distracted about him. His coat was crumpled, the creases down the front of his trousers were not really sharp, and his shoes were scuffed. His leather dispatch case looked worn, his umbrella was not as tightly rolled as it should have been, and wisps of hair protruded untidily from beneath his bowler hat.

"D'you think that's him?" whispered Queenie.

"Gotta be," said Wiggins. "Split up, quick!"

He hurried after the man, who was setting off in the direction of Oxford Street, and quickly caught up with him.

"Beg pardon, sir," he called out as he drew level. "Would you be Mr Harold Redman?"

"I am he. Why?"

Wiggins handed over the letter and gave the same story that he had given Sir Charles. Redman looked puzzled, but thanked him and tore open the letter at once. As he read it, he became agitated.

"Bad news, guv?" Wiggins asked innocently.

"Er, no... No..." He fished his watch out of his waistcoat pocket and consulted it, looking worried and distant. Suddenly remembering Wiggins, he handed him a sixpence, thanked him and set off at a brisk pace.

Wiggins signalled to the others, and the four of them followed Redman along the street, dodging between cabs and carriages and omnibuses as he threaded his way over Oxford Street and into Soho Square. He hurried across the garden in the middle of the square, past the little black-and-white pavilion at its centre, and out onto one of the narrow streets that led from it. Soho was one of the oldest areas of London, popular with immigrants and refugees from France, Italy and a host of other countries. So many of them had opened restaurants and shops selling food and other goods from their own countries that the Boys felt they could easily have been in a foreign land.

Redman's pace did not slacken until he

reached his goal, which turned out to be a café in a quiet side street. A bell jangled as he pushed his way through the door. It was hard to see inside through the heavy lace curtains that hung at the window, and in any case the glass was steamed up. Queenie looked up and saw the café's name painted above it. She pointed to it. LUBA'S, the sign read, and underneath: RUSSIAN TEA ROOM.

"Bingo!" said Wiggins.

RUSSIAN TEA AND BLINI

The Mayfair street was quiet. Too quiet for Beaver, Rosie and Sparrow, who were afraid they would be noticed while they watched and waited for Sir Charles to make a move. But when the black front door finally opened, it was the tough-looking manservant, Fredericks, who emerged. He stood on the edge of the pavement, looked up and down the road impatiently, then walked quickly away.

"What d'you reckon?" Beaver asked the other two. "Should we follow him?"

"He could be on a secret mission for his boss," Rosie suggested.

"That's right," said Sparrow. "He could be his henchman what he sends to do his dirty work."

"You go after him," Rosie said. "Me and

Sparrow will stop here and keep an eye open for Sir Charlie."

"Watch out for yourself, though," warned Sparrow. "He looks like he could turn nasty."

Beaver ambled off down the street and round the corner behind Fredericks, trying to look as though he was not actually following him, while Rosie and Sparrow settled down again to watch and wait. In the next street the manservant hailed a hansom cab and climbed into it. To Beaver's surprise, he took the cab straight back to his master's house, then held the door open as Sir Charles came down the steps and climbed in.

"Blimey," said Sparrow. "Must be nice to be rich. Old Charlie don't even have to call a cab for hisself!"

"Yeah," Rosie agreed. "Not when he's got a henchman to do it for him."

"Wonder what else he does for him. We better keep our eyes open." Sparrow turned to Beaver, who had just arrived back. "You stick with Charlie. We'll stop here and keep an eye on Fred."

They didn't have long to wait. The cab was hardly out of sight round the corner with Beaver trotting after it, before Fredericks came out of the house again. He looked carefully up and down the street, then set off at a smart pace, seemingly unaware of his two young shadows.

Outside Luba's Russian Tea Room, Wiggins fished out the sixpences he had just earnt and handed them to Queenie. "You and the others go in and get a cup of tea or something," he told her. "And have a good look around. See what Redman's up to and who he's talking to. I'll keep out of the way in case he sees me and twigs he's being followed."

"Can I 'ave a bun?" Shiner asked.

"Or a piece of toast," Gertie said wistfully. "I'd love a piece of warm toast with loads o' butter and maybe a wee drop of jam like my da used to…"

"Hold on," Wiggins interrupted sternly. "We ain't here to enjoy ourselves. We're here to do a job."

"Right," agreed Queenie. "Come on, you two. See you in a minute, Wiggins. D'you want us to send you out a piece of toast or somethin'?"

Wiggins pulled a sour face at her as she

pushed open the door of the café and went in with Shiner and Gertie. They were met with a thick fug of steam from a giant silver urn on the counter and clouds of sharp-smelling smoke from the cigars, pipes and cigarettes that many of the customers were puffing at. The place was only half full, but the noise was tremendous. Everyone seemed to be talking at once, gabbling and arguing at the tops of their voices in what sounded like several different languages. Those who weren't talking sat hunched over newspapers printed in a strange alphabet, which not even Queenie could read. The papers were attached to wooden rods with a hook at one end, and more copies hung from a rack by the counter so that people could borrow them to read while they ate and drank.

A bony woman in a black dress with a long white apron tied around her waist was collecting plates and glasses from the tables. Her dark hair was pulled back into a severe bun, and a pair of metal-rimmed glasses was clipped on her nose. She looked at the Boys with suspicion, as though she were expecting them to make trouble, and she blocked their way in, setting her hands akimbo.

"What you want?" she demanded in a thick foreign accent.

"We'd like three cups of tea and some buns, if you please," Queenie answered in her politest voice. "It's all right, we got the money." And she held up the two sixpences.

The woman's lip curled scornfully. She plucked one of the coins from Queenie's hand and pointed at an empty table.

"Sit!" she ordered fiercely. "There! No cup tea, no buns. This Russian tea room. You have glass tea and blini."

"What's berlini?" Queenie asked nervously.

"Blini is little pancakes. Is good. You will like."

The Boys sat down at the glass-topped table as the woman marched across to the counter. While she busied herself preparing their food and drinks, they looked around at the other customers. Two men at a corner table frowned in concentration as they hunched over a chess board. In another corner, Redman was talking urgently to a man with wild hair and an unruly black beard. They were speaking very quietly and glancing nervously round the room. They were clearly talking about the letter Wiggins had delivered, which Redman still held in his hand. Then he put it down on the table, smoothed it out and jabbed at it with his finger. The bearded man wiped his own fingers on his loose red shirt, then picked up the letter and examined it carefully. He shook his head, puzzled. After a few more words, Redman pulled out his watch, then got to his feet, quickly shook the other man's hand and hurried out into the street.

"We gonna follow him?" Gertie asked.

Before Queenie could answer, the waitress arrived back at their table. She set down three saucers on which stood tall glasses in silvery metal holders with curly handles, a large plate piled with small round pancakes, three little plates and finally a bowl of strawberry jam. The glasses were filled with clear, steaming liquid, each with a slice of lemon floating on top.

"Eat! Drink!" she commanded, and she stood watching to make sure they did.

"What's this?" Shiner asked, pointing to the glasses.

"Tea."

"Where's the milk?"

"No milk. Russian tea with lemon. Very good."

"Lemon?" Gertie said. "Sure and that sounds too sour for me."

"You put in sugar," the woman told her, pointing to a glass bowl filled with sugar lumps.

Shiner needed no second bidding. He scooped up a handful of lumps, which he dropped into his glass and stirred with the long spoon from the saucer, then popped another into his mouth, crunching and sucking contentedly. Gertie quickly did the same. Queenie just managed to get the last two lumps before Shiner emptied the entire bowl. The Russian woman shook her head, stern-faced, as Shiner turned to the blini.

"Is good, no? she asked, as he spread jam on the first one and took a bite.

"Mmm," he nodded vigorously, his mouth full. The little pancakes really were delicious, and in no time at all the plate was empty. The woman grunted her unsmiling approval and took it away.

"What we gonna do about…?" Gertie whispered once she had gone, jerking her head towards the door through which Redman had left.

"Wiggins'll pick him up," Queenie whispered back. "We'll keep an eye on that one," she said, nodding towards the bearded man in the corner. Then, to the Boys' delight, the waitress brought them a second plate of blini. Relieved to see that the bearded man in the red shirt was showing no sign of leaving yet, Queenie, Shiner and Gertie tucked in heartily, wondering hopefully how many more platefuls the waitress might bring them before they had to go.

Beaver had no trouble keeping up with Sir Charles's cab. To begin with it was slowed by heavy traffic, and then it was stuck behind a troop of cavalry soldiers, their horses' hooves making a deafening clatter as they walked steadily on. Beaver had no need to run and could enjoy looking at the white plumes bobbing on the Life Guards' tall silver helmets, their breastplates gleaming in the morning sunlight above their scarlet tunics, white breeches and thigh-length black boots. He watched the curved sabres in the soldiers' glittering scabbards swinging from their belts, and he shivered as he imagined them being used against the enemy in a cavalry charge.

Sir Charles's cabbie seemed content to sit behind the Life Guards, and Beaver was content to plod along behind them both, wondering why the cab didn't try to overtake them or turn off. They passed in front of a grand, brown stone building that Beaver recognized as Buckingham Palace, and continued along the Mall through St James's Park until they reached the open space of Horse Guards Parade.

The horses and men of the old guard, who had been on duty since the day before, were lined up on the parade ground waiting, the horses' heads tossing impatiently. As the new guard arrived and lined up to face them, a trumpeter sounded a silvery call and the ceremony of handing over began. Beaver watched, fascinated, as standards changed hands and swords flashed in salute. He imagined how good it would feel to be one of those proud soldiers. He was so fascinated, in fact, that he quite forgot what he was supposed to be doing until he suddenly realized that the cab had gone. He began to panic. What was he to do? He had lost Sir Charles.

Wiggins had ducked into a doorway as Redman came out of the Russian tea room. The man looked anxiously at his watch and set off quickly, almost breaking into a trot as he hurried through the Soho streets past the restaurants, shops and cafés, sometimes having to hop sideways into the road as an owner swished a bucket of water across the pavement to clean it. Wiggins dropped carefully into step a few yards behind, making sure there were always a few people between them but never enough to lose sight of his target altogether.

On they went, leaving Soho behind, then crossing Trafalgar Square. Still Redman hurried on, dodging through the traffic into Whitehall, a broad street filled with government offices, with Wiggins trailing a few yards behind. Finally, he turned off into the courtyard of an elegant red-brick building through a gateway with an anchor built into its arch. Wiggins tried to follow but was stopped by a uniformed marine, who asked where he thought he was going.

"Er, I'm with him," he stammered, pointing to Redman's retreating back as he disappeared into the building.

"A likely tale, I don't think," the marine scoffed. "On yer way, sunshine."

Wiggins shrugged. There was clearly no point in trying to argue. "What is this place, anyway?" he asked.

"Don't you know nothing?" the marine replied. "This is the Admiralty. Her Majesty's Board of Admiralty, if you want the proper title."

"And what goes on here?"

"Goes on?" The man stared at Wiggins as though he were an idiot. "Why, this is where they run the Royal Navy."

Wiggins sniffed and pretended to look around. "Where's all the ships, then?" he asked cheekily. He peered past the sailor, as though looking for ships. He didn't see any, of course. What he did see, however, was the back of a man standing in a tall first-floor window, consulting his watch. A moment later another man appeared beside him, looking flustered and apologetic. It was Redman. As the first man turned to greet him, Wiggins caught sight of his face and his jaw dropped. Sir Charles.

In an instant, the two men had disappeared from sight inside the building. Wiggins stood wondering about what he had seen. Were they in cahoots? Could it be that they were both guilty? That *both* were spies and traitors?

Wiggins was brought back to earth by the sentry, who asked what the matter was. "You look like you seen a ghost or something," he said.

"Something like that, yeah," Wiggins replied distractedly. He moved off down the street, away from the marine's gaze. A few yards further on, a mounted Life Guard in full uniform sat motionless on his horse, his drawn sword resting on his right shoulder. A small crowd of visitors to London stood looking at him. Among them, to Wiggins's surprise, was Beaver.

"What you doing here?" he asked.

Beaver hung his head in shame. "Sorry, Wiggins," he confessed. "I lost Sir Charles."

Wiggins shook his head slowly and tutted,

unable to resist teasing Beaver. "That was very careless of you, Beav," he reproached him. "Guess what, though? It's OK – I just found him."

Outside the Mayfair house, Rosie was wishing she had brought her tray of flowers with her. It would have given her something to do, and she might have earnt a few pennies, too. Sparrow passed the time by practising card tricks with the pack he always carried in his pocket. He was halfway through trying to produce four aces from nowhere, when the shiny black door opened again and Fredericks came out, now wearing a square bowler hat and a short coat. As he marched off down the street, Sparrow nodded to Rosie, scooped up his cards and set off after him. Rosie followed on the other side of the street.

Fredericks crossed Park Lane into Hyde Park and took one of the many footpaths towards the Serpentine, the big lake in the middle of the park. Without pausing, he strode past nursemaids with children and older people enjoying a gentle morning stroll along the bank. Unlike them, he obviously had a purpose in mind, and the two

Boys found it hard to keep up without running. The manservant finally slowed down as he reached the embankment carrying the main road through the park onto a long stone bridge across the water. The footpath continued under the road, through a narrow, arched tunnel in the embankment. After looking carefully around him, Fredericks slipped into this tunnel – and out of sight.

Sparrow didn't dare follow him into the tunnel – he would be too easily seen. Instead, he hurried up the bank, crossed the road and waited for Fredericks to come out on the other side. But to his surprise there was no sign of the tough manservant. Could it be, he wondered, that there was a secret passage down there? After a few minutes, he gave up and began to cross back over the road – only to see the man reappear, heading up the slope to the parapet of the bridge. Ducking behind a bush, Sparrow watched, intrigued, as Fredericks seemed to lean against the parapet for a moment, then turned and marched back the way he had come.

Sparrow scuttled across the road to rejoin Rosie. "What do we do now?" he asked. "Follow him, or wait till he's out of sight, then go under the bridge to see what he was up to?"

"Let's wait. He looks like he's goin' home."

"'Spect you're right," Sparrow said. "Job done, eh?"

"Yeah. But we gotta try and find out what that job was. And what he was doin' when he was up there on top. Looked like he was writing somethin' with a piece of chalk."

"Did it? I couldn't see – he had his back to me. Let's take a look."

Waiting until they were sure Fredericks had gone, Sparrow and Rosie clambered up the bank to the roadway. Sure enough, where he had been standing, something was chalked on the flat top of the parapet. It looked like two "V"s – or perhaps a "W".

"*V V? W?*" Sparrow said, puzzled. "What's that mean?"

"Wait a minute!" exclaimed Rosie. "Look at it the other way up."

"The other way… Oh, my word! It ain't a 'W' – it's an 'M'!"

"Right. 'M' for Moriarty!"

A Dead-Letter Drop

Sparrow and Rosie scrambled down the bank from the road and into the shadowy tunnel underneath. It was quite empty and they could see nothing that looked at all suspicious – no alcoves or gratings or doors that might have led to a secret chamber or passageway. Only plain stone walls.

"Don't look like many people come through here," Sparrow said, looking at the moss growing on the footpath.

"You can see where he walked," said Rosie, pointing to where Fredericks's feet had flattened it. The footprints showed that he couldn't have gone far under the bridge before he had stopped and faced the wall.

"Beats me what he was up to," said Sparrow, scratching his head.

"Yeah," Rosie agreed. "Hold on, though. Take a dekko at this." Crouching down to get a closer look, she pointed to a little pile of pale dust on the ground. She took a pinch of it in her fingers and showed it to Sparrow. "What d'you think that is?"

"Mortar," he said, examining it. Then he looked at the wall above. "Hello. What we got here, then? This bit looks like it's loose."

The joint between two of the stones, which Sparrow was looking at, was about three feet above the ground. The edges of the strip of mortar between them stood out very slightly, and he got his fingers around it and wiggled until he could get a proper hold and ease it out. He laid it down on the ground and poked his fingers into the gap where it had been.

"What you found?" asked Rosie impatiently.

"There's a space been hollowed out behind. And there's somethin' hid there."

"Let's see, let's see!"

After a bit of scrabbling around with his fingers, Sparrow eventually pulled out a slim package wrapped in waterproof cloth. He laid it gently on the ground and unfolded it to reveal a sealed envelope.

"It's a letter," he said excitedly. "A secret message!"

"Now then, lads!" Sarge greeted Wiggins and Beaver as they arrived at his lodge. "Back from patrol, are you?"

"Yes, Sarge. We've come to report."

"Right. Fall in, then!"

"Fall in what?" asked Beaver, puzzled.

"No, no! Not *in* anything. Get fell in!"

"He means line up," Wiggins explained, "like being on parade. It's what they says in the army."

"No talkin' in the ranks!" Sarge barked. "Stand to attention, there!"

"Sarge," Wiggins interrupted, "we're on a secret mission. We don't want nobody seeing us report to Mr Murray."

"That's right," added Beaver in a low voice. "It's very hush-hush."

"Ah. Yes. I was forgettin' that. Fall out. You'd better sneak through the Bazaar and go to him."

"Yes, Sarge."

"And try to make sure nobody sees you."

"Nobody sees you doing what?" asked a familiar voice behind them. Dr Watson was standing in the doorway of the lodge, regarding them curiously.

"Doctor!" exclaimed Wiggins, wondering how much he had heard. "What you doing here?"

"I might ask you the same question. I was passing by and thought I'd call in to see my old comrade Sergeant Scroggs."

"Well, fancy that," said Wiggins. "That's just what we're doing!"

"We've come to report— Ow!" Beaver stopped with a yelp as Wiggins kicked his ankle.

"Report?" Dr Watson asked.

"Report for duty," Wiggins said quickly. "To see if there's any jobs need doing around the Bazaar. Anything we can help Sarge with."

"That's very thoughtful of you," said the doctor.

"Oh, yes, sir," said Sarge. "They're good lads. Don't know what I'd do without 'em."

"Yes, Mr Holmes often says that." Dr Watson smiled at the two Boys. "I don't suppose you've managed to persuade Madame Dupont to change her mind and withdraw her complaint?"

"No, sir," Wiggins replied. "Not yet."

"But we're workin' on it," said Beaver. "Now we know Sarge wasn't seein' things, and that he wasn't drunk."

"You may *know* it, but can you prove it?"

"We can, sir," Wiggins told him. "And we will. But we're sworn to secrecy."

"Are you indeed?" Dr Watson raised his eyebrows in surprise.

"Yes, sir. Matter of national security," Sarge explained.

"Matter of life and death," Beaver added dramatically.

"Well, I'm dashed. Ghosts and state secrets and matters of life and death..." Dr Watson stared at them doubtfully. "Are you quite sure about all this?"

Before Wiggins could say any more, there was the sound of running footsteps and Rosie and Sparrow arrived, hot and out of breath.

"Wiggins!" Sparrow gasped. "We found a message – a secret message!"

"Sir Charlie's henchman left it under the bridge," Rosie panted. "For Moriarty!"

"Moriarty!" Dr Watson exclaimed. "What is that evil genius involved in now?"

"Dunno, Doctor," Wiggins shrugged, trying to put him off. "First I've heard of it."

"But it's true!" Rosie insisted, oblivious to Wiggins's warning look. "Ain't that right, Sparrow?"

"As I live and breathe," said Sparrow. "And here's the message, to prove it."

He pulled the waterproof package from his pocket and held it out to Wiggins, who snatched it from him and tried to tuck it out of sight as quickly as possible.

"I think you'd better tell me exactly what's going on," Dr Watson said, looking worried. "It sounds as though it could be very dangerous."

"But, we promised…" Beaver began.

"Whatever your secret is, you can trust me to keep it. I give you my word."

"That's good enough for me," said Sarge. "You can tell him."

"I may even be able to help you," the doctor added.

And so, with Beaver chipping in a few extra

details, Wiggins quickly explained the situation to Dr Watson, who listened very carefully, then blew out his cheeks with a low whistle.

"My word," he said. "If this is true…"

"Course it's true!" Wiggins protested.

"Forgive me. I didn't mean to doubt you, my dear Wiggins."

"Good. You'd best come and meet Mr Murray and let him tell you hisself. We gotta give him this letter anyway."

With Sarge keeping watch, Wiggins led the other three Boys and Dr Watson through the Bazaar to Mrs Pettigrew's boarded-up shop. He gave three short knocks on the door followed by another two, the signal they had agreed with Mr Murray, who let them in and closed the door quickly behind them.

"I thought you promised not to tell anybody," Mr Murray admonished when he saw the doctor.

"This ain't just anybody," Wiggins replied. "This is Dr Watson. He works with Mr Holmes."

Murray's face cleared. "Mr Sherlock Holmes?" he asked. "Then you are welcome, Doctor. I presume the Boys have told you about my situation?"

"They have. It is a great pity Holmes is not here. He would have relished a case like yours. I shall do my best to contact him, but when he is working under cover he is almost impossible to locate."

"That is as it should be," said Murray. "In the meantime, it seems the Baker Street Boys have something to report." He turned to Rosie and Sparrow, who were bouncing up and down with impatience. "Yes?"

"Yes!" Rosie cried. "We found a secret message!"

"What Sir Charles's henchman hid!" Sparrow added. "Show him, Wiggins."

Wiggins pulled the letter from his pocket and handed it to Murray, who unwrapped the waterproof cloth and examined the envelope carefully.

"There is no name or address written on it. And it's firmly sealed. You haven't tried to open this?" he asked.

Rosie and Sparrow shook their heads.

"Good. We shall need a little steam. Fortunately, I was about to make myself a cup of tea, so we're halfway there already." He pointed to a kettle which was heating up on a small spirit stove in a corner of the shop. "As you can see, the good Sergeant Scroggs has provided me with a few home comforts. Now, while we are waiting for the water to boil, tell me how you found this letter."

Rosie and Sparrow recounted all that had happened, and how they had seen Fredericks chalking a mark on the bridge and then discovered the hiding place.

"Well done!" said Murray. "That's what is known as a dead-letter drop. A hiding place where a secret agent can leave or pick up messages without risking being seen meeting the other person. The chalk mark would be a sign that there is a message waiting to be collected."

"That's devilish clever, and no mistake!" exclaimed Dr Watson. Then he turned to Rosie and Sparrow, puzzled. "But how could you know it was for Moriarty?"

"Because the sign that Fredericks chalked on the bridge was a letter 'M'," said Rosie.

"'M' for Moriarty!" cried Wiggins. "Of course! Well done."

"Who or what is Moriarty?" asked Murray.

"Professor Moriarty is an evil genius," replied Dr Watson. "Holmes calls him the Napoleon of crime. He regards him as his most fearsome opponent."

"You have encountered him before?" Murray asked Wiggins.

"We've crossed swords with him a few times."

"And won?"

"Yeah. But he's a slippery customer. Always gets somebody else to do his dirty work so you can't pin nothing on him."

"Perhaps this time it will be different," said Murray. "Now, let's see what Sir Charles has got to say to him."

Steam was now puffing out of the boiling kettle. Murray held the letter over the spout and moved it to and fro.

"What you doin'?" Beaver asked.

"The steam will melt the glue on the envelope, and then we can peel it open without cutting the paper," explained Murray. "D'you see?"

"Be careful you don't scald yourself," Dr Watson warned. "Steam can be dangerous stuff. Hotter than boiling water, you know."

Murray picked up a knife and slid the blade under the flap of the envelope, working it gently along until he could peel it open. There was a note inside: a single sheet of paper folded once. He unfolded it and read aloud what was written on it: *"Spaniards Sat 3."*

"Spaniards?" asked Wiggins. "I thought it was Russkis we was after."

"So did I," said Murray, frowning deeply. "This is confusing. Three *what* sat *where*?"

"It might be a code," suggested Beaver. "You know, when words mean somethin' different."

"Very possible," Murray agreed. "In which case we're lost without the key or a code book. Unless it's something else. There could be secret writing, perhaps..."

He held the sheet of paper up to the light and looked at it very closely. "No," he sighed. "Not even a watermark."

Next, he held it over the spirit stove. "Let's try a little gentle heat," he murmured, taking care not to scorch the paper. "No, nothing. If he *has* used a secret ink, it is not one that reacts to heat. I need to examine the surface more closely, to see if there are any tiny scratches from a pen. If only I had a lens…"

"This any help?" asked Wiggins, digging into the inside pocket of his coat and producing his magnifying glass.

"Good heavens," said Murray, impressed. "You really are a detective, aren't you?"

"Mr Holmes give me that," Wiggins said proudly.

Murray peered at the note through the powerful lens, then shook his head and handed it back to Wiggins.

"No," he said. "This paper can tell us nothing more. We must get it back to its hiding place before anyone discovers its absence. Now – Mrs Pettigrew must surely have had some glue here, for doing up parcels…" He rummaged around a bit, found what he was looking for in a drawer in the shop counter, and sealed the envelope again with great care. Then he wrapped it in the waterproof cloth and handed it to Sparrow.

"There," he said. "Now hurry and put this back *exactly* where you found it. It must look as though it has never been touched. Off you go!"

Sparrow and Rosie opened the door a little way, looked cautiously through the crack to make sure no one was watching, then dashed back towards the park.

"I shall leave too," said Dr Watson, "and see if I can locate Holmes. When I do, I shall inform him of your case, and I have no doubt he will wish to take it on."

"Thank you, Doctor," said Murray, holding out his hand gratefully. "But remember – not a word to anyone else."

Watson nodded, shook Murray's hand, then slipped quietly out of the door and hurried away through the Bazaar.

"Now," said Murray, turning back to Wiggins and Beaver, "you have told me about Sir Charles, but what about Redman? Did you deliver my letter to him?"

"We did," Wiggins answered. "I give it to him myself."

"And how did he react?"

"He looked bothered, then he went charging off to a caff in Soho."

"Do you know the name of this caff, er, café?"

"Luba's Russian Tea Room."

"Ha!" exclaimed Murray. "Luba's! I know it. It is a meeting place for Russian exiles."

"What's an exile?" Beaver asked.

"A person who has been forced to leave his own country and live somewhere else," Murray told him.

"Who forces 'em?"

"Their government, their police…"

"Why?"

"Usually because they're dangerous revolutionaries."

"You mean they want to blow things up and kill people?" asked Beaver incredulously.

"Some of them do, yes."

"Oh, crikey," said Wiggins, worried. "I sent Queenie and Gertie and Shiner into that caff."

"It's all right," Murray reassured him. "Those revolutionaries only want to kill people from their own government."

"So they wouldn't want to kill *you*? Or your

brother if they thought he was you?"

Murray looked serious for a moment. "Not unless…" he began, then stopped.

"Not unless what?"

"One of them might – if he wasn't a real revolutionary, but an undercover agent working for the Russian secret police."

"You mean just pretending to be a real revolutionary so he could spy on the others?" said Wiggins.

"Exactly. Such a man would not hesitate to murder anyone who could expose him to the people he was spying on."

"Like Queenie and Shiner and Gertie," said Beaver. "If he sees 'em watching him, he'll think they're gonna blow his cover! And then…"

Wiggins was already on his feet and heading for the door. "C'mon, Beav," he cried. "We gotta get 'em outta there afore it's too late!"

A HORNET'S NEST

Queenie, Shiner and Gertie had already left Luba's Russian Tea Room. The bearded man had sat in his corner for a while, staring at the letter Redman had given him. Then, quite suddenly, he seemed to make up his mind about something. Folding the letter and stuffing it into his pocket, he got to his feet and crossed the room to where a woman sat alone at a table, her rich chestnut-coloured hair falling across her face as she scribbled intensely in a notebook. He leant down, whispered something in her ear and jerked his head towards the door. She looked up, startled, then quickly gathered her papers and followed him out, pulling a black cloak around her shoulders.

Shiner went to stand, ready to dash after them, but Queenie laid her hand on his arm.

"Take it easy, now," she whispered. "We don't want to look like we're followin' 'em."

Trying to look casual, the three Boys drained their glasses, then strolled to the door. As they passed the waitress, she reached out and pinched Shiner's cheek between her finger and thumb.

"You come back soon," she said. "I give you more blini." And she almost smiled.

Blushing deep scarlet, Shiner escaped to the street. Queenie and Gertie couldn't help giggling as they followed him out.

"She's taken a proper shine to you," Queenie teased.

"Taken a shine to Shiner, she has," Gertie added with a chuckle.

Shiner scowled furiously and stared past them at the bearded man and the woman, who were standing in a doorway a few yards away, talking hard. The man looked carefully over his shoulder, then took the letter from his pocket and handed it to the woman, who adjusted her spectacles and read it, then stuffed it into her handbag and hurried off down the street without a backward glance.

"C'mon," whispered Queenie. "Let's see where she takes it."

"What about *him*?" Gertie asked.

"I'll stick with Blackbeard," said Shiner, glad of the chance to be free from their teasing. "You two tail 'er. See you back at HQ."

As the two girls set off after the woman, the man walked back past them. For a moment Shiner was afraid he was going back into the café, but to his relief the man continued along the little street and out into a bigger one beyond.

Shiner trailed after him as he turned under an archway, crossed the busy Shaftesbury Avenue and plunged into another area of small streets and ancient alleyways. When he turned into one of these, Shiner hung back for a few seconds, afraid of being seen, then hurried after him. But suddenly there was no sign of the man – he must have sped up and turned into another street. Wondering what to do next, Shiner was halfway along this road when a strong arm shot out of a narrow passage, grabbed him round the neck and pulled him into the darkness. A rough hand clamped over his mouth to stop him crying out.

"Got you," snarled a deep voice. "Why you spy on me? Who send you?"

After running all the way from Baker Street, Sparrow and Rosie were quite out of breath by the time they got back to the bridge over the Serpentine. There were more people in the park than there had been earlier, and Sparrow had to wait a few minutes before he could enter the tunnel without being seen. Rosie kept a lookout while he slid the letter back into its hiding place and replaced the loose piece of mortar. Then they found a spot under a nearby tree where they could sit on the grass and watch everything.

For what seemed like a long time, all was quiet and peaceful. A few people passed through the tunnel: a young couple strolling arm in arm; a nanny pushing a baby in a large wicker pram and a nurse pushing an old man slumped in a wheelchair; a constable on patrol from the nearby police station; two elegant ladies carrying parasols and walking a fluffy white poodle on a lead. None of them seemed at all like spies. Then Rosie spotted something that made her sit up.

"Look!" she cried, pointing up at the bridge.

Sparrow looked – and saw it too. A familiar black carriage had stopped on the roadway above the tunnel.

"It's him!" he gasped. "Moriarty!"

They scrambled to their feet, but before they could even start to run up the bank, the coachman had whipped up the horse, and the carriage had sped away. By the time the two Boys reached the roadway, it was completely out of sight. They both knew they had no chance of catching it, and they turned back, feeling desolate. Rosie stopped to look at the chalk mark on the parapet.

"Somebody's rubbed it out!" she cried.

"D'you think that means…?" Sparrow began.

"Dunno. Let's go and see."

They careered back down the bank and into the tunnel. Sparrow ran to the loose piece of mortar and eased it out. He poked his fingers into the hole and felt about. There was nothing there – the message had gone.

The woman from the tea room strode through the streets, her black cloak billowing out behind her, clutching her notebook and papers under her arm.

Queenie and Gertie had no difficulty following her – because she was tall, they could easily see her flowing chestnut hair above the heads of the other people, even when the street became quite crowded. After a short distance, she turned off into a quieter road and entered a tall block of flats. Through the glass of the door, they could see a uniformed hall porter greet her with a smart salute. Everything looked extremely respectable.

"D'you think that's where she lives?" Gertie asked.

"Looks like it," Queenie answered. "And there ain't no way we'd get past that doorman. We'll just have to hang about and keep our eyes open."

"Oh, not again," Gertie groaned. "Watch and wait – that's all we ever seem to do on this case."

"Ain't much else we can do for now."

"I know. But it's not very excitin', is it?"

They had not been watching and waiting for very long, however, when the woman came out again, still carrying her notebook. As they followed her this time, she strode back along the busy street, then went into the post office. Leaving Gertie on guard outside, Queenie pushed through the heavy swing doors and found herself among lines of people waiting to hand over letters and parcels to the clerks behind the long counter. At first she could not see the woman, but then she spotted her standing at a separate counter under a sign that said TELEGRAMS AND TELEGRAPHS. She was writing a message on a form, which she handed to the clerk, who read it quickly, counted the number of words and held out her hand for payment. Queenie wished she could see who the telegram was for, but she couldn't get close enough to look. Then she had to duck behind a line of people to keep out of sight as the woman turned from the counter and left the post office.

Outside, Queenie signalled to Gertie and they both began tailing the woman again. She led them round the corner, past several rows of bookshops, to a huge stone building set back from the road behind high black railings. The two girls watched as she walked up the steps leading to the entrance and in through the great wooden doors.

"Cor!" said Gertie, staring up in awe at the enormous stone pillars supporting a great portico filled with classical carvings. "What sort o' place is that?"

Queenie thought it looked like the picture of an ancient Greek or Roman temple which she remembered seeing in one of her mother's books, but the sign on the railings said THE BRITISH MUSEUM. "I've heard of that," she said.

"Museum?" Gertie queried. "Now what on earth could she want in there?"

"Dunno. Let's go and find out."

"They'll never let you and me in, will they?"

"Don't see why not," said Queenie, pointing at a small group of schoolchildren who were following their teacher up the steps. "Come on."

They scurried across the forecourt, tagged on behind the children and soon found themselves inside the museum. Their mouths dropped open as they looked around them at the amazing objects on display. Straight in front was a white stone statue of a helmeted Greek warrior brandishing a sword and shield. To one side stood an Egyptian mummy in a brightly painted sarcophagus. Gold cups and plates gleamed and glistened in a glass-fronted showcase. Queenie would have loved to stop and look at everything properly, but they could see their woman disappearing round a corner and had to hurry after her.

The woman clearly knew exactly where she was going, and she marched on with barely a glance at the wonders all around. Queenie and Gertie just about managed to keep pace with her as she passed by great pieces of marble carved into horses and chariots, and ancient Greek ladies dressed in flowing robes that were so lifelike it was hard to believe they were made of stone.

She eventually halted by a big door and disappeared through it, but when the girls tried to follow, they were stopped by a man in a dark blue uniform and peaked cap.

"You can't go in there," he told them firmly. "Not unless you've got a ticket."

"You mean like a train ticket?" Gertie asked. "Why? Where's it goin' to?"

The man was not amused. "It's not going

anywhere," he said. "That's the Reading Room."

Peeping past him through the glass panels in the door, Queenie could see an enormous, circular room. The walls, right up to the great dome of the roof, were lined with thousands and thousands of books, some of which had to be reached by iron staircases and galleries. Below, dozens of people sat at long desks, curved to fit the shape of the room, reading and writing busily. The woman took her place at one of them, nodding a silent greeting to those nearest to her.

"What they all doin'?" Queenie asked.

"Studying. Thinking. Writing," the attendant told her. "They're very clever people. Scholars and professors and suchlike."

"Will you just look at all 'em books!" gasped Gertie. "I never knew there was so many books in all the world."

The man gave her a superior smile. "We've got a copy of every book that's ever been printed in this country," he said proudly, stroking his heavy moustache. "But they're not for the likes of you. Now hop it, both of you! And don't touch anything on your way out. I'll be watching."

Wiggins and Beaver ran all the way to Soho and arrived, puffing and panting, outside Luba's Russian Tea Room. There was no sign of Queenie, Shiner or Gertie either outside or inside the café, or in any of the streets and alleys near by.

"I'm worried, Beav," Wiggins admitted. "I'll never forgive myself if anything's happened to 'em."

"Don't fret," Beaver tried to reassure him. "There's three of 'em. They'll be OK if they stick together."

"Yeah, I s'pose so. Well, there ain't nothing we can do here now. Better go back to the Bazaar and wait for 'em to show up."

After another quick look around the area, just to make sure, they made their way back to HQ in case the others had returned home and were waiting there for them. But the secret cellar was empty. So, with heavy hearts, they hurried round to the Baker Street Bazaar to report to Murray in his hideout.

They had only just closed the door behind them when there was another knock on it, again in the secret code, and Sparrow and Rosie tumbled breathlessly in.

"It's gone," Rosie gasped. "Somebody's took the message!"

"And now Moriarty's got it," Sparrow added.

"Did you see him?" Wiggins asked. "Did you see Moriarty?"

"No," Rosie admitted, "but we seen his carriage."

"And you didn't follow it?"

"No. He drove off at a good lick. We never had no chance of catchin' it."

"Forget this Moriarty fellow for the moment," Murray cut in impatiently. "Did you see who actually took the message?"

"No," said Rosie. "They was inside the tunnel, see."

"But the only people what went through it all looked respectable," Sparrow added. "None of 'em looked like spies."

"Well, they wouldn't, would they," said Wiggins. "Not if they didn't want nobody to know."

"Quite so," Murray agreed. "But tell me about them, all the same. Describe them to me, if you can remember."

"Course we can remember," Sparrow said scornfully. "We're the Baker Street Boys, ain't we? Mr Holmes learned us what to do."

Between them, Sparrow and Rosie managed to recall and describe all the people they had seen passing through the tunnel in the park. Murray shook his head sadly.

"You're quite right," he said. "It could have been any of them. They all sound perfectly respectable."

"That's how they looked," said Rosie. "There was even a copper."

Murray sat up sharply. "A policeman? You didn't mention him."

"He'd be a park policemen," said Wiggins. "The Royal parks has their own police force, you know."

"I 'spect he was on his way to the police station," said Sparrow. "It's only just round the corner from where we was. He wasn't on duty."

"Why do you say that?" asked Murray.

"He didn't have his armband on. When a copper goes on duty, he puts a striped band on his sleeve, don't he? By his wrist."

"That's correct," agreed Murray. "You're a sharp lad to have spotted that. I'll wager that's our man. He must have collected the message, then handed it over to Moriarty or his coachman."

"Well done, Sparrow," said Wiggins.

"D'you reckon he weren't a proper copper?" Beaver wanted to know.

"You mean somebody pretendin' to be one?" asked Rosie. "Like in disguise?"

"Possibly," Murray replied. "Or a proper copper gone bad. That's why I didn't want to go to the police – I don't know who I can trust."

They were still thinking about this when Queenie and Gertie returned and told them what they had seen in Luba's Russian Tea Room, and how they had trailed the woman.

"She ended up in the British Museum," Queenie said. "Cor! What a place that is. All them carvings and statues and gold and mummies and stuff."

"What was she doing there?" Wiggins asked. "Meeting somebody? Leaving secret messages?"

"No, she went in a sort of library."

"There were millions and millions of books,"

Gertie added. "Sure and I never thought there was that many in the whole wide world!"

"Ah, yes," said Murray. "That'll be the Reading Room. A lot of revolutionaries go there to study and write their own books.

"Is that all she did?" Wiggins asked Queenie.

"No, before the museum, she went to the post office and sent a telegram," Queenie replied. "I couldn't see who it was to, but she looked like it was somethin' urgent."

"Excellent," Murray told her. "We seem to have stirred up a real hornet's nest."

"No, no," said Gertie, "there weren't no hornets. I seen hornets and I don't like 'em. They can sting you somethin' rotten!"

"What's a hornet?" asked Sparrow.

"It's like a wasp, only bigger and nastier," Wiggins said.

"If you get stung by hornets," Beaver added seriously, "you can die."

"Oh dear," cried Rosie. "You don't think...?"

"Hold it!" Wiggins held up his hand. "There ain't no hornets. It's just a saying. Right, Mr Murray?"

"Quite right, Wiggins. If you poke a stick into a hornet's nest, they all come flying out looking for trouble. And that's what our revolutionary friends from Luba's are probably doing."

"Yeah, but what are *we* gonna do now we've stirred 'em up?" asked Sparrow. "I don't much fancy gettin' stung, even if it is only a sayin'."

"Well," said Murray, "now that we're all back together…"

"Hang on," Queenie butted in. "We *ain't* all together, are we? Where's Shiner?"

THE HANGED HIGHWAYMAN

The black-bearded man from the café shoved
Shiner into a room and slammed the door shut
behind him. The boy heard a key being turned
in the lock and then the sound of the man's footsteps clumping across the bare boards of the
landing and down the stairs. He hurled himself
at the door and hammered on it with his fists,
shouting at the top of his voice, "Lemme out!
Lemme out!" But the footsteps carried on until
another door closed at the foot of the stairs, and
then there was silence.

The room seemed to be in the attic of a tall,
old house. It was dingy, dusty and dim – the
only light seeped in through a small skylight in
the ceiling, with glass so grimy it was impossible
to tell if the sky above was blue or grey. The only

furniture was a single iron bedstead, a rickety wooden chair and a cheap chest of drawers with three legs and a couple of books propping it up where the fourth leg should have been. A large tin trunk sat in one corner of the room, battered and dented from years of use and plastered with old shipping labels.

Shiner looked around desperately for a way of escape, but there was nothing. The skylight was too high for him to reach, even if he stood the chair on top of the trunk or the chest of drawers. And he knew that if he did manage to reach it, he probably wouldn't be able to open it – and even if he got that far it would only lead out onto the steep roof. He worked his way carefully round the bare room, knocking on the walls in the hope that one of them might be hollow – he had heard that in some old buildings the attics and lofts joined up, in which case it might be possible to break through into the house next door. But these walls were all solid.

Angry at himself for allowing Blackbeard to catch him, he let out a scream of rage and kicked at the walls and door until his toes hurt. Then, as his temper cooled, he threw himself down on the bed, wondering fearfully what his captors would do with him. He had no doubts now that he was in the hands of a dangerous gang of revolutionaries. And he had no way of escape.

By the evening, Queenie was starting to get quite worried about her little brother. She knew he could usually take care of himself, but she also knew he often did things that got him into trouble. She wondered if that was why he had not come home for his supper. Even though he had eaten a pile of blini in the tea room, he must be hungry by now – the other Boys were ravenous, and Shiner always had the biggest appetite of them all. Queenie had been too busy to find anything to cook, but Murray had given her some money to buy pies for all of them as well as for himself, and they had taken theirs back to HQ to eat.

When they had finished and Shiner still hadn't returned, Queenie decided she would have to go and look for him.

"I'll come with you," Beaver volunteered. "In case you need backup."

"Me too," said Rosie, jumping up.

"And me," Gertie joined in. "I was with you when he went off after Blackbeard."

"Right," said Queenie. "We can start at the tea room. That's where we last saw him. You comin', Wiggins?"

Wiggins shook his head. "No, I got some thinking to do. 'Sides, somebody oughta stop here, case he comes back while you're out."

Sparrow had already left for his job at the theatre, so once the others had rushed out, Wiggins was alone. He settled down in his special chair to do some hard thinking. He had a nagging feeling at the back of his mind about the strange message, *Spaniards Sat 3*. It was still a puzzle that he couldn't solve, but there was something vaguely familiar about it – he simply couldn't remember what it was. After a while, however, an idea came to him, and he hurried off to see Murray at the Bazaar.

"I bin thinking about your brother," he told him. "You said whoever murdered him did it 'cos they thought he was you."

Murray nodded sadly. "Yes," he said. "It should

have been me. It was my fault he was killed."

"No, it weren't," Wiggins said. "You can't help looking like your twin. But the thing is, if the murderer mistook him for you, he must have seen him somewhere, right?"

"Yes, of course."

"So, if we knew where your brother had been …"

"…we'd know where the murderer could have been, and that might give us a clue!"

"Exac'ly."

"You're a clever chap, Wiggins, but how do you think we're going to find that out?"

"Well, in Madame Dupont's tableau in the wax-works, your brother is at his desk, right?"

"Right."

"And what's on that desk?"

"Well, the gun, of course…"

"And what else?"

"Pens and … a book. His diary. By Jove, Wiggins – you could have something there! The diary should tell us what Alwyn had been doing and where he'd been."

"Exac'ly! The waxworks is shut for the night

now, so if I get the key from Sarge, I could nip in there and borrow the diary. We could read it and put it back in the morning, afore they open, and nobody would know."

"Wiggins, my friend, you're more than clever – you're brilliant!"

"Ta very much," said Wiggins with a broad grin.

Queenie, Beaver, Rosie and Gertie peered through the windows of Luba's Russian Tea Room but could see nothing. The café was dark and deserted, with a closed sign hanging inside the door. They stepped back and looked at the upstairs windows, but there were no lights there either. For the next hour, the four Boys combed the streets of Soho, searching every alley and doorway, but they could find no sign of Shiner.

"I'm sure he'll turn up," Beaver said, trying to comfort Queenie. "You know your little brother. Remember how he turned up in the Limehouse laundry, when we thought we'd lost him?"

"That's right," said Rosie, trying to sound cheerful. "He saved my bacon then, and no mistake."

"Sure and I'll never forget the way he climbed up that crane," added Gertie. "I couldn't have done it better myself. He's a brave lad, so he is."

"Yeah. Too brave sometimes," Queenie replied. "Too brave for his own good. Always has been."

"Come on," said Beaver. "Let's get back to HQ. Wiggins'll know what to do. And you never know – Shiner might be there waiting for us."

But of course Shiner was not waiting for them at HQ, and nor was Wiggins, who at that very moment was creeping into the Dungeon of Horrors to get the diary from Alwyn Murray's desk.

Even though Wiggins was getting quite used to the Dungeon, it still felt spooky. Thinking he could hear a rustling sound behind him, he looked back over his shoulder, and in doing so he bumped into the highwayman's skeleton, setting it swinging eerily in its gibbet. He hurriedly brushed past it, trying not to look at the grinning skull with its empty eye sockets under the black three-cornered hat. Grabbing the book from the desk, he retreated as fast as he could.

* * *

Shiner woke up with a start to the sound of footsteps on the stairs. Bored with sitting alone with nothing to do, he had lain down on the bed and fallen asleep, but now he quickly came to his senses and sat up. The room was dark, but he could see a sliver of light under the door and hear a key being turned in the lock. He thought fast – if he was quick enough when the door opened, he might be able to dive past Blackbeard and make his escape down the stairs. He hopped off the bed to be ready, but when the door did open there were two people standing there, Blackbeard and the chestnut-haired woman. Between them they completely blocked his way, and Shiner knew he stood no chance of getting past. The woman raised the paraffin lamp she was holding, to see better, and stared at Shiner.

"It is a child!" she exclaimed in a strong foreign accent. "A street urchin. What you do, Ivan, locking up innocent children?"

"He is no innocent," Blackbeard spat. "He was following me."

"Hah! He probably wanted to pick your pocket."

"'Ere!" Shiner protested. "I ain't no dip!"

"Dip?" the man asked, puzzled.

"Cor blimey, don't you know nothin'? A dip's a pickpocket. And I ain't no thief, so you better watch what you're sayin'."

"Hmm," the woman mused. "He is sharp, this one. You are right, Ivan – perhaps he is not so innocent."

She looked steadily at Shiner. "If you are not dip, what are you?"

Shiner looked steadily back at her, determined to give nothing away. "I'm a shoeshine boy. I clean shoes."

"Why you follow my friend? You want shine his shoes?"

"Well," said Shiner, looking down at the man's scruffy boots, "they could do with a good rub up…"

"Where your brushes? Your boot polish? No, you don't want clean his shoes. So why you follow him? Someone send you to spy on him. On *us*. Who? Tell me."

Shiner shook his head stubbornly. "No," he said. "Can't."

"Can't? Or won't."

Shiner shrugged but still stayed silent.

"Very well," the woman snapped. "You stay here till you tell. Come, Ivan!"

And with that, she left the room. Blackbeard followed, slamming the door and locking it.

Shiner was left alone again, and the attic room seemed darker than ever.

Glad to be out of the Dungeon, Wiggins hurried back to Mrs Pettigrew's shop and handed the diary to Murray, who opened the book and began to read.

"Is it real?" Wiggins asked.

"Yes," said Murray, visibly upset. "This is my poor brother's handwriting. I can hardly bear to look at it."

He blinked back a tear. Wiggins felt uncomfortable, watching his distress.

"Listen," he said. "It's getting late. I'm going back to HQ, to see what the rest of the Boys've bin up to."

"Good idea. I'll need a little time on my own to read this carefully."

Wiggins opened the door and squinted out to make sure the coast was clear. "Right," he said. "I'll be here first thing in the morning to put it back afore Madame comes to open up." And he slipped quietly out into the night.

When the Boys started getting up the next morning and Shiner had still not come home, Queenie was worried sick.

"I'm goin' back to that caff," she announced. "To see if anybody knows where he might be."

"Be careful," Beaver warned. "It might be dangerous."

"I don't care. I gotta find him."

"I'll come with you," said Wiggins. "But I gotta go back to the Bazaar first."

"We'll all go to the caff now," said Gertie. "We'll see you there."

When Wiggins arrived back at Mrs Pettigrew's shop, Murray was not looking happy. "I think I know where he was seen," he told Wiggins.

"Where?"

"The fair on Hampstead Heath." Murray opened the book at a page he had marked and began to read aloud: *"A splendid day spent enjoying all the fun of the fair. Little Sarah squealed with delight at the merry-go-round. Evie was intrigued by the Ghost Show and especially our very first glimpse of the latest invention, moving pictures."*

"Moving pictures?" Wiggins said. "Cor, I'd like to see that. But anyway, now we know where they was…"

"I'm afraid it doesn't really help us."

"Why not?"

"They went there on Bank Holiday Monday – along with half the population of London."

"Oh, yeah," Wiggins said. "I see what you mean."

"Thousands and thousands of people from all over the city."

"And it could have been any one of 'em."

"Yes. Ah, well, the diary was a good idea. Not your fault it was no use in the end."

"I'm sorry about that. Now let me put it back afore anybody notices it's missing."

Murray handed the book to Wiggins, who headed for Madame Dupont's waxworks once again. Now that it was getting light, the Dungeon didn't seem quite so spooky. He replaced the diary on the desk and turned to leave. As he did so, he noticed that the highwayman's hat had fallen off. He must have knocked it last night when he bumped into it in the dark. He bent down to pick it up, pausing to straighten the sign beside the exhibit – and stopped, staring at its words:

The body of Black Jack Duvall, hanged at Tyburn in 1740 for highway robbery, was displayed in this gibbet on Hampstead Heath, where he operated from the notorious tavern known as The Spaniards Inn.

"Blimey!" Wiggins gasped, hardly able to believe what he had read. "Spaniards!"

BLACKBEARD'S

"I got it!" Wiggins burst excitedly into Mrs Pettigrew's shop. "I found the answer!"

Murray sat up, startled. "What the...?" he exclaimed. "What are you talking about?"

"I know what 'Spaniards' means!"

"You do?"

"It's a pub. Or it was in 1740."

"It still is. It's quite famous. Of course!"

"D'you know where it is?"

"Yes. It's—"

"On Hampstead Heath, right? Where your brother went to the fair."

"My goodness! But how...?"

Wiggins quickly told him about the sign next to the highwayman in the Dungeon.

"That's amazing," Murray said. "But we still

don't know if the two things are connected."

"They must be," Wiggins replied. "All we gotta do is find out how."

Murray smiled at his confidence. "Oh, is that all? And what about the other part of the message?"

"Yeah, well … maybe if we go up to Hampstead and have a sniff around…"

"You may find it crowded. It's holiday time again, and the fair will be on. Besides which, you don't even know what you're looking for."

"That's true," Wiggins admitted. "This calls for a bit more thinking about."

"It's a pity Mr Sherlock Holmes isn't around – from what I've heard of him, he'd be able to work it out."

"That's the trouble with Mr Holmes. He's never here when he's needed. We have to manage without him most of the time."

"Do you think you can manage without him this time?"

"Course. But I'll have to think about it a bit more. I gotta go now."

"Where to?"

"We lost one of the Boys. Looks like some of

your Russian revolutionaries might have took him."

"That's terrible! Some of these reds can be quite ruthless. I couldn't bear it if anything dreadful were to happen to one of you on my account. We must find him before it's too late."

Queenie and the others were waiting outside the Russian tea room when the stern-faced waitress arrived to open up for the day. She looked at them with suspicion.

"More of you, huh?" she asked. "What you want? Where my friend who like blini?"

"That's what we want to know," Queenie told her. "He didn't come home last night."

"He is lost?" She sounded dismayed.

"What, Shiner? He couldn't get lost round here," Gertie said. "Not in a month of Sundays."

"Knows his way around, does our Shiner," Sparrow added.

"If he didn't come home," Beaver said, "it must have been 'cos he *couldn't*. And if he couldn't, he must've been locked up or somethin'. So if he—"

"Wait," said the woman, interrupting him.

"One moment." She unlocked the door of the café and ushered them inside.

"Now," she said as she closed the door behind them, "why you think Luba know where your Shiner is?"

"Who's Luba?" asked Queenie.

"I am Luba. This my tea room."

"Oh, we thought you was just the waitress."

"Waitress, cook, bottle-washer, I am everything. Now tell me why you think I know about Shiner."

"'Cos he was followin' one of your customers," Gertie blurted out.

"Why?"

"We're not allowed to tell you," Beaver said.

"Then I cannot help you."

Queenie thought hard. She did not want to put Murray in danger – but if Shiner already was, she had to do everything she could to rescue him. She took a deep breath. "All right," she said. "We might as well come clean. We're the Baker Street Boys, and we're tryin' to help a friend of ours find out who murdered his brother."

Luba stared at her scornfully. "You think I have murderers in Russian tea room? Why?"

"'Cos when we was followin' one of the suspects yesterday, he come in here. Our friend's just escaped from Russia, and if they spot him, they'll kill him."

"Who will?"

"The Russian secret police." Beaver lowered his voice to a confidential whisper. "It's all to do with spies and secret agents and stolen plans and stuff."

"Ha!" Luba let out a hollow laugh. "You think my customers work for Okhrana?"

"What's Oker ... whatever you said?"

"Okhrana is secret police of Tsar."

"What's Tsar?"

"Not what – *who*. Tsar is Emperor of Russia. He is tyrant. We hate him. But we hate Okhrana more. They spy on us, even in London."

Gertie suddenly had an awful thought. "What if," she said, "Blackbeard thinks Shiner's spyin' on him for the Okarina thingy?"

Queenie and the others were aghast.

"Who is Blackbeard?" Luba asked.

"The geezer what Shiner was trailin'," said Gertie. "You know, him as was sittin' in the corner over there when we was in yesterday." She pointed to the table.

"Ivan!" exclaimed Luba, narrowing her eyes. "I know him. He is wild man. Come!"

She headed for the door, ushering the Boys before her.

"Where we goin'?" Queenie asked.

"Ivan's house!" she replied. Then, as they opened the door, she stopped suddenly. "Wait!" she called, then dashed across to the counter, scooped up a handful of blini from a glass case and stuffed them into her coat pocket.

"My little Shiner will have hunger," she said. "These from yesterday, but he not mind."

Wiggins arrived just as Luba was locking the door behind them. "Where you lot off to?" he demanded.

"Madam Luba knows where Shiner might be," Beaver said.

"Madam Luba?"

"I am Luba."

"Pleased to meetcha." He raised his hat as he had seen Mr Holmes and Dr Watson do when they met a lady. "I'm Wiggins, captain of the Baker Street Boys. What they been telling you?"

"Enough to know we are on same side. Come. There is no time to lose. We talk while we walk."

Luba led the Boys through Soho and into the warren of little streets beyond Shaftesbury Avenue, telling Wiggins what had happened and listening to him as he explained about the Boys' mission. At last she stopped outside a small old house with a battered front door that had once been painted red. She hammered on it with her fist, and shouted, "Ivan! Ivan Ivanovich! Open up!"

After a minute or two, a man's sleepy voice from inside called, "What you want? Who is there?"

"Is Luba. I must speak with you! Open door!"

There was the sound of bolts being drawn back and then the door was opened a little way. Through the crack, the Boys could see a dark eye under a bushy eyebrow peering out at them suspiciously. Luba snorted and pushed the door wide open, to reveal Blackbeard. He looked startled to see the Boys and tried to close the door again, but Luba shoved him back and stepped inside.

"What you do, crazy man?" she demanded fiercely. "You kidnap child. Lock him up?"

"He was spying on me. Spying for Okhrana!"

"No, he wasn't!" Queenie shouted. "He was followin' you 'cos he thought *you* was spying for the Oki-whatsit."

"I do not understand."

"Never mind for now," Luba said. "Where is boy? What you do with him?"

"He is safe, locked in attic."

"Bring him," she ordered sharply. "Now!"

Blackbeard scuttled away upstairs, unnerved by Luba's ferocity. She marched into the nearest room and the Boys followed her. It was a bare room, with worn lino on the floor, a sofa against one wall and four hard chairs around a wooden table. On the table were piles of pamphlets and handbills, some in English, some in Russian, all printed in lurid red ink, echoing the colour of the flag hanging over the empty fireplace. The days and dates on a calendar hanging on another wall were also printed in bright red, in English this time, and some of the numbers had rings around them. Wiggins strolled over to look more closely at the picture on the calendar, which was of a foreign city filled with elegant white buildings and churches whose strange domes looked like golden onions gleaming in the sunlight.

"Is that Russia?" he asked Luba.

"Saint Petersburg," she answered. "Our capital city. Is beautiful, no?"

"Yes," he agreed. "I wouldn't mind going there."

"Hmm. Is pity it is home to so much cruelty, so much misery."

Before Wiggins could ask her any more, Blackbeard came back, dragging Shiner by the arm and thrusting him roughly into the room. Shiner's face lit up when he saw the Boys, but he did his best to hide his relief.

"What you lot doin' 'ere?" he asked gruffly, trying to shake off Queenie as she rushed to give him a hug.

The Boys grinned. This was the Shiner they all knew.

"Well, he's OK, at least," said Beaver. "No need to ask."

Luba stepped forward, wagging her finger at

Shiner and looking as stern as ever.

"You are very bad boy," she scolded him. "You must thank your friends for saving you. They were very worried."

"Oh, right. Thanks."

Luba shook her head in mock annoyance.

"I suppose that will have to do," she said, and pointed to the table. "Now, sit. Eat."

She pulled the blini from her coat pocket and piled them on the table in front of Shiner. This time he made no effort to hide his delight. As he tucked into the little pancakes – watched enviously by the other Boys – Luba smiled fondly at him, then turned back to Wiggins.

"You must tell Ivan everything," she said. "He will help you. He has many friends."

Wiggins hesitated. "I dunno," he said. "I promised..."

"You can trust him. The Okhrana are his most bitter enemies."

"They send secret agent here," Ivan growled. "Assassin to murder me and my friends."

"Have you told the police – *our* police?"

"They cannot help. They not believe us. We do

not know who he is, or where he is. Only that he is very cunning."

"Blimey," said Beaver, "sounds like it could be the same geezer what killed Mr Murray's brother."

"Yeah, it does."

"There has been killing?" Ivan asked. "Tell me."

So Wiggins explained everything that had happened, and Ivan listened very carefully.

"This is our man. I have no doubt it is work of Okhrana," he said when Wiggins had finished. "You have done well, but is not enough. We know there is to be meeting. We think we know where. But we do not know when."

"If only we could work out what the rest of that message means," cried Wiggins in frustration. "Three *what*, sitting *where*?"

He paced the room, deep in thought, then stopped in front of the calendar, hoping the picture of Saint Petersburg might give him some kind of inspiration. But it was not the picture that did it for him – it was the days and dates beneath it. He spun round in triumph.

"Got it!" he cried. "Look! Mon, Tues, Wed – it

ain't 'three' anything 'sat' anywhere. 'Sat' is short for *Saturday*!" He tapped the calendar with his finger. "And three can't be the date, 'cos Saturday is the ninth. It's got to be the time. So it's three o'clock on Saturday, at the Spaniards pub on Hampstead Heath!"

"Brilliant!" shouted Beaver. "Wiggins – you done it again!"

The rest of the Boys cheered. Luba smiled. Ivan nodded, then held up his hands for quiet.

"Very clever," he said. "Well done. There is only one problem."

"What's that?" asked Wiggins.

"Saturday is today. If we are to catch villains, we have no time to lose."

"Right, let's get moving, then!"

Leaving Ivan and Luba to collect up some of their friends, Wiggins and the Boys rushed back to Baker Street. As they arrived, panting, at the gates of the Bazaar, Sarge came out of his lodge, looking bewildered.

"What's goin' on?" he asked. "What's the rush?"

"We gotta get Mr Murray. We're going to the fair!"

THE GHOST SHOW

Selwyn Murray was startled when the Boys burst in on him without warning. He leapt to his feet, certain that his enemies had tracked him down and were about to murder him, so he was relieved to see Wiggins's excited face appear round the door.

"Wiggins!" he exclaimed. "What are you doing? Someone might see you!"

"Don't matter if they do," Wiggins replied. "Not now."

"What do you mean?"

"We know where they're going."

"Where?"

"The Spaniards – three o'clock this afternoon. *Saturday* at *three*. Get it?"

"Of course! Sat 3. Well done!" He pulled out

his watch. "But it doesn't leave us much time."

"You're right," agreed Wiggins. "And if we're gonna catch 'em red-handed we'll need the coppers there."

He turned to the other Boys, who were crowded behind him in the doorway, and rapped out his instructions: "Shiner, you know all about the Russians. Rosie, you know about the secret message. So you two go to Dr Watson, tell him where we're going and ask him to get on to Inspector Lestrade. Off you go, now! The rest of you, come with me and Mr Murray."

"How we gonna get to Hampstead?" asked Beaver. "It's too far to walk, ain't it?"

"It is indeed," Murray answered. "And we don't have time to wait for a train or an omnibus. We'll go by cab. Run and tell Sarge to find us a four-wheeler, quick as he can."

The driver grumbled at having to squeeze six people into his cab, but Murray pointed out that half of them were small and offered him extra money to take them all.

"And there'll be another ten shillings for you,"

he promised, "if you get us to The Spaniards Inn before three o'clock. It is a matter of national importance."

"Make it a pound and I'll have a go," the man replied.

"Very well. A pound it is. Now drive!"

Encouraged by the idea of so much money, the cabbie whipped up his horse and soon had them careering through the streets, past Lord's Cricket Ground and the elegant villas of St John's Wood, towards the long hill that led up to Hampstead Heath. It was a bumpy ride, and the Boys had to hang on tight to stop themselves being flung about inside the cab, but they all found it exciting, if a little scary.

Before they reached Hampstead, however, the poor horse began to get very tired. Its flanks were soaked with sweat, skeins of white saliva hung from its mouth and it slowed down almost to a walk. When they saw a stone horse trough by the side of the road, the driver pulled over and stopped to give it a drink of cool water while Murray and the Boys waited in an agony of impatience. Wiggins pulled out his pocket watch.

"We ain't gonna make it," he groaned.

Murray checked his own watch, then leant out of the window. "This is urgent!" he called to the driver. "Matter of life and death. We've no time to lose."

"I don't care how urgent it is," the driver replied. "It ain't worth killing my Betsy."

"He's right," said Gertie. "If she don't have a drink we shan't get there at all."

At last the driver patted the horse's quivering neck. "That'll do, girl," he said. "Not far to go now. Then you can have a rest." He climbed back onto his seat and jerked the reins. The horse responded with a steamy snort and set off again at a smart pace.

Although it was on the edge of London, Hampstead looked and felt like a village. And because this was a holiday, it was full of people who had come out of the city to enjoy the fresh air of the Heath, an area of unspoilt countryside filled with trees and ponds and green hills that were perfect for getting away from the hustle and bustle. Unfortunately, there were so many people strolling through the streets that the cab containing the Baker Street Boys and Selwyn Murray had to slow down again to get through. As it passed the ancient church, the clock was already striking three.

"Listen!" Queenie cried. "We'll be too late!"

"How much further is it?" Wiggins asked.

"At least half a mile. Maybe a mile."

"We could run that," said Beaver.

"Easy!" agreed Sparrow.

"And it'd be quicker," added Gertie.

"Right," said Murray. "Out you get!" He opened the door and called to the cabbie to stop. "Here," he said, giving him a handful of money. "Good man. You did your best. Thank you."

The Boys tumbled out of the cab.

"That way," Murray shouted, pointing down a side street. "We can cut across the Heath."

It wasn't easy going – the ground was uneven and hilly – but they dashed on towards the top, making good progress. On Murray's advice, they headed towards the music and screams of pleasure which they could hear in the distance, since the fair was always held near The Spaniards. And so they pressed on. The Boys were fit and used to running, and they soon left Murray far behind as he stopped because of a stitch, holding his side in pain but waving them on.

Soon they reached the first stalls and sideshows of the fair. Just in front of them on the other side of a narrow road, beyond a small toll-keeper's cottage, they could see a white, three-storey building with a sign board on its front: THE SPANIARDS INN. They ran towards it, halting just in time before they were run down by a black coach that emerged from the inn's yard and drove off at speed.

"Look!" Sparrow shouted, pointing at the door of the carriage. It had a monogram painted on it, a curly letter "M". As the carriage passed them, the Boys caught a glimpse of the shiny, domed head and sunken eyes of the man inside. And then it was gone, rolling down the hill and out of sight.

"Did you see him?" cried Queenie. "I could swear he was laughin' at us."

"We're too late," moaned Beaver. "He's gone."

"Yeah, but what about the geezer he was meeting?" said Wiggins.

"That's right," Gertie agreed. "He might still be in the pub."

"Stay here," said Wiggins. "I'm going to have a dekko."

"But how will you know who he is?" Queenie asked.

"Dunno. Have to wait and see."

Wiggins pushed open the door of the pub and went in. It took a moment for his eyes to adjust to the dim light, made even darker by heavy black beams overhead and low ceilings stained brown by centuries of smoke from countless cigars and pipes. Through the fug of smoke he could see that the main room which he had entered was half full of men sitting at tables or in alcoves, chatting and drinking. None of the people he could see as he walked through looked suspicious, and he was about to leave when he noticed a doorway at the other end. Putting on a cool face, he ambled nonchalantly over to it and stepped through.

It was a small room with a table in the middle, on which stood a bottle of brandy and four glasses, one of them empty. Three men were sitting around the table, deep in conversation.

One was a powerful-looking man with deep-set dark eyes, long, slicked-back hair and a pointed black beard, whom Wiggins had never seen before. The other two were Sir Charles White and his manservant, Fredericks.

The man with the long hair glared at Wiggins and waved him away.

"Clear off, boy!" he snarled in a heavy foreign accent. "Get out of here!"

Sir Charles and Fredericks glanced round casually, then suddenly recognized Wiggins.

"The messenger boy!" Sir Charles exclaimed, then snapped his fingers at Fredericks. "Get him!" he barked.

Wiggins did not wait to be "got". As the three men leapt to their feet and rushed towards him, he turned and raced back the way he had come, dodging between the drinkers in the bar and diving out through the door.

"Run for it!" he shouted to the other Boys. "They're after me!"

"Who?" Beaver asked.

"Where to?" Queenie wanted to know.

"Them!" Wiggins yelled as the three men

followed him out of the pub. "To the fair! Lose yourselves in the crowd!"

"There are more of them!" shouted Sir Charles, pointing at the other Boys with his silver-topped black cane. "I want them all."

Without waiting to be told twice, the Boys ran from The Spaniards, crossed the road and headed into the fairground. The three men pursued them, with Sir Charles shouting instructions to the other two and directing them with his cane. Murray, having now got his breath back, arrived just in time to see the chase and hobbled after the men, unseen by Sir Charles or Fredericks. As it was only mid-afternoon, the fair was not really busy yet and the crowds were not thick enough for the Boys to lose themselves in.

"We gotta keep 'em running round till the inspector and his men get here," Wiggins panted.

"And Blackbeard Ivan and his lot," Queenie added. "They'll know what to do."

"Just don't get caught, any of you," said Wiggins. "Now, scatter!"

All seven Baker Street Boys ran in different directions. The three men split up and tried to follow. The chase wound in and out of hoop-la and roll-a-penny, hook-a-duck and skittles, and dozens more sideshows and stalls. They ran around the tall helter-skelter, where girls screamed and clutched their skirts to stop them flying up as they corkscrewed down the slide; they hopped on and off the gallopers and round-abouts and swing-boats; they ducked behind the huge wheels of traction engines that puffed out steam and smoke as they powered the rides and the lights and the organs blasting out merry music. They passed the little German band that they had seen near the Bazaar, marching and playing hopefully, trying to make itself heard above the general din. It was fighting a losing battle but was still managing to collect a few pennies from young men eager to impress their girls with a show of generosity.

The Boys were starting to enjoy the excite-ment of what was turning into a great game of tag – but it was a dangerous game, with serious penalties. When the dark-eyed man finally out-witted Queenie and caught her, Beaver heard her scream and ran to her rescue. But although he was easily the strongest of the Boys, he was no match for the powerful foreigner. Without letting go of Queenie, the man shook Beaver off, threw him to the ground and was just lifting his foot to kick him when he was seized from behind. It was Ivan and a bunch of his revolutionary friends, including Luba and the chestnut-haired woman.

"Orlov!" Ivan growled. "I should have known it would be you."

"You coward!" spat Luba. "Why don't you pick on somebody your own size?"

She grabbed the man's arm and Ivan delivered a hard punch to his solar plexus, then leapt on top of him and pinned him to the ground with the help of his friends.

"Is he from the Okey-cokey?" Queenie asked.

"Yes," replied Luba. "I knew him in Russia. He is Okhrana agent and spy."

"And murderer," added Beaver. "When the coppers get him he'll be hanged."

"No, no!" gasped the man as he caught his breath. "I have killed no one!"

"Yes, you have," Queenie accused. "You killed Alwyn Murray."

"I am not assassin," he protested. "Not murderer. It was not me!"

"Well, who was it, then?"

Gertie was still running nimbly through the fairground, but Fredericks had spotted her and was on her tail. As she passed the coconut shy for the second time, he stepped out from between two stalls and grabbed her by the arm. She struggled and tried to wriggle free, but it was no use.

"Leave her be!" a loud Irish voice suddenly roared. "Take your filthy hands off moi girl!" The shout came from a big man with a mop of ginger curls who was running the coconut shy. Fredericks took no notice and tried to drag Gertie away, but the red-haired man snatched a wooden ball from his stall and hurled it with all his might. It flew like a rocket, with deadly accuracy, and hit Fredericks on the back of his head, knocking him out cold. He fell to the ground as though he had been poleaxed.

"Every ball a coconut!" the Irishman bellowed triumphantly, running forward with his arms outstretched.

Gertie spun round and let out a great shriek. "Da!" she screamed. "Oh, Dada, is it really you?"

"It is, it is!" he cried, enveloping her in a great hug. "Oh Gertie, my little Gertie! I been searchin' high and low for you since they let me out of jail. I thought I'd lost you for ever!"

And they hugged and kissed and held each other tight as though they would never let go, weeping tears of joy at being reunited.

Unlike his two companions, who had rushed around the fair like maniacs, Sir Charles was hunting his prey by stealth. He was determined to catch Wiggins himself, and planned to take him by surprise. Keeping out of sight, he crept between the stalls and tents until eventually he spotted the leader of the Baker Street Boys by the massive, ornate facade of what looked like a full-size mobile theatre. Wide steps led up to the ticket booth and entrance, where a placard announced: *Next performance 15 minutes.* The gaudy sign over the front, surrounded by pictures of ghouls and spectres of all sorts, proclaimed it to be the Ghost Show.

As Wiggins stopped before it, Sir Charles leapt

out of hiding and confronted him. Before Wiggins could run, Sir Charles took hold of his cane, pulling it apart to reveal a gleaming steel blade, which he now pointed at him.

"Blimey," said Wiggins. "A sword-stick!"

"Yes," hissed Sir Charles. "And it is razor-sharp. So stand still and do exactly what I tell you."

"Not on your nelly!" Wiggins replied. And he spun round and bounded up the steps through the curtained doorway.

Sir Charles let out a curse and rushed after him. As the theatre was between shows, the stage was empty and there was no audience in the auditorium. But it was filled with long benches and Wiggins was able to dodge Sir Charles by clambering over and around them more nimbly than the older man. Then one of the benches tipped over and Wiggins stumbled and fell. Before he could get to his feet again, Sir Charles was standing over him, the sword pointing at his chest.

"Now," he demanded. "Tell me – who sent you?"

"I did!" boomed a new voice, echoing hollowly through the theatre.

Sir Charles looked up to see Murray standing on the stage, glaring down at him with a face like thunder. All the blood drained from Sir Charles's own face as he stared in terror.

"No!" he gasped. "It can't be! It's not possible – you're…"

"Dead?" Murray taunted him.

"Yes. I *know* you are. I… I…"

"Killed me?"

Sir Charles was trembling with fear as he answered. "Yes."

"Say it again. Louder."

"I killed you. You can't be here… This is some sort of ghost show trick. Well this time I'll make sure!"

And with that, Sir Charles dropped his sword, reached into his pocket and pulled out a revolver. Raising it in front of him he took careful aim at Murray and squeezed the trigger.

There were two loud bangs at almost the same moment. The first was the gun going off; the second was the shattering of a very large mirror. Suddenly the stage was empty apart from the shards of broken glass. There was no sign of

Murray. Sir Charles spun round in disbelief as another new voice spoke up behind him.

"Yes, Sir Charles. It *was* a ghost show trick. All done with mirrors. Now if you don't mind, I'll take the gun." It was the leader of the little German band speaking. But the voice was that of Sherlock Holmes. He reached out and took the revolver, then handed it to Inspector Lestrade, who was standing beside him.

"Sir Charles White," pronounced Lestrade, "I arrest you for the murder of Mr Alwyn Murray and his wife and child."

Sir Charles glared furiously at him, quite unrepentant. "It was a mistake," he snarled, "a ghastly mistake. How was I to know—"

"That I had a twin brother?" asked Murray, emerging from where he had been standing in the wings, with Sparrow by his side.

"You!" hissed the murderer.

"Yes. You thought I was rotting in a Siberian prison camp after you betrayed me to the Russians. But I escaped, to see you brought to justice – with the help of my young friends from Baker Street."

Eureka!

After Orlov and Fredericks had been arrested – with Fredericks nursing a painful lump the size of a pigeon's egg on the back of his head – the Boys and their new Russian friends gathered outside the Ghost Show. Sir Charles glowered furiously at Wiggins as Lestrade and his men hauled him out of the show and marched him away in handcuffs.

"How did you know we was in there?" Wiggins asked Murray.

"Sparrow saw him chase you inside," Murray replied. "We decided to go through the side entrance to take him by surprise."

"Well, you did that all right. But how did you know what to do? How did you know about the mirrors?"

"I seen it afore," said Sparrow with a big grin.

"We had a ghost show at the theatre once. Dead good, it was."

Wiggins was impressed. "You did well," he said approvingly.

"You all did well," said Mr Holmes as he removed his musician's cap and peeled off the false nose, eyebrows and heavy moustache. "I have followed your progress with great interest."

Dr Watson, who had only just arrived with Shiner and Rosie, shook his head in amazement as he watched the transformation from German bandsman to internationally renowned detective.

"Good heavens, Holmes!" he said. "I've seen many of your disguises, but this takes the biscuit. To think that I've passed you in the streets several times and never guessed…"

"I know," said Mr Holmes with a smile. "You even put sixpence in my collecting box on one occasion."

"So I did," laughed Dr Watson.

"Because we played your favourite tune," added the detective.

"Ha! And I wondered how you knew. But what were you doing?"

"I have been on a secret mission for my brother, Mycroft, who as you know holds a high government post. He suspected that someone had been stealing plans to a secret new vessel – capable of operating beneath water – and selling them for a great deal of money to the agent of a foreign power."

"Russia!" exclaimed Wiggins.

"Precisely."

"Orlov," declared Luba. "He is secret agent. Now you have him."

"But we don't have the plans," said Mr Holmes. "We need to recover them in order to safeguard the secret and prove his guilt."

Throughout this conversation Gertie's father had been standing to one side with his arm around his daughter, holding her tight as though afraid she might disappear again. He cleared his throat and spoke up.

"Would you be talkin' about that Russki feller with the little pointy beard?" he asked.

"That's him," replied Mr Holmes. "It would appear that he has been living among your people, using the fairground as his cover."

"He has, he has! I always thought there was somethin' fishy about him, but I couldn't fathom what it was."

"P'raps he's got the plans hid in his caravan," said Beaver. "You could show us which van is his and we could search it."

"You could," said Gertie's father, "but I doubt you'd find anythin' there."

"Exac'ly," agreed Wiggins. "First place anybody'd look."

"Right. But I reckon I know where they might be. A couple of days back I was out on the Heath in the middle o' the night, lookin' to catch a rabbit or two for the pot…"

"Not poachin' again, Da?" Gertie teased.

"This is no private estate," he said defensively. "It's public land and there's thousands o' rabbits runnin' wild out there for the takin'. Anyways, I was settin' my traps when I hear somebody comin', tippy-toeing like a leprechaun in the dark—"

"Orlov!"

"Who's tellin' this story? You or me?" said Gertie's da gruffly, but his eyes were twinkling as he spoke. "Aye, you're right, it was your man.

He didn't see me, I made sure of that, but I seen him. He was carryin' a spade and a smallish box. I saw him mark out a spot, then dig a hole and bury the box."

"You didn't look to see what was in it after he'd gone?" asked Wiggins.

"None o' my business. And whatever it was, I didn't want to get mixed up in it. I never liked the look o' that feller."

"Well, like it or not, my friend, you're mixed up in it now," Mr Holmes said. "Do you think you could find the place again?"

"Sure and don't I always need to know where my traps are? I've got one set not three feet away from that very spot."

Gertie's father fetched a spade from his own van and led them out of the fairground and across the Heath. To the Boys it seemed like a wilderness, but the Irishman knew exactly where he was going. Using various trees as markers, he eventually arrived at a secluded spot, where he pulled back the lower branches of a bush to reveal a newly turned patch of ground. Once he started to dig, it was only a few seconds before the clink of metal on metal could be heard. After a few seconds more he had pulled a black tin box out of the ground and was brushing the dirt from its lid.

"It's locked," he announced. "Shall I smash it open?"

He went to raise his spade, but Mr Holmes stopped him.

"No need for violence," he said. "If you will permit me, madam?" He stepped across to Luba, pulled a hairpin from her head and handed it to Wiggins. "Now, my young friend, let's see if you can remember what I taught you about locks."

Wiggins took the hairpin, inspected it, then carefully bent it out of shape. Concentrating hard, his tongue peeping out from between his lips, he slid the end of the pin into the lock on the box and began to move it around, up and down and from side to side, wiggling and twisting it gently. At last there was a satisfying *click* and a smile spread across his face as he lifted the lid. Mr Holmes nodded his approval and bent over the open box to examine its contents.

"Eureka!" he said, smiling.

The Boys stared at him.

"I reek of what?" Wiggins asked, sniffing.

"No, no. You don't smell of anything. What I said was 'eureka'. It's ancient Greek, meaning 'I have found it'."

Wiggins laughed. "Eureka. Yes, we have eureka-ed it, ain't we!"

"Unless I am very much mistaken, these are the missing plans. Which means that Sir Charles White must be the traitor who stole them and sold them to the Russians, through Orlov." Mr Holmes turned to Murray and held out his hand. "I congratulate you, Mr Murray. Your suspicions were correct and I am deeply sorry that you suffered such a grievous loss because of them."

"Thank you, sir. You are very kind."

"Wait a minute," said Beaver, looking worried. "What about the other bloke – Mr Redman?"

"Completely innocent," said Mr Holmes. "All he has done is support a group of Russian exiles – our friends here – who seek justice and freedom from tyranny for their homeland."

"But how does Moriarty come into it all?" asked Queenie.

"In his usual way, I have no doubt. He finds someone who desperately needs money or is greedy for more than they have, or someone who has a guilty secret that would ruin them if it were to come out. He then turns them into his puppet, doing whatever he wants while he pulls their strings. But he always operates out of sight, in the shadows, where no one can touch him."

"One of these days we'll get him," said Wiggins.

"One of these days, maybe. But now it's time to go home. You have done well once again, and you deserve your usual reward. Where shall we hold our feast this time?"

"There's only one place we *could* have it," piped up Shiner.

"That's right," agreed Queenie. "Luba's Russian Tea Room!"

Luba's usually stern face broke into a wide, beaming smile. "Yes!" she promised. "I make you real Russian banquet. You eat so much you will not be able to move!"

As an extra reward before they returned home, Murray took the Boys back to the fair and paid for them to go on all the rides and into all the side-shows. In fact, because Gertie's dad worked on the fair, most of the showmen let them ride for free, which made it all the more special. The one thing they couldn't see, of course, was the Ghost Show, which was now out of action. They found the owner busy clearing up the broken mirror, but when Murray and Wiggins went to apologize, he seemed remarkably cheerful.

"Don't worry," he told them. "I've been plannin' to make some changes anyway. The old ghost shows have had their day. I'm goin' to show something new, the latest invention – movin' pictures. They'll be the wonder o' the modern age. Folk will flock to see 'em, just you wait and see. Moving pictures! They're the future!"

Murray wished him luck, then turned to Wiggins. "Time we were heading back," he said. "We still have something to do – something very important."

Madame Dupont was in the Dungeon of Horrors, carefully cleaning the models at the end of the day with a feather duster. She was just tidying the hair on the waxwork of Alwyn Murray, when she heard a sound behind her. She turned – and found herself looking into the identical face of Selwyn Murray. She let out a scream, dropped her duster and fainted.

"Would you like a glass of brandy?" Wiggins asked her when she had come round.

"Ooh, yes, please," she said, still shaking. "I need one!"

"Just like Sarge did," Wiggins reminded her.

"I am very sorry," said Murray apologetically. "I really didn't mean to give you such a shock."

"But you… You're real? Not a ghost?"

"No, a twin. Real flesh and blood."

"It was this Mr Murray what Sarge saw the other night," Wiggins told her. "So he didn't see a ghost and he wasn't drunk."

"At least, not until afterwards," added Murray. "I'm afraid it was all my fault."

Wiggins brought Madame Dupont a glass of medicinal brandy, and between them he and Murray explained everything. Murray assured her that Sarge had played an important part in the unmasking of the real murderer of his brother and the capture of a Russian spy, and Wiggins persuaded her to relent and let him keep his job. When they told him the news, Sarge was delighted – but decided that this time it was probably better not to celebrate with a drink.

Later that evening, the Boys celebrated with the banquet that Luba had promised them in the Russian Tea Room. She had pushed the little tables together to make one long table down the middle of the room, and it was heaped with dozens of dishes piled high with different foods in the best Russian tradition. All the food was delicious, and the Boys ate and ate until even Shiner could eat no more.

After they had finished their meal, there was a moment of sadness when Gertie left, though all the Boys were happy to see her reunited with her father. Queenie and Rosie both sobbed their hearts out, and even Wiggins and Beaver found themselves blinking back tears. The six of them stood in the doorway to the café and waved goodbye as Gertie walked off down the street, having promised to come back and see them whenever the fair was in London. Each of the other Boys secretly wished that it was him or her going home with a father or mother, but it made them all the more glad to have each other.

Queenie noticed Luba looking wistfully at Shiner.

"Why are you so fond of my brother?" she asked.

"When I was young," Luba said, "I also had little brother. He look just like Shiner."

"Where's your brother now?"

"He took sick and die, many years ago, in Okhrana prison camp. But every time I look at Shiner, I see him." She squeezed the boy's shoulder. "You come see Luba again. Any time, yes? I give you lots blini, and tea with plenty sugar lumps. OK?"

Back in HQ, the Boys crashed wearily into their beds and were soon all fast asleep. All, that is, except for Queenie and Beaver. Although she was tired out after the events of the day, Queenie could not help staring at Gertie's empty bed with a mixture of sorrow and happiness. She was also watching Beaver as he took an exercise book and sat down at the table, sucking his pencil, ready to start writing. Tiptoeing across to him, she looked over his shoulder at the empty page.

"Can't think what to call this one?" she whispered.

"It's hard to choose," he replied. "There's so much that's happened, what with spies and traitors and secret messages and murders and twins and everythin'."

"Well, it all started with a ghost in Madame Dupont's Dungeon, didn't it? So how about 'The Haunted Horrors'?"

Beaver thought for a moment, then nodded. "Yeah. 'The Case of the Haunted Horrors.' That'll do nicely."

And he bent over his exercise book and began to write.

THE SPANIARDS INN AND HAMPSTEAD

THE SPANIARDS INN is a real pub on the northern edge of Hampstead Heath. No one is sure how it got its name, but at nearly three hundred years old it is one of London's oldest inns. During the eighteenth and early nineteenth centuries it was well known as the haunt of highwaymen and cut-throats preying on travellers heading into or out of London across the Heath: the notorious Dick Turpin is said to have been one of them. The inn is supposed to have had a number of secret tunnels leading from its cellars onto the Heath, to allow highwaymen to escape unseen in the event of a raid by the law.

Hampstead still has the feeling of a village, even though it is now simply part of north-west London. The Heath remains a largely natural and unspoilt open area where city dwellers can enjoy walking, swimming in one of its natural ponds, and various other leisure activities. A travelling fair has traditionally been held there for centuries and still takes place on most public holidays, attracting large crowds.